Sign up for our newsletter to hear
about new and upcoming releases.

www.ylva-publishing.com

Other books by Wendy Hudson

Four Steps

WENDY HUDSON

MINE TO KEEP

Dedication

To Lynsey, for everything

Acknowledgements

Thanks to the Ylva team for their continued support and hard work making this happen.

Love and thanks to Andrea Bramhall, friend, editor, and personal pep squad. I couldn't do this without you.

To fellow writer pals Michelle Teichman, Angela Brooks, and Lee Winter—always available for rantings, ravings, and random musings.

For pretending not to be bored with my incessant book chat, a ton of thanks to the work wife, Susan, and all my colleagues on the day job.

Thanks to the locals of Biggar, Hopetoun's inspiration, for the warm welcome when I visit and the stories that you've shared.

My family and friends have been hugely supportive and it's a great feeling knowing they're behind me. Love you all.

And Lynsey, by my side through it all—the good, bad, and ugly. We just keep doing what we're doing, and I can't wait for the next chapter.

PROLOGUE

He sat below a patch of leafy birch trees, the late spring sun glittering down through the yellows and greens. The paper in his hand remained unread. Instead, he watched as his wife wandered the garden, their five-month-old daughter in her arms.

Starlings danced overhead, their chatter loud and shrill. He saw her stop to point skywards at them, murmuring in his daughter's ear. They were both smiling, a rare sight, and he closed his eyes a moment to log the memory and enjoy the calm.

Her voice brought him back to the garden. "I'm going to head up to the house. She needs feeding."

He nodded and gave her a half smile, then leant his head back against the trunk and shook open the paper.

A shriek snapped his head up from the sports page. He saw her in mid-flight, arms curling around his daughter as they tumbled towards the paved footpath. He was on his feet, moving with arms outstretched, nowhere near close enough to catch them. The thud of impact forced his eyes closed again for a moment. The blood rushed in his ears and his heart pounded double speed as the world righted itself.

There was no sound from the baby, only cries from his wife. Blood trickled from a gash on her forehead, matting the blonde, downy hair on his daughter's head.

He knelt down and pulled at his wife's arms. "Let her go, you stupid fucking bitch. What have you done? Let me see her." Eventually, he prised his daughter free and bundled her into his arms.

Her face was white, eyes wide open, and there was a small smear of blood on her chin. It only seemed to be a graze, but he touched her all over, feeling her head for bumps, her limbs for awkward angles. All the while she stared back at him, still and quiet with shock.

"Is...is she okay? I'm so sorry." His wife stayed sat on the ground, holding a sleeve to the cut on her head.

He glared down at her. "No thanks to you. What the fuck? I know you're useless, but now you can't even walk up the path without falling over. What if she'd bashed her head? Eh?"

"She didn't. I'm sure she didn't. I protected her. Let me see her." She made to get up, but he hugged his daughter to him and moved away.

"You protected her? Are you an idiot? You could've killed her." Spittle flew from his mouth as he screamed the last sentence. A cry came from the bundle in his arms, and he realised how tight he was holding the child.

"Calm yourself." She was on her feet now, dusting off her flowered dress. "It was an accident. Obviously, I didn't do it on purpose."

He breathed heavily, fury building towards his wife at her casual manner. "Oh really? There seems to be a lot of those lately. Can you really be that clumsy?"

He watched her eyes narrow. "What the hell are you talking about?"

"Don't play the fucking innocent. You've wanted to hurt her from day one. I can see the way you look at her, jealous she gets all my attention now."

"That's absurd. That's your own crazy insecurities talking. I love my daughter." She held out her free arm. "Give her to me."

He jiggled on the spot as the small cries continued. Smoothing a hand over the back of the baby's head, he tucked her close under his chin. "No fucking chance. And don't you dare put this on me. What about when I get home from work and she's screaming her head off, while you sit and watch shit on the telly?"

"Christ." She heaved a sigh and looked off to the distance before closing her eyes. When she looked back, her frustration with him was palpable, and that irked him more. "I've explained that to you. She's fed, watered, dry, and safe. It's about her learning to self-soothe."

He watched her wince as she swapped sleeves, the blood from her head soaking through it almost immediately. "Safe? Are you fucking kidding me? You bloody bashed her face on the pavement. For all I know, this kind of shit goes on all the time when I'm not here. How the hell am I supposed to go to work and trust you to take care of her?"

He watched her look at the baby in his arms and then up at him. She looked him square in the eye and spoke through gritted teeth, "Keep pushing me, and it'll be an empty house you come home to."

Wrong answer.

The blood roared in his ears, and he glared right back at her, neither of them backing down. She'd lose. She always lost, but it didn't stop the bitch from trying. Constantly undermining him, insulting him, threatening him. Needling away at him, pushing and pushing, over and over, until the roar was overbearing and he had to let it loose. He made to move towards her, never breaking her stare, until a small hiccup from his arms drew both their attention to the wriggling bundle.

The noise in his head calmed, but he knew he couldn't let her away with it. It was one threat too far, a kick to the sorest part of his soul. And the bitch knew it. She was asking for it.

He spoke quietly, injecting some concern into his tone. "I'm taking her inside. Stay here. I'll bring something for your head."

She didn't argue, only moved to sit on the grass, watching him go. Once inside, he laid his daughter in her playpen, checking her over once again. He drew some warm water into a bowl and dipped a soft cloth in it to gently clean her chin. She smiled up at him, and he cooed along with her, washing the blood from her hair before placing her favourite stuffed bear in her arms. "Daddy will be right back, sweetheart. You're safe now."

He marched outside, down the steps to the path, never breaking his stride until he was over her, looking down at her pathetic face. He spoke low as the anger simmered. "Do you really think I'd let you leave?"

She huffed out an exaggerated breath, a half smile on her face. "What are you going to do? Lock me up like you did with your first wife?"

That caught him off guard. He stepped back. "What the fuck are you talking about?"

"Oh, don't play dumb with me. She wrote to me, you arsehole, back when we first got together. Only, I was too stupid to believe her. I thought she was being a typical jealous ex. Because my sweet, handsome husband would never do something like that."

"She's a liar." He seethed inside, the fire in his stomach burning up through his chest as the anger became desperate to boil over.

4

She stood and closed the gap between them. "No. You are—"

His vision blurred and the rest of her words were muffled, then cut off. His hands were moving of their own accord, wrapping themselves around her throat, squeezing tighter and creating the blessed silence he craved.

Then the fire was in his groin as her knee connected with it. He tumbled sideways, howling at the sky and clutching himself. As his focus returned, he could see her running away. Away from the house, away from him. The pain disappeared as he zoned in on her. Back on his feet, he picked up speed as he ran her down.

The river came into view as he grabbed a handful of her hair. Then he was dragging her, her screams barely penetrating his mind. He knew what needed to be done.

Twenty feet. Fifteen. Ten. He didn't stop. Not even when they reached the river's edge. She clawed at him as he waded in amongst the reeds. The frigid water quickly soaked them both.

Then the screams stopped.

He watched her panicked eyes stare up at him through the murkiness. They were mesmerising, and he couldn't tear his own gaze away. Faint clouds of blood dispersed themselves from her head, and her feet thrashed as he pushed her deeper until she connected with the muddy river bed.

She couldn't stop him now.

She was meant to be different from the last. His salvation. His second chance. Fuck, he had tried his best to make it work. To at last have the family he deserved. But she had failed him at every turn, just like his disappointment of a first wife. Back then, he had allowed himself to be pushed around

5

and had given up the day she had eventually walked out. Well, not this time.

This time he was in control, and she would obey him.

Her life was his to take.

With his knee on her chest and a vice grip around her neck, he watched captivated as the breath left her in garbled bubbles. They forced their way out, furious at first, until time stretched from seconds to minutes, and she was finally, blissfully still.

When she was limp and lifeless, he hooked his arms under hers and waded out further. The river rose to his chest and the current pulled at his feet, but he stood firm. Her glassy eyes still chided him, dared him to do his worst.

Well, he had this time. She'd used the last of her chances. He released her body to the river and set himself free.

"Let's see you take her away from me now."

CHAPTER 1

Erin's tears mimicked the fat raindrops battering her windscreen. They came out of nowhere more and more lately, and she had resigned herself to go with it. "Better out than in," as her mother would say.

One more nugget of wisdom to add to the list she'd grown up with. Not for the first time, she questioned setting off on this journey and ignoring the last bit of advice her mother had offered.

She flipped the wipers to top speed and slowed the car, approaching a left turn as directed by the satnav. Trees enveloped her from either side, their branches low, forming a dark tunnel for her to follow as she approached the hotel driveway. She saw the sign for Cornfield Castle and made her way carefully up the winding hill that climbed to her destination.

The castle rose before her as she approached the crest, an imposing shadow warmed with brightly lit windows and lanterns adorning either side of its grand entrance.

She parked in a space to the left side and took a moment, allowing the quiet to wrap around her with the darkness. Through the few remaining tears, she concentrated on the dashboard clock until finally, they stopped, and it changed from an orange blur to clear numbers. Another tissue was added to the pile on to the passenger seat before she braced herself against the downpour and ran around to the boot to retrieve her case.

The gravel crunched and she skidded slightly as she hurried to the entranceway, and the bulky case bumped against her shins and thighs. Warmth poured over her the moment she stepped over the threshold. A woman smiled through the glass door as she approached reception.

"Miss Carter, I presume?"

Erin dropped her bag and leant on the desk in relief. "Yes, it's Erin. You got my message then?"

"I did. Your room is waiting, and by the looks of it, you're ready for it."

Erin attempted a smile and eyed the woman's badge. "Thanks, Ann. More than ready."

Ann passed her the booking form to sign. "You're welcome, dear. Give me a second, and I'll call George down to take your bag. He's doing the security rounds. Do you want a tea or coffee to warm you up? There's stuff in your room, but it's only instant, I'm afraid."

This time, Erin's smile was real. "You read my mind. And real coffee sounds perfect."

Ann pointed to her left. "You'll find Abigail closing up the bar. Tell her I sent you. I'll call when George appears."

Erin thanked her again and headed around the corner as directed, taking in her surroundings for the first time. An imposing mahogany display cabinet stood to her right, filled with broken pottery pieces, silverware, and jewellery. An assortment of history that made no sense to her but clearly meant something to the castle.

She restrained herself from reaching out to touch the wallpaper—it had a furry-looking design, the same as she remembered from her grandmother's dining room. A memory of catapulting peas and mashed potato at it made her chuckle, and she realised it was the first laugh to escape her in weeks.

Longswords, their handles patterned and ornate, crossed above an arched doorway that she guessed led to the bar. It

8

was past midnight, and her footsteps made no sound on the blue-and-green tartan carpet. She smiled when she noticed it, a prerequisite of traditional Scottish hotel bars, along with tartan curtains to match.

The room was dark apart from a couple of spotlights shining above the bar. The clinking of bottles came through a doorway to the side of it. She took a stool to wait for someone to appear whilst lustily eyeing the coffee machine.

The embers in the fire were barely hanging on, but the room was warm and a small sense of relief seeped into her with the heat. She could smell peat in the air, along with a mustiness you only found in a building that had survived the test of time. It wasn't unpleasant—rather, it was reassuring having the solidity of the castle around her.

The clinking continued in the stockroom, joined by a soft voice that drifted over her, singing in Gaelic. Erin considered knocking on the bar, but the melody was a soothing antidote to the drama of her day, and it cast a spell. She felt her shoulders sag and relax and allowed her eyes to close a moment.

"Can I help?"

Erin jumped, spinning on the stool from her view of the fire to a girl decked out in chef whites, holding a crate of bottles. "Sorry. Abigail? Ann sent me from the front desk, said you could help me out with some coffee?"

If Abigail was embarrassed to be caught singing, she didn't show it. She merely eyed Erin for a moment before dumping the crate, turning to the machine, and switching it on.

"What are you after? Latte? Cappuccino? I can do decaf if you prefer?" She turned back to Erin. "That's if you want any sleep tonight."

"Decaf is perfect. Strong and black, please." Erin smiled her appreciation. "Sorry to put you out. I got a puncture on the way here, so I've spent the best part of the night soaked, waiting for a recovery truck. So much for summer, hey?"

Abigail waved her away. "You're fine. I'm only restocking for the morning. Our bar guy had to leave early, so I offered."

"I did think that was an odd uniform for bar staff." Erin indicated the whites.

Abigail set the steaming cup in front of Erin. "Aye, I'm the head chef, but I'm residential, so I help out here and there when needed."

Erin watched as she pulled out the grips that held her cap in place and let wavy blonde locks fall free. She rolled her head from side to side and gave the back of her neck a rub, closing her eyes in what Erin imagined was satisfaction.

She returned to the machine and spoke over her shoulder. "Mind if I join you for one?"

Erin shrugged. "You're the one that lives here. I don't mind. That's so cool, by the way, living in a castle."

Abigail leant against the bar, cradling the coffee cup in her hands. She blew on it and spoke through the steam. "Sometimes. It can be weird living where you work, but it has its perks too."

"Such as?" Erin sipped her coffee. It ran smooth across her tongue, and she would have groaned if it weren't for the girl holding her attention across the bar.

Abigail smiled and took a sip of her own before answering. "Well, for a start, there's no commute, the fridge and bar are always stocked, and I get the chance to have coffee in the middle of the night with pretty strangers."

Erin felt the heat rise in her cheeks and heard her mother in her head telling her to take the compliment and not be so awkward all the time. She coughed but managed not to look away. "Thanks. I think. Assuming you meant me, that is?" So much for the not being awkward.

Abigail laughed. "Yes, I meant you, but I'm sorry, I've made you uncomfortable. Not used to girls complimenting you?"

"Yes. I mean, no," Erin stuttered. "I mean, there's no need to be sorry. I find I'm always surprised, that's all. As you can see, it makes me excruciatingly self-conscious." She shook her head in defeat. "Feel free to leave now. You've fulfilled your coffee duty, and I won't be offended."

Abigail smiled mischievously. "Nah. I'd rather watch you squirm. Call it payback for you catching me singing."

"See, I knew I should have called out or something to let you know I was here. Sorry, I didn't mean to embarrass you. I was enjoying it. You sing beautifully."

"I tell her the same thing, but she doesn't believe me."

They both turned in unison to the doorway. A tall, rangy teenager stood against its frame, stooped in the way of someone used to ducking under things.

A bar towel flew his way, and he caught it easily. "George, I've flipping told you about creeping up on people.

He threw the towel back. "Not creeping. I didn't want to interrupt your smooth skills in operation."

Now it was Abigail's turn to redden. "I hate you, little brother."

George crossed the room with his hand out. "George Miller. At your service, Miss Carter." He gave a small, theatrical bow, blond hair flopping across his face. "I see you've met my charming sister. Has she even asked your name?"

Erin could see the resemblance. The unruly blond hair and light sprinkling of freckles across their noses, along with the same slightly crooked grin gave it away. George was ridiculously tall and scrawny, not yet grown into his body, whereas Abigail seemed to have peaked at a curvy five-and-a-half feet. There seemed a reasonably big age gap between them. Erin guessed six or seven years.

She pretended to take a moment to think. "Do you know what, George, she didn't."

Abigail blushed harder, and Erin couldn't help but laugh along with George.

"Erin Carter," she offered in Abigail's direction. "In case you were wondering."

Abigail clattered her empty cup into the sink. Her mutterings were indecipherable, and Erin thought George would probably get more than a towel thrown at him later.

"Right, I need to get this place locked up. Erin, it was nice to meet you. George, show our guest to her room."

Erin was faintly disappointed when Abigail disappeared back through to the stockroom, leaving her to drain the last of her coffee before following George back towards the reception area. "Will she be upset with you?" she asked.

George merely shrugged. "I'm used to it. It comes with the territory of living and working with your big sister. Don't worry about it. She's prone to bouts of grumpiness."

He lifted Erin's case easily from behind the front desk and collected her key. "You're in room nine, which is at the top of the castle. It sits between two of the turrets. It's pretty cool. We normally give them to folk staying a while. You are staying a while, aren't you?"

Erin followed him up the wide, sweeping staircase, taking in beautifully rich tapestries hanging either side, adorned with colourful clan crests. Each one was interspersed with a variety of stuffed animal heads, which never failed to creep her out. "Aye, well, maybe. We'll see."

He eventually stopped at door nine, handing her the key. "Breakfast is served until nine thirty. Dial zero if you need anything day or night, and lastly, sleep well."

Erin smiled her thanks. "Cheers, George. Goodnight."

He loped away, and she let herself into the room, flipping a switch that illuminated multiple ornate lamps positioned around the space. She leant back against the door and sighed in relief. The tears came from nowhere. Five minutes ago, she'd been unexpectedly laughing and semi-flirting, and now she was a blubbering mess. Again.

"Shit." She swore aloud at her own stupidity and wiped at her eyes with a sleeve. "Sorry, Mum, but I'm getting really tired of this."

The suitcase stared at her, begging to be unpacked. But the call of the bed was stronger, and she couldn't ignore it. Only her shoes, handbag, and jacket made it off before she flopped diagonally across its plush surface. She was asleep before the thought of removing the rest of her clothes could even enter her mind.

CHAPTER 2

Sunshine poured in through the window, pulling Erin from the peaceful doze she'd slipped into finally. After passing out the night before, her sleep had been fitful, plagued by nightmares she fought with her subconscious to avoid.

She'd passed the darkest hours of the night ritualistically, visiting places locked away from her in waking hours. Then the cold had awakened her as the dawn chorus sang, forcing her under the blankets. After that, real sleep had been elusive.

Erin reluctantly peeked out over the covers and squinted towards the offending light, cursing herself for not closing the curtains the night before. She rubbed the sleep from her eyes, and they watered, blurred, and eventually refocused on the room around her. Still fully clothed, the sheets tangled around her legs caused a small tantrum as she tried to extricate herself.

Finally free, she crossed to the large sash window, unlocked it, and raised the bottom half. The hit of damp, fresh air washed over her as she stood, eyes closed, and allowed it to cleanse her of the nightmares. With her head tilted to the sun's warmth and the hint of summer that it promised, a semblance of calm found her.

The phone rang, jolting her from the moment. It was shrill in an old-fashioned way, kind of how her grandmother used to be. She crossed the room and hooked a finger under the receiver on the fourth ring. "Hello." Her voice broke, and she cleared her throat. "Sorry, I'm not long awake."

"Good morning, Miss Carter, it's George. We haven't seen you for breakfast this morning, and I wanted to let you know service is finishing up."

"Wow, what time is it?" She never wore a watch, or any jewellery for that matter, save a pendant left by her mother that hung low under her T-shirt. She looked around for her bag and the phone that would be in its pocket.

"Nine fifteen. There's no rush. I wouldn't normally call and disturb you, but I know you missed your dinner reservation last night as well. There's a few spots for a late breakfast around the area, but trust me, you're going to want to try Abby's eggs."

Erin scrubbed a hand over her face. "It's okay. I appreciate it, George. Give me fifteen minutes to shower and change, if that's all right?"

"Absolutely. We'll see you soon."

She replaced the phone in its cradle, smiling at the small-town, friendly service she'd received since arriving. She couldn't imagine a city hotel being thoughtful enough to call if she missed breakfast. They'd more than likely be delighted to have saved the money.

As the hot water pummelled Erin's tired shoulders, she allowed herself to go back to the nightmares, to the darkened rooms and the raised voices, muffled through the hands she had held firmly over her ears.

These were the only memories she had of her mum and dad together, although the words they had shouted and screamed never took form. The arguments never reached a resolution in her mind. The only clear moments were of herself in the places she hid: the attic, the wardrobe, under the stairs, or her bed. When the real-life nightmare had started, Erin had tucked herself away until her mum would eventually find her. With the house finally quiet, she would hold Erin, and they would rock together for what felt like hours, soothing each other.

She hadn't understood it all back then. If she were honest with herself, she still didn't. One day, not long after her sixth birthday, she and her mum had left the house. Since then, neither her dad nor his legacy were ever spoken about again. As years passed, the urge to ask questions had diminished. As they had moved house to house, town to town, Erin had gradually stopped looking for places to hide in case he came back.

Now her mum was gone, too, and the old feelings and fears had all returned in full force. She was back in those dark places from her dreams—her nightmares—desperate to get out.

Terrified that the haunting was only just beginning, after weeks of torture, she had resolved to take control and deal with it. In her usually orderly world, it made no sense to allow a shadow the power to dictate her every thought and dream.

This wasn't how she intended to live her life, in a constant state of mental paralysis, closed off to everything and everyone. She had to find a way to end it once and for all if she was ever going to find a trace of normality amongst the chaos.

So here she was, in a small town in South Lanarkshire, with a thousand questions tripping over each other, vying for her attention.

Her rumbling tummy brought her back to earth, spurring her into action. She dried and dressed quickly in skinny jeans and a light-grey sweater. After tugging on her favourite worn navy Converse, she brushed out her short dark hair and tucked it behind her ears still damp. It would kink as it dried, but flyaway hair was the least of her worries.

Finally, she picked up the shiny silver Mackintosh rose pendant and rubbed a thumb over the pattern before she looped the long chain over her head and tucked it under her top.

"You can do this, Carter, c'mon. It's time." Notebook under her arm, she took a calming breath. Time to face people. Time to find some answers.

CHAPTER 3

The scent of bacon made Erin's mouth water as she descended the last of the stairs. Her stomach growled again, complaining at the lack of sustenance she'd provided it the past few days.

George greeted her at the dining room doorway with a crooked smile. "Good morning, Miss Carter."

"Please, call me Erin. Only my students call me Miss Carter."

"You're a teacher?" George looked her up and down surreptitiously. "I wish there were teachers who looked like you when I was at school. I might not have ditched classes so often."

As clumsy as the compliment was, she'd heard cruder and decided to appreciate his attempt. "You're sweet, George. Thanks."

He studied her a moment longer, and she shifted on the spot before asking, "Em, breakfast?"

"Oh, right. Yes, this way. I saved you the best table by the window. Although the early rush is over."

She followed him, winding her way through the mostly empty tables. Given the time, the majority of guests had already eaten and left. A few remained, taking their time over coffee and a newspaper.

He seated her in a large bay window away from the stragglers. The occasional beam of sunshine streamed in, warming the spot. "Here's the menu. I'll be back in a few moments to take your order. Tea or coffee in the meantime?"

He was all propriety again, and she went with it. "Coffee, thanks."

He nodded and left her alone with the menu. The view immediately distracted her, and she scanned the vista before her. An ornate fountain spouted water playfully not far from where she sat. She watched as droplets caught in the wind and broke free from the cycle, spraying in the same direction as the leaves that tugged on their branches.

Behind it, the sun played peek-a-boo with fast-moving clouds, its warmth immediately missed on her face every time it ducked away. The hills were lush green, dotted with sheep and the criss-cross of stone walls, the shadows of the clouds moving over them as if within touching distance.

A river cut through the landscape—the Clyde, she knew— meandering its way over a hundred miles from the Daer Reservoir to the Firth of Clyde. She'd travelled its route from Glasgow to where she sat now in Hopetoun, and it gave her a small measure of comfort. She was still in touch with home, however empty it might be now.

She jumped as George appeared at her shoulder with a pot of coffee in hand. "I never get bored of the view here."

"I can see why. It's beautiful."

He poured her coffee and set the remainder of the pot on the table. "Have you decided what you want?"

"Sorry, no. I was distracted. How about you ask Abigail to surprise me with some kind of chef's breakfast special? Is that okay?"

He raised his eyebrows but smiled. "Sure. Should I tell her it's a request from you?"

Erin was confused. "Of course. Is that a problem?"

"No, no. Not at all. Won't be long."

With that, he headed back to the kitchen, leaving Erin scratching her head. Had it been presumptuous to request some kind of special breakfast treatment? She hadn't meant to be rude or difficult. It was merely to avoid making a decision.

The last remaining guests left, and she was alone with her coffee and the view. She poured a second cup and pulled out her notebook to read over her notes on the area.

"Are you researching something?" Abigail stood in her whites, holding a plate and peering curiously at Erin's scribbles.

Erin closed the book and moved it, making room for the plate. She shook her head. "More like someone." She scanned her breakfast, liking what she saw. "Eggs Benedict?"

Abigail nodded. "It's a classic for a reason. Enjoy."

"It looks delicious. Thanks." Erin couldn't wait to tuck in but caught Abigail's arm as she made to walk away. "Oh, and sorry if I made you go out of your way. I didn't mean to be cheeky asking for something off menu."

Abigail smiled. "Not at all. It's actually on the menu, so it was no trouble. If you want something a bit more inventive, I suggest you have dinner here tonight. I'll try and impress you properly."

George appeared to refill her pot. "First coffee and now dinner? You're not hanging around, big sis, even by your standards."

Abigail turned to swat his head, and Erin couldn't help but laugh despite her blushing. "Get back in the kitchen, you little arse, before I hang you."

They watched George go as he rubbed the side of his head. Abigail turned, brushing down her whites self-consciously. "I'm sorry about him. I didn't mean anything ulterior with dinner. I figured you're here for a while, and honestly, I get tired of the menu sometimes, so it's purely selfish getting to cook something different."

Erin shook out her napkin and looked up. "Sit if you want."

Abigail looked surprised, as was Erin. Since when did she invite company?

"You sure? You're the last order, so I have a few minutes."

"Aye." Erin nodded towards the chair opposite her. "You're kind of making me uncomfortable hovering like that."

Abigail smiled and seemed to breathe out a small sigh of relief. She slid into the chair. "Does this mean you don't think I've been highly inappropriate?"

Erin popped the top of a perfectly poached egg with her knife and took a bite. This time, she couldn't help the small groan that escaped. "If dinner is anywhere near as good as this, then invitation accepted." She went in for another bite.

Abigail swiped her forehead dramatically. "Phew." She poured herself a cup of coffee and nodded in the direction of the notebook. "Who is the 'someone' you're researching? If you don't mind me asking."

"I don't. But I also don't want to spoil my breakfast getting into it."

"Oh." Abigail looked disappointed.

"It's someone from a long time ago. I heard he might be in the area, so I thought I'd try my luck."

Erin had no more to offer at this point, and the last thing she wanted to do was discuss her past over breakfast with a stranger. The tears were at bay so far today, but any mention of her mum and she knew there might be no controlling their reappearance.

Besides, she liked Abigail. There was a relaxed vibe about her, a calmness that Erin felt in her presence that she enjoyed. Dredging up shadows from the past was only going to ruin that effect.

"Fair enough. Do you at least need any help getting around the area? Anywhere in particular you need to know about or get to?"

Erin thought for a moment, then shrugged. "I think the internet and my satnav have it covered right now, but that'll probably only get me so far. I'll let you know." She felt Abigail study her over her coffee cup but didn't meet her eye. Afraid she might start inappropriately spilling her guts, she concentrated on the silky sauce and eggs on her plate.

"So, what do you do when you're not researching mysterious people?"

Erin was glad the conversation had returned to the mundane. "I'm a maths teacher. Secondary school, up in Glasgow."

She watched Abigail's nose crinkle. "I hated maths. My teacher was a witch of a woman who I swear would have used the cane if she was still allowed."

Erin laughed. "I think every school has one of those. I'm not that teacher—well, most of the time."

She again felt scrutinised under Abigail's gaze and continued to busy herself, pouring more coffee and buttering toast. Eventually, the gaze left her and moved to the view.

Erin could hear the distant clinking of someone washing up and the footsteps of other guests on the stairs. Otherwise it remained quiet in the dining room, and she sighed as a feeling of peace flowed through her once again.

She joined Abigail staring out the window, but it failed to hold her attention. The woman quietly humming to herself across the table was far too distracting. Her hair was caught up in the chef hat again, small wisps poking out from under it, tickling her forehead. As Erin watched, Abigail tucked a thicker lock behind her ear. Erin counted four tiny silver hoops in it, piercing their way down to a shiny star stud in the lobe. Her skin looked smooth and clear under the freckles. It was lightly tanned, but in a natural way. She wondered if maybe Abigail and George had Scandinavian blood in them.

Abigail turned her way and Erin quickly looked down at her plate, hoping she hadn't been caught staring.

"You don't like to talk much, do you?"

Erin wiped her mouth with the napkin, giving herself a moment. It was an observation she was used to hearing. The fact was, silence didn't faze her like it seemed to do most people. She was comfortable in it. Relished it, in fact.

After the torrid few years that were the beginning of her life, she had learned to embrace the quiet wherever it presented itself and sought it out the rest of the time. She had an uncanny ability to retreat and zone out from whatever surrounded her, to the point where she didn't always realise she was doing it until someone was irritably snapping their fingers in her face.

It was her first line of defence, and not something she ever felt the need to apologise for.

Erin found having conversation forced upon her by strangers tantamount to assault. On a train, in a shop or bar, sitting in a park. And what was with taxi drivers and their ridiculously personal questions? It was jarring and presumptive in a way she couldn't explain.

That wasn't how she felt now. She didn't have the usual urge to defend herself from Abigail. In this sunny room, she sat with a beautiful woman, sharing a glorious view over a delicious breakfast. She was merely appreciating the moment and savouring what she had assumed was amicable silence.

"Sorry. I was just enjoying the quiet." It was out of her mouth before she realised how Abigail might take it. Given she had been the one who had broken it.

Too late.

Abigail's cup was back in its saucer. "Sorry, you should have said. I didn't mean to disturb..." She was on her feet mumbling an apology.

"No, no." Erin shook her head and held out a hand to stop her, but Abigail was already on her way back towards the kitchen. "Abby. Stop." Erin got to her feet and followed, catching her by the wrist. Abigail stopped as requested and stuffed her hands in her whites. "I didn't mean it like that. I meant I was enjoying the quiet with you. Not to mention my wonderful breakfast. You're right. I don't talk much, but I wouldn't have asked you to sit with me if I hadn't wanted you to."

Abigail studied her again, tilting her head as if that would help see Erin better and gauge if she was telling the truth. "You're sure."

Erin smiled to reassure her. "I'm very sure. Sorry. I think something, but I don't always say it very well."

"You called me Abby."

Erin was confused. "Sorry?"

"Only my friends call me Abby."

Now Erin did feel awkward, unable to tell what she meant by that statement. They might have only just met, but Erin felt as if this was someone she would want on her side, someone who could maybe help her navigate the local waters. "Oh. Is it okay for me to call you Abby?"

"Aye." Abby continued her retreat to the kitchen.

"Hey, wait." Erin wanted to be sure they were cool. "Is the offer of a culinary treat still good for tonight?"

Abby stopped in the doorway. "Of course. I enjoy cooking for my friends." She winked, and Erin knew all was well. "Book yourself a table for seven, and I promise you a treat." She slipped through the door before Erin could respond.

Erin sat back at her table. Picking up her cup, she ran over the last few minutes quickly in her mind. She wondered if Abby offering to cook something special for a guest who hadn't long arrived was unusual. *Was I flirting? Was she?* It had been so long, she couldn't be sure.

No. That wasn't flirting; I barely said a word to her. Or if it was, it was the worst attempt in the history of romance.

She chastised herself. The last time a woman had caught her attention in this way was, well, she couldn't even remember. But the timing was impossible. Another emotional complication into the already jumbled mash-up of her life was not what she needed right now. Besides, there was no reason to think Abby had considered anything else.

~ ~ ~

Abby's cheeks burned. *What a bloody idiot.* A pretty face appeared and nothing but silliness seemed to prevail in her brain.

But what a pretty face it was.

She could have killed George. Always fricking turning up and stirring the pot. It was hard enough to meet someone in sleepy, back-of-nowhere Hopetoun, never mind with him always peering over her shoulder. Thank the stars he hadn't stuck around for the whole show at least. He'd have been relentless.

She clattered a stack of clean plates back on to their shelf and surveyed the kitchen.

Done.

She whipped the tea towel from her shoulder and hung it on a rail, before discarding her apron, hat, and jacket into a laundry bag in the adjoining utility room.

Her thoughts returned to the quiet stranger. Mysterious in her reasons for visiting, Abby had felt the sorrow emanating from her as soon as she had sat at the bar the night before. Her eyes had been red-rimmed, but even despite noticing the remnants of tears, Abby could still sense the oppressive weight that clearly sat tiredly on Erin Carter's shoulders.

Weary from the early-morning rush, Abby climbed the stairs to her room and stripped off the last of her whites en route to the shower.

Her mind turned to the menu for the evening, or to be more precise, the menu she would cook for Erin. An overwhelming urge to please this woman had descended from nowhere. Or was it the need to impress? Probably a mixture of both.

She checked herself. So a pretty girl had shown up—she might be nothing more than that, and she certainly wasn't volunteering any more information about herself. Who knew what or who waited for her back home, wherever that was?

Glasgow. She'd mentioned Glasgow.

How many times had someone waltzed through those doors and momentarily caught Abby's attention before they'd inevitably poured cold water on any ideas she had? She adjusted the water temperature until goosebumps pimpled her skin. *Yes, exactly like that.*

She'd roamed the castle's rooms and hallways her entire life, and spent the past ten years of it mostly in the kitchen. In all that time, despite the thousands of people who had crossed its threshold, only one had become more than a fleeting desire.

And look how that had turned out.

She held her face under the bracing stream and rinsed away the memories before they had a chance to take hold. There was no use giving in to maudlin what-ifs and maybes. They wouldn't change anything.

A fluffy bath sheet helped her rub the cold away, and she wrapped herself in it before flopping onto her bed. *Stick with the cold showers, Abby. There's no reason to think Erin's any different from the others.*

CHAPTER 4

Back in her car, Erin checked her list of destinations for the day. It was mostly made up of local establishments in the small town of Hopetoun, a few miles from the castle.

She had never imagined anything would prompt her to make this journey. That she would feel the need to put a face to the silhouette lurking in her dreams. But then, she had always imagined her mum to be invincible. Amelia had been Erin's rock, her protector, the constant in her life, no matter what, who, or where.

Now she was alone.

Alone in her grief. Her home. Her whole fucking life.

She didn't know what there was to gain from finding her dad. Answers, maybe? She could take a guess at why they had left him. That her mum had finally said "enough" one day. She could understand that. But her mum had never answered the question of why he had stopped being her dad. And Erin couldn't help asking herself, what if he had changed?

She reassured herself that if the answers weren't there, if he was nowhere to be found, well, then she would be no worse off than she was right now. At least she'd have tried. But the closer she felt to finding him, the less that reassurance worked. The lost child inside of her imagined him opening his arms and scooping her into them, telling her it would all be okay, that she was safe again.

The adult in her told her not to be so fucking ridiculous. And weak. And pathetic.

When had she become so reliant on others? What she had told Abby was true, that she was happy with quiet, without complications and drama. She had her numbers and found comfort in them. Teaching maths, she had all the answers; they were facts, undeniable and constant. Her world was orderly, routine, with everything in its place.

Friends were unpredictable and often disappointing. Girlfriends even more so. She'd had a few of each over the years, but Erin had never had the inclination to pursue them—it had never felt right. So they'd eventually become tired of chasing her and faded away. She told herself if she were really interested, if they were "the one", then it wouldn't have felt like such hard work to make the effort to spend time with them.

Moving so much as a child hadn't helped. There had never been time to build a foundation, never mind a whole structure. Then, as she'd gotten older and moved again, and again, the people she met had already done that groundwork. They had best friends, exes, memories together, and nostalgia to keep a conversation going. There was no space for Erin, no openings. No room at the inn.

So, she had studied. She had lost herself in numbers and always found the answers there. Teaching had come naturally to her. She had the right temperament, and the kids changed yearly. They came and went as often as she had. It was also a universal profession that didn't tie her to one place any longer than she wanted to be there.

Although she had settled in Glasgow for now, there was still no need for attachments or sentiment. Sure, she had colleagues, would enjoy the odd Friday-night pint with them, and attend the required social events. But they weren't friends. She had no pets to warm her old tenement flat. Nothing to welcome her with a wagging tail or a disgruntled meow when she came home at night. Not even a paltry goldfish. There was nothing and no one to rely on her. And no one she relied on in return.

Except her mum.

At the end, Erin had attempted to have her questions answered and had tentatively asked about her dad.

"Why are you asking this now?" Amelia tried reaching for a cup of water, and Erin caught the wince of pain at the small movement.

She manoeuvred the tray closer over the hospital bed and topped up the cup before handing it to her mum. "I'm sorry. The last thing I want to do is upset you, but…"

"But what?" Amelia cut her off. "He was a waste of space then, and I can guarantee you he's no different now." She slammed the cup down and the thin plastic cracked.

Erin pulled tissues from a box and mopped up the leak. "I'm sure you're right, Mum. I can't help it. It's the not knowing that's bothering me the most. I just feel like I need to find out for sure. For myself."

"All you'll find is disappointment. Mark my words." Amelia stilled Erin's hands and gripped them tight. She pulled her closer until their eyes were level. "I've given you a good life, haven't I? Done my best for you?"

"Yes, Mum, of course. This isn't about me and you." Erin perched on the side of the bed and kept hold of her hands. "It's only about me. About what happens when…"

She couldn't say the words. Saying them made it real. The thought of losing her only real tether to the world was too big to comprehend. She wasn't ready for it to be real.

Amelia held her eye and softened her voice. She reached out a feeble arm and cupped Erin's cheek. "You don't need him, Erin. You're strong. You're my daughter, remember. You'll find your own way, with me in your head and the beautiful person you are in your heart."

Erin remembered how frail her mum had felt in her arms as she had wrapped her in a hug. The chemo—futile though it was—had exhausted her. The strength had still been there in her eyes and the conviction in her voice had never wavered, but her body had lost the battle.

It was their only conversation about the man she had called "dad". Amelia hadn't wanted to spend her last days talking about someone who had hurt and abused her. She had wanted to enjoy some of her favourite things one last time and had asked that Erin help her do that.

Her last word on the subject had been her only concession to Erin's questions.

"The last I heard, he was living south of Glasgow. Somewhere near the Borders."

Erin blew out a breath in an effort to curb the tears as she fumbled with the satnav, eventually tapping in the postcode for Hopetoun Secondary School. Curiosity had half-heartedly got to her in the first few months after her mum had died, and Google had been the obvious first step.

She'd found a multitude of Graeme Carters on the electoral register, but only a few fitted the age range. A trawl of Facebook profiles hadn't produced a picture she recognised.

Then a LinkedIn page had caught her eye. A Graeme Carter was listed as working as a maths teacher in Hopetoun. It had no picture and didn't seem to be active, but it had been too much of a coincidence. The possibility that she might have unknowingly gone into the same work as her dad had unnerved her, made her wonder what other similarities they had.

So, she made a decision to find him. Good or bad, she had to know. And the town of Hopetoun seemed the most probable place to start. One phone call to the school later, all they would confirm was he no longer worked there. She checked the electoral records and there were no matches in Hopetoun. So, maybe he didn't vote. Or he lived in one of the other numerous small villages in the area.

Truth be told, she needed an excuse to get out of Glasgow. The long school summer holidays stretched out before her, and for once the quiet of her flat offered no comfort. It was suffocating.

The satnav finally acquired satellites and plotted her route. It was Saturday and the school would be closed, but it was central in the town and as good a place as any to start.

~ ~ ~

The narrow roads wound their way for a couple of miles before opening up as Erin approached Hopetoun. It was a typical sleepy Scottish town. A meandering high street lined with pubs, cafés, a flower and book shop, hair salon, post office, and bank, amongst other small businesses plying their wares. A few small stone cottages still remained along one section. She imagined they were once desirable as the centre of the village, but were now noisy and blackened with pollution from the cars and trucks that bumped their way through town towards the motorway.

The secondary school was set a few streets back, but she parked up outside the bank. The sun shone and called her outside to walk. The streets were busy with local folk running errands, enjoying coffee together, and window-shopping while the weather permitted.

She left the main street and took a narrow lane that led to the school. It was modern and utilitarian, the playground tarmacked and devoid of inspiration. She had lost count of the playgrounds she'd set foot on in her early years, always on the periphery, always the new girl.

A mural ran the length of one wall, depicting historic Scottish figures, their serious faces bearing down on those who passed. It wasn't until her later years that Erin had found the relevance in these people and their contribution to the world, the wisdom they were still able to impart, defying time and mortality.

She tried to imagine her dad walking through the front gate, briefcase in hand, greeting children as he passed. *Would he wear a tie? Was he popular with the kids?* Instead, all she saw was a faceless figure, the indistinguishable figment of her imagination. It had been foolish to think being close to somewhere he had maybe worked would somehow unlock the memories of his face, his mannerisms, his voice. She sighed aloud in frustration and retraced her steps along the lane.

Back on the high street, she strolled slowly, getting a feel for the place, taking it in. People stopped to talk to each other or raised a hand in greeting across the road. This was somewhere people knew their neighbours, had family that spanned generations, and knew the name of the person serving them in the shop or the pub. There was hope to be had in that. Maybe someone would remember her dad.

A small boy cried ahead of her as he was tugged past the ice cream shop by someone she could only assume was his mum, harried with another child strapped to her back. She struggled with bulging shopping bags in one hand, doing her best to hold on to the little boy with the other.

Erin shook her head, muttering, "Suck it up, kid. You can't always get what you want."

"Sorry?" The question was directed Erin's way. His mum had heard her speak.

"Uh. Nothing. Sorry, I was talking to myself."

She was rewarded with a suspicious eye cast up and down before the woman continued tugging the boy and carried on her way. She threw glances back at Erin, compelling her to duck into a shop out of uneasiness.

A bell above the door announced her arrival, and she smiled at its old-fashioned charm. At the chime, a lady who looked to be well past normal retiring age observed her over gold-rimmed glasses from behind the counter. "Morning."

Erin gave her a small nod. "Morning." She looked around and found herself in the post office. Lost for a reason to be in the place other than to ask questions, she skirted away from the counter and perused the magazines, wondering how to approach the subject. A science periodical she recognised came to hand. She took it and approached the old lady.

"Can I get you anything else?" The lady beeped her gun over the barcode and looked at Erin expectantly.

"No, that's all, thanks." Erin fumbled for her purse, suddenly nervous about asking real people questions about her dad.

"You're a new face around here. Visiting family?" The lady bagged her magazine and put her hand out for the money Erin finally freed from her purse.

"Aye. Something like that. I'm actually looking for family."

The lady's eyebrows rose and she counted out change back into Erin's hand. "Maybe I can help. I reckon I've seen every face to live around these parts come through my door over the years. What's your name?"

"Erin. Erin Carter. Did you ever know a Graeme Carter?" Erin heard her voice rise in pitch on saying his name out loud. She felt optimistic that it would be recognised by the lady, but also fearful. She hadn't prepared for the very first person she would speak with to know exactly who she was looking for. It couldn't be that easy.

And it wasn't.

"Naw. Can't help you there, love. I know a few Carters around this way, but no Graeme. There's James that owns The Rose pub, and Carter's dairy farm out towards Lymington. None of them is a Graeme, but might be worth asking them. Sorry."

That Erin breathed a sigh of relief at her response was something she'd have to think about later.

She took the proffered bag with her magazine. "Thanks anyway. It was a long shot."

"No problem at all. I'm Mary by the way. Who is this Graeme, anyway?"

Erin was already backing towards the door. "Oh, a distant relative. Thought I'd look him up while I was through this way."

Mary nodded, accepting her answer, but Erin was sure her shiftiness hadn't gone unnoticed. "Well, if you've got any more questions about the area, you come see me."

Erin smiled. Whether the offer was from kindness or nosiness she wasn't sure, but she appreciated it nevertheless. "I will. Thanks." She opened the door and the bell chimed again. It was almost closed behind her when she heard her name. She stuck her head back in anxiously to find a thoughtful-looking Mary.

"Did I forget something?"

Mary shook her head. "No, but I seem to remember there was an Eddie Carter stayed way out past the golf club. Where the river Tweed comes through this way. He and his wife Marie bought up an old croft house. She passed though, about seven or eight years ago, bless her. Word is, she had a baby girl die at only a few months old and couldn't cope with the grief. Took a walk down to the river one day and never came back. Jumped off a bridge, apparently. No one's seen Eddie since. He used to play at the rugby club."

Erin's heart broke a little hearing the story. To lose a child and wife in that way, she couldn't comprehend it. She felt her own grief bubble up to the surface but swallowed it back, returning Mary's sad look. "That's terrible."

"Aye, it is. James up at The Rose played rugby with him. It might be worth asking if he knows a Graeme."

"I will do. Thanks again, Mary. I'll stop by if I have more questions."

Back on the pavement, Erin breathed again. She looked up and down the street, deciding her next stop, then walked across to her car still parked outside the bank.

She wasn't ready for more people, for questions asked or answered. She stopped in the café for a takeaway sandwich and cup of coffee, hurried to her car, and slammed the door. Erin cocooned herself in its safe space. She glanced back and forth between the direction of the castle and the hills. Her decision was made in seconds. The fields and hills beyond Hopetoun called.

CHAPTER 5

"That Erin's a looker." George sat on a kitchen stool, noisily munching an apple.

Abby flicked her tea towel at his legs. "Sod off."

"What?" He held up his hands, all innocence. "I'm only saying."

"Well, don't." Abby continued to busy herself with a steaming pot of Loch Spelve mussels, cooking off the garlic and white wine, before pouring in a little fresh cream. Lunch service was slow, most folk out and about, taking in the sights, making the most of the unpredictable sunshine. But for once she was grateful. It gave her more time to think about the evening menu for Erin.

"Do you think she's gay?" Pieces of masticated apple escaped from George's mouth, and Abby turned up her nose at him and the question.

She threw a cloth his way. "Clean that up."

He obliged but wasn't distracted. "She doesn't give much away, but I reckon I can find out."

"George." Abby stood, hands on hips, giving him her best big-sister glare. "Leave the girl alone. Besides, why does it matter?"

He hopped down and discarded the apple core into the food waste bin. "Erm, maybe because I saw the way you checked her out last night. Oh, and you're cooking 'something special' for her tonight." He did the finger quotes thing, knowing it irritated her.

"So? She's been here five minutes, and the offer just kind of happened. I mean, she seems sad. Doesn't she seem sad to you? It felt like a nice thing to do. That's all."

"She does seem sad. But still. I'm thinking her pretty face also had something to do with the offer."

Abby removed the enamel pot from the heat and sprinkled in fresh chopped parsley before replacing the lid and sliding the finished dish George's way across the counter. "Table six. Get out of my kitchen."

He chuckled and grabbed some mitts, and then picked up the hefty pot with ease. "You're only adding fuel to my curiosity by avoiding the question."

"That's not even a saying, idiot. And I'm not avoiding it because there's nothing to avoid."

"Yeah, yeah." His smirk stayed in place as he backed out of the kitchen door. "Sometimes, you forget I know you."

He was gone before she had a chance to throw another insult his way. Unfortunately, she had to admit he was right. Abby wasn't in the habit of offering the strangers who passed through their doors special treatment. But he was wrong about her motivation.

Okay, maybe he wasn't all wrong. The pretty face definitely helped. And those eyes. If ever the word "brooding" required pictorial form, Erin's eyes were it. It was as if she was constantly grappling with a problem, the answer never quite within her reach.

Abby wanted to ask what the question was. She wanted to smooth her brow and offer to help. As they'd sat in silence at breakfast, the melancholic shield surrounding Erin had been hard to ignore. Abby didn't have a single coherent reason why, but she wanted to tap her finger on it and ask to be let in.

"Aw shit," she cursed at the empty kitchen. "Damn you, George."

~ ~ ~

The drive had done Erin the world of good. She'd trundled at a steady speed along the back lanes, windows open and the radio blaring. She'd taken random turns until she reached a river. Was it the Clyde or the Tweed? She wasn't sure and didn't really care. She wasn't even sure what direction she'd started in.

Her favourite DJ's soothing voice introduced track after track of funk and soul, and her mood mellowed with the music as Candi Staton belted out "Suspicious Minds", and Erin couldn't help but sing along. She had made a decision of sorts, created a mantra for her own mental health and fortitude.

There is no need to rush.

The first step had been taken; she had made it to Hopetoun. Step two had also commenced. Talking to Mary may have been hard, but she'd survived. If she were to find her dad, then there would be other Marys, other questions, and she would survive them too. There was no need to rush to step three. But when or if she did, it didn't mean she had to take it.

There is no need to rush.

One step at a time.

Simple but effective pearls of wisdom to hold on to that she knew her mum would approve of. She would also probably add fifty more along the same lines.

Eventually, she punched the address into the satnav for the hotel and was surprised to be less than ten miles away. She took her time winding through the lanes back to it. Now the rest of the afternoon stretched before her, with nothing to do until dinner at seven.

The quiet murmur from the hotel lounge invited her in. Couples and lone travellers were scattered around the large ornate room, sipping on hot drinks and pints, a few looking up as she entered but otherwise paying her no attention as she took an armchair close to the unlit fire.

A guy she didn't recognise took her order and returned with a glass of cold Pinot Grigio and a smile before leaving her to it. She pulled out her notebook and turned to an empty page.

It didn't take long to jot down the information Mary had provided. She wrote the word "related" with a question mark next to James and Eddie Carter's names, along with The Rose as her next stop for questions. The rugby club, Carter's dairy farm, and Marie Carter's death and baby, were also added to the list. The former two might help her—the latter were mere morbid curiosity.

George sauntered into the room and caught her eye, speaking briefly to the barman before heading her way. "Can I join you?"

She wasn't particularly in the mood for company, but his friendly face was hard to turn away, and she figured he was working so wouldn't linger. "Sure. How're you doing?"

He nodded and his hair flopped down over his eyes. He brushed it away, and she wondered how it didn't annoy the hell out of him. "Yeah, good. On a break and thought I'd say hi. How's your day been?"

She glanced at her glass. "Well, I'm drinking wine at three in the afternoon, otherwise not bad."

He leant pointy elbows on his knees and gestured towards the notebook. "The research not going well?"

She furrowed a brow and then remembered Abby. "You've been talking to your sister?"

"Aye, sorry, she wasn't gossiping or anything. There's not a lot goes on around here, and she was more wondering out

41

loud to me at what you might be down this way for. Plus, we don't get many people booking rooms with no check-out date."

Erin sighed, picked up her glass, and leaned back into the soft cushions of the chair. "It's okay. It's not really a big secret or anything. I'm looking for a relative, that's all. Someone I haven't seen in a long time."

"Maybe we can help. We're local, born and bred, and know most folk from working in this place."

"Maybe..." She studied him a minute wondering how much to tell. Deciding it couldn't do any harm, she picked up her notebook. "Do you know James Carter down at The Rose?"

George was nodding before she finished her sentence. "Aye, he served me my first legal pint. Plays for the local rugby club and puts on some epic barbeques in the summer whenever there's a big sporting event on. Is that who you're looking for? You related?"

She didn't answer his question, merely underscored rugby club, noting it higher up the list as a potential place to visit. "Do you know if he's related to an Eddie Carter who used to live around here?"

It was the first time she had seen his expression anything but affable. The look of worry was fleeting but unmissable on a face so naturally open. He leant his chin in one hand and tugged at an earlobe irritably. "Can't say I know an Eddie Carter. What have other folk been saying?"

"I only know what Mary at the post office told me. She says he was married to a woman called Marie and lived out near where the Tweed flows through. Apparently, they had a baby who died young. Then Marie committed suicide and Eddie left town."

George shifted towards the edge of his seat and sat a little straighter. "Ah yeah, I've heard the stories. I was pretty young when it happened though. Don't remember it really, to be honest, and I've never heard James talk about him. I'm not sure anyone really knows the whole story about Eddie. I don't think he was born around here."

Erin noted that down. "And James is local?"

George was on his feet, and she saw him cast a furtive glance towards the doorway. "Oh yeah, been here all his life, same as a lot of folk."

The James/Eddie lead didn't seem promising, but Erin thought it best to follow up anyway, given their shared surname. "You ever meet a Graeme Carter?"

George thought for a moment, then shook his head. "Nope, doesn't ring a bell. Listen, I need to get back to work."

She wondered at his change in demeanour, from light to flight in a matter of moments. "No worries, George. Thanks anyway."

He started to leave but turned after a couple of steps. "So, who's this Graeme Carter?"

There's no need to rush.

Too many questions. Time to go. Erin had the sudden urge to retreat to her room. Hide from the world and everyone in it.

"Oh, no one." She faked a yawn and stood up with him. "I think I'm still tired after yesterday. A nap before dinner is probably a good idea."

He glanced at her unfinished wine but didn't question it. "Aye, of course. I'll leave you to it. And listen, Erin, be careful, eh? A stranger asking questions might make some folk round here twitchy."

"Really? Why?"

"Ah...you know...small town. People are always suspicious of outsiders. Just take care, yeah?"

"Of course. I'm not here for trouble."

"Cool." He pointed to the notebook resting on the arm of the chair. "Don't forget that."

She forced a smile of gratitude. "Thanks. I'll see you at dinner." She scooped it up and tucked it away in her bag before heading for the stairs and the solace of her room.

CHAPTER 6

"C'mon, peanut, time for bed."

The blonde head of his daughter didn't lift from where it hovered over her latest work of art. "Aw, five more minutes, Daddy, I'm almost done."

He smiled, observing the pink tip of her tongue stuck out to the side while small hands moved furiously over the sheet of paper with an orange felt pen. "Okay, you can have five, but it had better be worth it."

The head lifted, rewarding him with a beaming smile. "The best yet."

He moved around the room picking up discarded toys, placing dolls and stuffed animals back on their shelves, and returning a cornucopia of cars, puzzles, and crafting tools back to their home in a trunk under the window.

He ran a finger along the edge of the trunk as the lid closed. He remembered the afternoon he'd painted it white before handing over the brush to his five-year-old daughter to decorate. Flowers and butterflies had been her favourite things then, resulting in swirling blobs of mixed colours that had dried thick and uneven. She'd been so proud of herself, and he had been unable to refuse when she'd asked to give the chest of drawers the same treatment.

Now eight, her artistic skills had markedly improved, and he surveyed the pictures covering every inch of space on the wall opposite the door. He thought he knew them by heart, and it had become a game between them, closing their eyes and calling out an animal before guessing where it could be found on the wall. The latest creation would add another giraffe, by far her favourite to sketch. He sought out the others, markers for how she had improved since those early stick-figure drawings.

He crossed to the chest of drawers and opened one. "What's it to be tonight? Monkeys or bears?" He knew the answer, but also knew she preferred to pick herself. It was the monkeys that had inspired her current nickname.

"Monkeys of course, Daddy. It's always monkeys on Saturday." She jumped up triumphantly, presenting him with her finished piece. "Jelly, the giraffe. What do you think?"

He took it from her and held it at arm's length, stroking a finger and thumb across the bristles on his chin whilst she bounced on her heels, waiting impatiently for his critique. "I think you've got yourself another masterpiece. Where shall we put it?"

Another grin broke out, showing her slightly crooked baby teeth, minus one along the bottom. That one had cost him an extra bedtime story when it had fallen out along with a flood of tears.

She scanned the wall and pointed to an area that represented her penguin phase. "There, make it look as if Jelly is peering down on the wee penguins."

He laughed and positioned the picture as instructed, lifting her into his arms when it was done so they could take in the latest addition together. "We're going to have to start on another wall soon."

She rested her head on his shoulder and spoke into his neck. "Maybe you can take some for your walls, Daddy. I can help you put them up." She said it quietly, and he knew she was testing the water, testing the rules of the house.

He dropped her back to the floor and took her by the shoulders. "We've talked about this, peanut. And you know exactly why that can't happen. I know you're a brave girl, but brave won't keep you safe. Only I can do that." He turned her towards the bathroom. "Now it's teeth-cleaning time, so go and get brushing."

She did as she was told without another word, and he pulled out the monkey pyjamas. "Don't forget, I want a clean face and hands too."

"Yes, Daddy," she called out around the froth of toothpaste.

He sat on the edge of the bed and smiled when she reappeared, pink cheeked and flashing her teeth again as proof of cleaning. A picture of innocence. She automatically sat on the cushion he placed on the floor between his feet, and he smelt the soap waft from her fresh face. He brushed long strokes through her fine golden hair, untangling it after a day of play.

Done with that, he plopped the folded pyjamas on her head; it was their signal he was done and she could get up. She jiggled about unbalanced, getting ready, while he scanned the bookshelves alongside the bed. "What's it to be tonight then?" He stuck with her artistic theme of the day. "*The Giraffe and the Pelly and Me?*"

Her head popped through the monkey-covered top, and she gave an excited screech of yes through the hair covering her face. He helped free her from it and did up the top button, eliciting giggles with their nightly ritual of side tickles. She eagerly crawled under the covers as he pulled them back, tucking her favourite stuffed bear in the crook of an arm before settling expectantly for the story.

47

Her eyes closed before he reached the halfway mark, but he finished the book anyway, knowing she would still be vaguely listening whilst fighting off dreamland. He set the book aside and smoothed her hair, taking a moment to watch her sleep.

After placing a light kiss on her forehead, he slowly extricated himself from her side. "Goodnight, peanut. I love you."

He crept to the door, switching off the large light so all that remained visible was the soft purple glow of the night light on her face. As the door creaked closed behind him he didn't miss the sleepy murmur of, "I love you too, Daddy," before he pulled it tight and slid the heavy bolts into place.

CHAPTER 7

The nap was an outright lie. Erin had never been able to nap. Instead, she stripped and indulged herself with a long, steaming bath, eating half the biscuits left on the tea tray with rapidly wrinkling fingers.

Now she sat in the middle of the floor with her case, contemplating her minimal wardrobe and wishing she hadn't packed in such a rush. Eating dinner alone didn't exactly call for diamonds and tiaras, but Abby was cooking for her, so she figured some effort on her part should be made. She thought about Abby and her stomach stirred as raindrops began to patter the window in time to her heartbeat.

She wondered if Abby's intentions with dinner really were innocent. In Erin's experience, probably not. Still, it wasn't every day a pretty girl offered to cook for her, and despite knowing very little about Abby, she was inexplicably disinclined to say no. Abby had sparked a hint of curiosity in Erin, and she imagined a little distraction might be a welcome antidote after all, given her current dreary situation.

As she discarded items, she hung them in the wardrobe and straightened up her room. Eventually, she decided on skinny blue jeans and dressed them up with her favourite black shirt and boots. She looped her pendant back around her neck and added small silver hoops to her ears before tucking her hair behind them. She assessed herself in the mirror, and her shoulders dropped in a sigh. Tired and pale. She would have to do.

The same barman served her a second glass of wine, and she sat by the window, waiting to be seated in the restaurant.

She wasn't surprised when George appeared to walk her through. "I hope you're ready for a culinary treat."

Erin thought of how her stomach had reacted to thoughts of Abby earlier and wondered if it had been only hunger. "I'm starving, so more than ready."

He'd saved her the same table as that morning, but the view wasn't so enticing. Clouds had rolled in low off the hills, casting a murky mist over the hotel grounds, the fountain barely a shadow now. Typical, unpredictable, Scottish summer weather. "Thanks, George."

He attempted a graceful bow. "I'll be right back with your starter."

A few minutes later, it wasn't George who appeared with the small plate, but Abby, serving her for the second time that day. Her cheeks were tinged pink with the heat of the kitchen, and wisps of damp hair had escaped her hat, curling around her face. "Thought I'd pop out quickly with this and say hi."

Erin's smile was genuine. "Hi."

Abby held her gaze a moment before sliding the plate in front of her. Only when she stepped back from the table did Erin move her eyes from Abby to the plate. "Wow, this looks amazing."

Abby grinned at the compliment. "To start with tonight, Miss Carter, we have a pan-roasted breast of guinea fowl, with a parsnip puree, toasted pine nuts, and a blackberry jus." She rocked back on her heels, hands behind her back, clearly pleased with herself.

"It smells incredible, Abby. Thank you so much." The same as her brother, Abby half bowed, half nodded before heading back to the kitchen.

Erin's tongue tingled as the flavours of the first bite assailed her senses. It was delicious, and the spicy Malbec she'd chosen complemented the game and sweet blackberry perfectly. George delivered the next two courses, and she ran out of compliments to send back to the kitchen. Thoroughly stuffed, the comfy sofas of the lounge called, and she dropped into one with a satisfied sigh.

She'd withstood the urge to open her notebook over dinner, but now it stared back at her from the table and she couldn't resist any longer. She opened it to the first page, where a stack of pictures topped with one of her mum looked out at her. A six-year-old Erin sat in her lap, grinning up at her in delight. It had been taken not long after they had left her dad, and she remembered how her mum had hugged her so close as the camera had clicked, whispering in her ear how much she loved her.

A tear leaked free, but Erin quickly wiped it away at the appearance of Abby in the doorway. Her whites were gone, and Erin realised it was the first time she had seen her out of them. She looked relaxed in dark blue shorts and a simple, green V-neck T-shirt, her blonde curls swept up high into a ponytail. She smiled widely at Erin and headed her way, bypassing the armchair opposite to join her on the sofa.

"So?" she asked. Her eyebrows rose in expectation, waiting for Erin's verdict on the food.

"Abby, it was fantastic. Every, single, bite. I feel very privileged right now."

Her face flushed at Erin's words. "Excellent. I'm glad you enjoyed it." She glanced down at Erin's lap. "Is that you and your mum?"

Erin had forgotten she was holding the notebook, the picture in view. She made to close it but changed her mind, instead offering the photo to Abby for a closer look.

"Aye, I was six there. Her name is Amelia." She watched Abby scrutinise it, her eyes seeming to move over every inch of the photo.

"You were a cute kid. What happened to all that hair?"

Erin laughed. "My teens happened. I cut it all off at fifteen and never looked back."

Abby looked up from the picture then, her eyes travelling over Erin. "I think the short cut suits you. Also very cute."

Erin couldn't hold her eye and merely mumbled a reply as she busied herself putting the pictures back inside the book. "Thanks."

She heard Abby chuckle and eventually looked up to find her still staring. She glanced down at the notebook again, and Erin knew there were questions coming.

"Are you going to tell me who it is you're looking for or remain a woman of mystery? George said it was some family member, but I'm thinking there's more to it than that."

Erin closed the book and set it aside, picking up the last of her wine. She took a couple of sips, sizing Abby up. There was no denying how attractive she was, but there was more to her than that, and Erin could feel herself being drawn in. She felt more at ease around her each time they talked. She was maybe a little more forward than Erin was used to, but given her own reticence in social situations, that was probably a good thing.

Stop overthinking it. She's simply a nice girl looking for some company. You're here alone, for who knows how long. What's the harm?

She held up her glass. "Want to join me for one?"

If Abby was surprised by her invite, she didn't show it. Instead, she sprang up from the sofa and took Erin's glass by way of an answer. "Shall I get us a bottle to share?"

It was asked with a little more hope in Abby's voice than the usual nonchalance, which made Erin smile. "Aye, why not."

When Abby returned with the wine, she took her seat on the sofa again, a little closer than before. As she poured, she said with a mischievous sideways glance at Erin, "I charged it to your room."

"What? You mean ingratiating myself with the chef doesn't get me free wine?"

For a moment, it looked as if Abby believed she was serious before she nudged Erin with an elbow. "Aye, all right, I'm kidding. It should come with some perks, I suppose."

Erin laughed. "I take it you're finished for the night?"

"Not only for tonight, that's me done for the next few days." With her words, Abby seemed to relax back deeper into the sofa, clearly relieved to have some time off.

"You mean chefs actually get days off?"

Abby gave her a half smile. "It's been known to happen. When your parents own the hotel you work in, it helps."

Erin was surprised. "Ah, that's why you and George live as well as work here?"

"Yeah, something like that."

She didn't elaborate and Erin didn't ask her to. In her world, families were complicated, and she knew she wasn't alone with that. "The wine is definitely on you in that case." Erin took a sip. It was a Fleurie, and the delicate hint of peach tingled on her tongue. "I love Beaujolais."

Abby clinked their glasses together. "Me too. And it's a deal. If that's all it takes for your company, I have access to a whole cellar full of wine."

Erin didn't miss the meaning behind Abby's words and decided on safer territory. "So, what's your big plan for the next few days then? Are you heading away anywhere? Catching up with friends? Boyfriend? Girlfriend..." Erin felt her voice trail away and actually couldn't believe she'd asked that question out loud. So much for safer territory. She avoided looking at Abby, waiting for a response, until Abby burst out laughing.

"What?" Erin was confused. "What's so funny?"

"Aw, I'm sorry. I think that's the longest sentence I've heard pass your lips and it was oh-so-smooth."

Erin blushed but couldn't help the smile that came with it. "What? Oh, you mean the boyfriend question. I didn't mean it like that. I was only being polite asking about your plans..." She knew she was covering nothing and trailed away in her attempt.

Abby continued to chuckle. "Sure you were. And to answer your polite question, there's no boyfriend." She paused to take a sip of her wine, and Erin was drawn to her lips as the tip of her tongue ran between them. Then they were moving again. "No girlfriend either."

Erin refocused her gaze to a speck of lint on her jeans and picked it away. "Oh. Okay. Cool."

Abby waved her glass in Erin's direction. "And we're back to one word sentences."

Erin poked a tongue out. "Another glass of this and there'll be no shutting me up. You've been warned."

"Challenge accepted. I'm still waiting to know who you're down here looking for."

Erin tried to swerve it again. "And I'm still waiting to know what you're up to on your days off."

"Touché, smart arse." Abby topped up their glasses. "To be honest, my plans mostly revolve around sleeping, reading, and walking. Unless you have any other ideas?" She winked over her glass, and Erin did her best to curb another flush of colour.

"Sorry, I'm too busy being mysterious, searching for ghosts."

Abby laughed. "Ah, I knew it. There is more to the story. C'mon, give me the gossip. It's so goddamn dull and boring around here."

"Ah, so you're only interested in the gossip then?"

Abby half choked on her wine. "Wow, way to put a girl on the spot."

Erin stuttered, realising the perceived innuendo behind what she had said. "Oh no, I didn't mean that. I meant..."

Abby's hand on her knee stopped her. "Hey, I'm kidding."

Left unsure of what else to say, Erin reached for her notebook again. "I'm looking for my dad."

Abby seemed taken aback by her bluntness. "Oh."

"Yeah. Oh." Erin pulled out another photo and handed it to her. "This must be twenty years old now. I haven't seen him since I was six."

Abby studied the photo. If Erin expected to see recognition there, she was disappointed. "What's the deal? Why did he leave?"

"It wasn't so much he left, more that my mum took me and moved us across the country without telling him."

"I take it she had her reasons?" Abby handed the photo back, and Erin snapped the book shut on it.

"I don't remember much, but I know he wasn't exactly husband of the year. Or father, for that matter. Mum would never speak about it, only reassure me she'd done the right thing, and I was best to forget him and that time in our lives."

"But you haven't." It was a statement more than a question.

"No. Well, actually yes, to a degree. I have these nightmares…" Erin caught herself. Why on earth was she suddenly spilling her guts to this girl? She was practically a stranger, and apart from the mild flirting and obvious interest she'd shown Erin, there was no reason to trust her. Or think she would be interested in Erin's woes. For all she knew, Abby was merely having fun with a guest passing through, someone she never had to see again.

Abby rolled her hand, gesturing for Erin to continue, and she found herself unable to hold back. The emotions and the fears of the past few months tumbled out of her in a rush.

"I'm always in a dark place. It feels small, I feel small, and everything around me is muffled. I know there's shouting and it's my mum and dad, but I can't make sense of it. Then I'm blinded by light and my hands are getting pulled away from my ears, my face is being wiped of tears, and my mum is holding me so tight. We're curled up in this cramped space together. It's hot and smells musty, but I don't care because I can't hear his voice anymore." She took a breath and a gulp of her wine.

Abby's hand was back on her knee, and suddenly the small gesture was the only thought in Erin's mind. She looked up and held Abby's gaze. "Sorry."

Abby gave her leg a reassuring rub and lightly gripped her thigh. "What for? It's good to share."

Then the soothing comfort of her hand was gone and Erin wished it wasn't. "Maybe."

"Where's your mum now? Does she know you're searching for your dad?"

"No. She passed away a couple of months ago. From the little she said about him, I thought she would be against it. But then I found a note she had left me a couple of months after her death. She said maybe it was time. And now there's no one left but me and him I figured I had nothing to lose. Well, assuming he's still around somewhere."

Abby puffed out her cheeks and blew out a long breath, moving to top up their glasses again. "I'm so sorry about your mum, Erin. I can't imagine how hard that's been on you. And I'm sorry for making you talk about this when it's obviously still so painful." She passed Erin her glass back but held on to it as Erin's fingertips covered hers. "But I'm happy to listen if you want."

Erin pulled away first. What was the harm? It worked both ways—she never had to see Abby again either. "His name's Graeme. I know my mum was young when she had me, in fact, I'm pretty sure I'm the reason they got married in the first place. I think he's maybe late forties now, and as you've seen, the most recent picture is over twenty years old. I don't know much more than that."

Abby looked pensive, staring out of the window for a moment before turning her attention back to Erin. "How did you end up here?"

"Well, all my mum would say is last she heard he was somewhere near the Borders."

"Hmm…doesn't exactly narrow things down."

"No, it doesn't," Erin agreed. "But I did some searching on the internet and whittled it to a few possibilities. This one seemed most likely." She blew out a regret-filled laugh. "Then I promptly chickened out."

Abby didn't laugh at her glib attempt to reduce such a massive decision to nothing. "I can't say I blame you. It's a big deal after all this time. One that I'm sure would scare the crap out of me."

Erin smiled, grateful Abby could appreciate the magnitude of her decision to search for her dad.

"What made you eventually go for it?"

Erin thought a moment, but she knew exactly what had given her the final push. "There were letters. With mum's note."

"Ooh, now it's getting interesting." Abby turned in her seat to face Erin, crossing a leg underneath the other.

Erin swallowed. She knew the contents of the letters by heart, but even after reading them a hundred times over, it still didn't make them easy to talk about. God, she'd hated finding them, almost as much as she'd hated reading them.

Pale blue eyes searched hers, waiting for her to continue. A tear leaked free, and before she had a chance, a soft thumb brushed it away for her.

"Erin, you really don't have to talk about this. It's clearly too much. C'mon, let's stick to drinking wine, and I'll give you all the local gossip."

Erin's hand moved of its own accord and laid itself on Abby's wrist, squeezing it with appreciation. "Thanks."

Abby looked down momentarily, and Erin self-consciously pulled away. Seemingly unaffected, Abby shifted excitedly in her seat. "I have an idea. Why don't you come out with me tomorrow? I can give you the tour, help you familiarise yourself with the area." She clasped Erin's hand with both her own and gave it a little reassuring shake. "Maybe if you're feeling a bit more settled, that'll help with whatever comes next?"

Erin smiled. A day with Abby felt exactly what she needed. "You're on. Maybe it'll help." She caught sight of George in her periphery and instinctively extricated her hand from Abby's.

She looked sorry, but understanding crossed her face when she heard her brother's voice as he approached them.

"Ladies, you seem very cosy." He dropped into the armchair opposite, a smug look on his face.

Abby immediately went into defensive mode, an automatic state Erin didn't fail to notice she lapsed into whenever George was around. It was an alien reaction to Erin, having grown up a single child, although she witnessed it daily in her job. She had soon realised that siblings could be your biggest allies but also your biggest tormentors.

"Excuse me. Did you hear either of us invite you to join us?"

"Aw, don't be that way, big sis. I come in peace. Honest." He held up shovel-sized hands in acquiescence.

"Liar, you never come in peace. Not since the day you were born."

"Ouch. You see how she treats me, Erin?"

Erin laughed at the back-and-forth, amused as they played their well-rehearsed roles. It was strange how you could miss something you'd never had.

She decided to join in with the George bashing. "To be fair, we were doing okay here without you. And anyway, isn't it past your bedtime?"

Abby howled with laughter, and George opened his mouth once or twice but couldn't find a comeback. "Wow. When you actually talk, you really make it count."

Erin winked at him. "I think you should take the hint, George."

He unfolded himself from the chair, shaking his head. "Oh, don't you worry. I'm going." And with that he huffed out of the room.

"I think he fancies you."

Erin's head spun from the doorway back to Abby. "Don't be daft."

"I'm serious. He does this flick thing with his hair when he's nervous around a girl."

Erin shrugged her off. "He's a teenager, he fancies all girls."

"True. But at nineteen, he should really know how to talk to one already."

Erin smirked. "I'm sure with you as a mentor he'll be fine."

Abby squinted her eyes in a scowl but let the dig pass. Quiet descended while they finished their wine, watching as the barman added fresh logs and stoked the fire. It was late June but the nights still held a chill. A group of guests, dressed for night-time fishing, gravitated toward its flames for a last blast of heat to go with their order of port.

The warmth of the room, the wine, and the rich scent of Abby's perfume as she leant a little closer to Erin swept through her, making her eyelids feel suddenly heavy.

"I think I'm going to head to bed."

She caught the disappointment as it briefly crossed Abby's face, but it was quickly covered with a smile. "Sure. What time shall I see you in the morning?"

Erin glanced at the clock on the mantel—it was barely eleven. "Ten o'clock at the front door?"

Abby nodded, staying in her seat as Erin got up. "Perfect. I still get to be lazy and sleep in."

"Thanks, Abby." Erin hovered, sorry to leave, but knowing it was for the best. "And I'm not only talking about tomorrow." Before she could change her mind, she swooped and left a light kiss on Abby's cheek. "Goodnight."

She didn't look back. And wondered if Abby's cheeks were burning as hotly as her own.

~ ~ ~

They were. Abby's eyes skirted furtively around the room, wondering if anyone had noticed. She tipped the last of the wine into her glass, slipped off her pumps, and stretched out her legs, not quite reaching the other end of the sofa.

All around her guests continued with their evening. The group of men by the fire raucously and rapidly consumed a decanter of port between them. They joked and laughed, dispensing the banter from their system before the quiet enjoyment of night fishing.

A couple leant intimately across a small table together, fingers entwined, foreheads almost touching. They murmured words meant only for each other, eyes glassy with alcohol and the headiness of love.

Two older women sat curled up with books, happy in the ambient company of others, while engrossed in the world on their pages. Abby wondered at one of them, what was it that held her attention, as her face reacted animatedly to the words she read.

Meanwhile, Abby sat, content in her wine bubble as she committed the feel of Erin's lips on her cheek to memory, indelible and unique. *Seriously, what is it about this girl?*

She shook her head and quietly growled. She hated it when George was right.

CHAPTER 8

"Here, Eddie. Chuck us that box cutter."

Eddie obliged wordlessly, throwing the object slightly away from his colleague. He smirked when he failed to catch it. The crooked clock above his supervisor's office window seemed to tick slower tonight, and his brain was numb. Nine fifty p.m.— only ten minutes until his shift was over.

He waited for it.

"Oi, Eddie. You coming for a pint after?"

A few men nearby sniggered, and he avoided their eyes, merely shaking his head. He stacked the last box and climbed into his forklift.

He hated the back shift and the mindless morons who worked it.

"What? Your missus gonna put you across her knee if you're not home for bedtime?"

If only they knew.

He listened to them laughing at his expense and didn't imagine any of the jokes were new. It was as much part of the ritual as the punching in and out and hourly fag breaks. As he backed towards the loading dock, a parting "Weirdo fuck" reached his ears.

Bastards.

Well, let them have it. All their mockery stank of was unfulfilled lives and a pointless existence. He thought about what waited for him at home: His family. His daughter. The main reason for hating the back shift was it meant missing dinner and story time with her. At least with the night shift, she was already asleep and none the wiser to his absence.

With the lorry loaded, he signed the driver's sheet and headed for the rack of timecards.

~ ~ ~

He could hear the buzzing from outside the front door and panicked, wondering how long it had been going on. Through the front door, he threw his bag and jacket on the kitchen table as the speaker mounted on the kitchen wall buzzed again impatiently, three times, in quick succession.

As he reached the door, he could hear her tears and his heart sank. One. Two. Three bolts. He was in the room and she was throwing her arms around his neck.

"I...cut...my...self." His daughter choked each word out close to his ear, inconsolable in her pain and grief.

"I'm so sorry, peanut. I'm so sorry. Let me see." He tried to prise her off, but she only clung on to him tighter.

"Noooooo," she wailed. "You can't touch it. It hurts too much."

"Shush, shush." He attempted to sooth her, stroking her hair and back. "I won't touch it. I promise. But I need to see."

She clutched him tighter, but the sobs subsided slightly, and she leant back so he could see her face. It was red and blotched, and her disappointment at his absence was clearly visible. She held the hand with the offending finger behind her back, and he moved to take hold of it. But she shifted out of reach. "Promise again." Her voice was firm and asked for no argument.

He smiled. "Promise."

She drew the hand from behind her back slowly and offered it to him for inspection. A piece of toilet paper doubled as a makeshift plaster, blotting the blood.

"Can I take this off to take a closer look?" He pointed to the paper.

She clamped her eyes shut and held the finger closer. "Be careful."

And he was. He slowly peeled the paper away to reveal a tiny slice, no more than half a centimetre across the side of her forefinger. His heart slowed down in relief.

"Okay, Doctor Daddy says you're going to live." He looked up as she half opened one eye. The tears had subsided, but her cheeks were still streaked and damp. He wiped them. "But I'm going to get a second opinion."

He lifted her on to the bed and took her wrist gently, holding the offending finger up towards a shelf of teddies. Only her favourites lived there. "What does the gallery think? Will she live?" He waited a moment then began nodding his head as if hearing their reply. "They agree with Doctor Daddy, you're going to be fine."

She giggled, and he knew he was forgiven. "But we will need to perform minor plaster surgery before bed. Is that okay?"

As if on command, she lay on the bed and propped her hand on a pillow. Her favoured position for him to deal with the many cut fingers and scraped knees over the years. "Okay." She nodded with authority, ready for what came next, and closed her eyes again.

It only took a moment to retrieve the first-aid kit from the kitchen and administer a plaster displaying her favourite cartoon robot. "And we're done." He placed a light kiss on the tip of it.

She inspected his work from all angles and tried to bend the finger. "Can I still draw?"

He drew the covers over her and sought out her favourite bear. "The gallery says it might be a day or two, and I'd have to agree. I'm sure they'll entertain you in the meantime."

She huffed a little and shuffled down lower under the covers. "Why weren't you here?"

Not quite forgiven then.

"You know why, peanut. Daddy has to work sometimes. To buy you all those colouring pens and paper." He smoothed her fringe and pinched her nose. "But I promise I'm going nowhere until that finger is better, okay?"

She smiled and reached out her arms, and he lifted her up for a cuddle. "I love you, Daddy."

"I love you too, peanut."

He thought back to his shift. This was worth every miserable pint he missed down at the pub.

Fuck those guys.

CHAPTER 9

Erin leant against a pillar and closed her eyes as the sun broke through for a fleeting moment. The breeze still carried a chill and tickled her face with the scent of lavender. Rockeries around the front lawn were loaded with it, the purple vibrant against grey stone and evergreens.

She turned at the sound of voices and grinned as Abby appeared in the doorway. George loped down the front steps behind her, car keys in hand, and returned her grin. "Well, don't you look happy to see me?" He smirked Abby's way, and as was her habit, she swiped at his head, failing to reach it and clipping a shoulder instead.

"Shut up and drive, moron."

The plan was for George to drive them into town so both could enjoy a pint or two at The Rose once Abby had finished her grand tour. It would give Erin an opportunity to ask James Carter some questions with backup on hand. Abby knew him, so Erin wouldn't be that weird loner, showing up out of nowhere and asking questions at his door.

Abby hung her arm out of the open window as they meandered along country roads, her hand rolling up and down as it rode the waves of lukewarm air. Her tour had already begun with a history lesson on the castle. "It's been around since 1851 to be precise. It started as a smaller mansion until a rich Glasgow East India merchant decided to expand. It was him who wanted the French château look."

George chimed in. "He was our..."

"Shush, you," Abby chastised, flicking his leg with a sharp backhand. "I'm telling the flipping story."

Erin heard the expletives he muttered and laughed. "That got you told, George."

He puffed out an indignant breath. "As always."

Abby rolled her eyes. "You're so dramatic. Just drive and be quiet, okay?"

George saluted her and didn't say another word.

"Anyway," Abby continued, "where was I?"

As Abby chattered about the architect and other places in Scotland that he had designed, Erin couldn't help but smile at her enthusiasm for a place she clearly loved. She stole glances at her animated face and returned Abby's infectious grins when she looked back and caught her. "Well, it looks great still. It's obviously had a lot of love and attention. How did it end up in your family?"

"That's the bit George was about to spoil." She threw him a withering look which he did well to ignore. Instead, he mimed zipping his lips closed and gave her a wide-eyed "whatever" look.

Satisfied he was keeping schtum, Abby continued. "My dad's great-grandfather, Alexander. He was the merchant who bought it." She beamed over her shoulder at Erin's surprised look, clearly pleased with herself to have saved that little nugget of the story. "He had six daughters, and it's gradually been passed through the generations. Eventually, the family fortune dwindled, and so my dad had the idea of turning it into a hotel rather than some outsider buying it and doing the same."

"Smart." Erin nodded along, wondering at Abby's fortune to be able to recite one-hundred-and-sixty-odd years of her family's history. Erin barely knew anything more than what had occurred from the day she was born.

"And here we are." Abby clapped her hands together, then gave George a little shove. "Okay, you can talk now."

He manoeuvred into a spot at one end of the high street. "What, you mean now that we're here and you're about to ditch me?"

"Exactly. I win." She leant and planted a quick kiss on his cheek. "Later, little bro."

Erin gave his shoulder a squeeze as she climbed from the back seat. "Cheers, George. Maybe you'll get to win one day." She winked and slammed the door, missing his no doubt cheeky retort.

Abby stood surveying the street as Erin waved George off. She had already roamed part of it on her first trip to town, but Abby had insisted that seeing it was only half the story. She wanted to give her the gossip and recount the not-so-secret tales of the residents and shop owners.

"Okay, see the little flower shop over there?" Abby pointed to the colourfully pretty shop. "The woman who owns it used to be a teacher in Edinburgh."

Erin nodded. "I passed it yesterday. Why do I feel a story coming?"

"Well," Abby said, lowering her voice, "apparently she was pushed out of her post after an investigation into 'inappropriate relations' between her and a fifteen-year-old boy. Must be nine or ten years ago now. I hadn't long left school."

Erin's eyebrows rose. As a teacher herself, she knew how damaging that could be. "Was it true?"

"That's the sad part. It turned out the boy made it all up. I think a lot of the pupils had a thing for her, and he was bragging to his pals. Another teacher overheard and that was it. I guess the damage was done."

Erin shook her head in sorrow. "That sucks. Big time. I can't imagine what I'd do if it were me."

Abby's face showed the same remorse. "I know. Also, I'm convinced the woman she shares a house with now isn't there to make the rent cheaper. Which makes it even sadder."

Erin caught her meaning. "I wonder why she didn't tell them she was a lesbian."

"I suppose even such a short time ago it was still a big deal to be out and be a teacher." She shrugged. "I don't know. You're the teacher here. What do you think?"

Erin weighed it up. "I think I'd rather deal with that than be thought of as a paedophile. Although it's unfair she was even in the situation of having to choose. I mean, I don't exactly hide it from colleagues at my school, and I'm sure some of my pupils have guessed. But the goal is to keep personal separate from professional with the kids. Plus, you know how talkative I am about myself." She half smiled and nudged Abby with her shoulder.

"Oh yeah, you never shut up."

Abby linked her arm through Erin's. It was an affectionate gesture without assuming too much, and Erin didn't mind. They continued to slowly stroll the length of the street, stopping for coffee and sandwiches, and to pass the time of day with the locals Abby knew.

Abby surreptitiously pointed people out, telling her who they'd slept with, affairs, petty crimes, kids who'd gone AWOL, punches thrown outside the local on a Saturday night.

"I only know half the stuff I'm sure, what with being up at the castle the majority of the time. Old Mary in the post office is probably your go-to girl for the details."

Erin stopped, taking a seat on a bench next to a half whisky barrel overflowing with flowers. She studied the list of names opposite them, engraved on the village war memorial. "I've actually already spoken to Mary."

"Really? Did she know anything about your dad?" Abby plonked down next to her.

"No. She'd never heard of a Graeme Carter, but told me about another Carter family out by the river. Do you know the story? It was so tragic." Abby's shoulder pressed against hers, and the touch of warmth felt good as she stared down the street towards the post office. "Aye, I've heard about a hundred different versions of it though. That's the guy whose wife committed suicide. Postnatal depression, they said. Then he left town with the baby."

The differing version of events brought Erin's attention back to Abby. "That's not how Mary tells it. She says the baby died at a few months old, and that's why the wife killed herself?"

"Honestly, Erin. I doubt anybody really knows apart from the police and the family. Details are inevitably twisted or lost on the grapevine when it comes to these things, because everyone wants to believe they are the one that knows the truth. George would probably even tell you a different version from mine."

Erin stared into the middle distance, filing Abby's retelling away. She wondered what she would find with a simple internet search. "Yeah, you're right. Maybe we'll get more info up at the pub. Mary tells me the owner is also a Carter. I was hoping you'd be my friendly backup?"

Abby stood and took both Erin's hands to pull her to her feet. "What are we waiting for then? I'm gasping for a pint."

~ ~ ~

Erin carried two pints to Abby, who sat at a small round table in the corner of The Rose. She couldn't help slopping some over the sides and plonked them down unceremoniously, then shook beer from her fingers.

"The barman says James isn't around at the moment, but he'll be back later."

Abby took a swig of the cold local IPA. "Ah, that's good. And no worries, I don't mind hanging around for a while."

"Cool. Thanks." Erin followed suit, taking a long drink in an effort to steady her hands. She wasn't even sure she wanted James to return, if she was ready for more questions or answers. But sitting here with Abby was something she was happy to be doing, so she pushed thoughts of things that had not yet come to pass to the back of her mind. "Tell me, what would you be doing if you weren't sat here drinking beer with me?"

"Not a lot if I'm honest. Most folk I grew up with have moved away. Not many of the younger generation want to stick around a sleepy little town like this. Although they'll no doubt migrate back when they start having kids and need their parents to babysit."

"So, why do you stay?"

Abby's expression was wistful. "I guess I've never had an offer good enough to make me leave."

That made Erin wonder about exes, but by the time she'd taken another sip of her beer, the safe part of her brain told her to leave it alone. "What about the friends that have stayed? What does Hopetoun offer for fun?"

"Ah, well, you get the odd guest that's up for a laugh and a drink at the hotel." She tilted her pint in Erin's direction as proof. "And there's a friendly gang that come in here on a

Saturday night. Mixed in age, but all good banter. I'm not off on a Saturday often, but when I am I normally pop in. George tags along too these days, now he's legal. It's truly hilarious watching him crack on to girls."

Erin could imagine the stick Abby would give him. It probably didn't help the poor sod knowing his big sister was watching. "You mentioned hill-walking last night. Do you prefer to walk alone?"

Abby shrugged. "Most of the time these days. I used to go out a lot with my best friend, Hannah. Then she moved closer to Edinburgh for work, and now she's off travelling the world with a girl she met on the job a while ago. She's a police officer."

"Sounds amazing for her. But you don't sound impressed?"

Abby pulled a face that seemed torn between wanting to deny it and wanting to be truthful. "I'm happy for her, honestly. I just miss her, that's all."

"Has she been gone long?" Erin sipped away at her beer, realising how little she knew so far about Abby and how much she enjoyed listening to her talk.

"Almost nine months now. It was meant to only be for a few months, but I guess exploring the big wide world with the woman you love is more tempting than real life."

She looked a little lost then, away with her thoughts, and Erin wished she could make her feel better. "She'll be back before you know it." It was hollow sentiment, but Erin didn't think anything she could say would help.

"Maybe." Abby shrugged again, and it seemed to indicate the end of the conversation.

They were quiet a moment, allowing Erin to take in their surroundings. It was only mid-afternoon, so most of the tables were empty. Worn brickwork was exposed around sash windows, which, unlike the cottages, clearly benefitted from a regular clean. Numerous photos adorned one wall, varying in age. Local sports teams, signed pictures of famous folk who'd passed through, newspaper cuttings about events at the pub.

An old guy in a Harris Tweed flat cap sat at a high stool at one end of the bar, eyes glued to the horse racing on the TV. She watched him throw up a hand in disgust before violently scoring something out in his newspaper. A few lads played the bandit machine, knocking back pints and giving each other good-natured abuse.

It felt like a local. Well taken care of and comfortable. So different to the soulless bars taking over Glasgow, devoid of warmth with their contrived attempt at character.

A middle-aged guy, broad shouldered and compact, strode through the swinging front doors, greeting the lads as he passed. He lifted the polished mahogany at the end of the bar and slipped through behind it, nodding to the barman.

"Is that James?" She gestured his way for Abby's benefit.

"Oh yeah, that's him. Ex-rugby player and doesn't like you to forget it. Nice enough guy and a good laugh. He treats his regulars well."

Erin picked up their now-empty glasses, a surge of bravery taking hold, no doubt spurred on by the alcohol. "Fancy another round?"

Abby got up with her. "Sure. I'll come with you."

They headed towards the bar, and James made no secret of eyeing Erin up and down. "Afternoon, ladies. What can I get for you?"

Erin's mouth suddenly went dry. What if this guy had known her dad? What if he was related even? If she was right and the former teacher at the school was her dad, surely he would have drunk in the pub? And could it be random that he would happen to pick a small town with so many Carters as residents?

Abby cleared her throat and gave Erin a sideways glance, taking the empty glasses from her. "Hey, James. Two more pints of the IPA, please."

He returned her smile, but his gaze flitted back to Erin before turning his attention to pouring the pints. "What brings you in here this time of the day? And who's your friend?"

"Day off." She handed a ten pound note over and waited for her change before continuing. "This is Erin. She's staying up at the castle. She's also a Carter."

"Oh yeah?"

He aimed the question at Erin, and she took a sip of the beer before finding her voice. "Aye. I'm actually down here looking for someone. Mary up at the post office said you might be the guy to ask."

"Och, old Mary. Thinks she knows it all when she only ever knows half. Who are you looking for?"

"Graeme Carter." The name still felt so unfamiliar on her lips. "I think he was maybe a maths teacher at the secondary school."

She watched his eyebrows furrow in thought. "Graeme Carter, Graeme...oh, wait you mean Eddie?"

Erin was confused. "Eddie? No, his name was Graeme."

"Aye, aye. His first name was Graeme, but he went by Eddie. Think it was a middle name or something."

"Wait." Erin put a hand up, thinking a moment. She mentally scoured the notes in her book. A middle name for her dad was something she had never known. "Mary said there was an Eddie lived down towards the River Tweed, past the golf course. She said he lost his baby and wife and moved away? Is that the same guy?"

"Naw, see, I told you, Mary only ever has it half right. Eddie worked at the school, that's true. And him and Marie did have a wee one, must be eight or nine years ago."

Erin was trying to take it all in, that Graeme and Eddie might be the same person. She was cautious though, remembering Abby's earlier warning about stories in the town differing from one person to the next. "So what happened?"

"Well, Marie did take a one-way walk to the river, but nothing happened to the baby girl. There was a missing person's investigation when Marie disappeared. It was over a month or so before someone found her washed up on a bank a fair few miles from here. In bad shape, from what I hear. Barely recognisable."

Erin couldn't speak. The wheels were turning and running her in a direction she couldn't quite fathom. She could feel Abby tense next to her, staring her way, but she couldn't bring herself to meet her eyes. A hand found hers under the bar, and she gratefully returned its grip.

James continued, unaware of the impact his words were having. "There'd been storms and the river was running fast and high. Eddie said he'd come home from getting the messages to find the baby screaming with a cut on her face and Marie nowhere to be found. During the enquiry, the doctors agreed with him about the depression, said she'd been on some heavy medication for years. They thought maybe she had an accident with the baby and that's what made her snap. There was no note or proof it was suicide, so I think it was marked as death by misadventure."

Erin took a gulp of her pint mindlessly. The realisation she could have a half-sister somewhere had her emotions tumbling through her chest. She wondered if her mum had known.

Abby asked the question she was unable to get out. "So what happened to Eddie and the baby?"

James shrugged. "I think Eddie sent her off to live with an aunt up in the Highlands, said he couldn't take care of her alone. As far as I know he still lives out there alone, never comes to the town, quit his job at the school. I haven't seen him in years."

Erin's head snapped up at that. "Wait. He still lives here?"

Another customer came to the bar and held up his empty glass in James's direction. James put up a hand but started to edge towards him. "Couldn't tell you. Like I said, haven't seen him in years, so he could be long gone."

Erin found herself immobile with shock. It was Abby who thanked James before taking hold of Erin's elbow and steering her back towards their table. "Sit."

Erin did as instructed and knocked back half her pint in one. "Fuck."

"Fuck indeed."

"What if it's him, Abby? What if it's actually him? And did you hear that? I could have a sister. I don't think I'm ready for this. Actually, what the hell am I doing here?"

"Whoa, slow down, sweetheart. Take a breath. I'll be right back."

Erin stared into her pint, watching the bubbles fizz their way to the top. Could this really be happening? She felt drained at the prospect of trying to sort through the myriad of questions in her jumbled mess of a mind. But this was it, this was what she'd come looking for. Could she really turn her back on it now? She thought of her mum, of the strength she had instilled in Erin from the moment they had left her dad. One way or another, she knew she was in this now to the end. Whatever the end might be. After everything James had just said, there was no going back.

Abby reappeared. "Here." She handed Erin a whisky and a slip of paper. "Get that down you, then talk to me."

"What's this?" Erin opened the piece of paper. "His address? Fuck, fuck, fuck." She dropped the note and rocked back slightly on the stool, rubbing clammy hands along her thighs.

"Hey, calm down." Abby's tone was whispered and soothing. "It's only an address. It doesn't mean you have to go there, and there's no guarantee he's even living there anymore. James gave it to me along with the whisky. On the house. He said he's sorry to have laid everything out there the way he did. He didn't realise Eddie could be your dad."

"It's fine." It wasn't, it really wasn't, but Erin tucked the paper in her back pocket and knocked back the whisky. She sucked in her teeth as it scorched her throat. "Wow, that's terrible whisky."

Abby laughed. "You didn't really think he'd give us the good stuff for free?"

Erin couldn't find her own laugh, but she smiled as best she could at Abby. "I'm glad you're here."

"You want to get out of here? Go somewhere else to talk?" Abby was already pulling her phone from her pocket to call George. "I know a pretty cool castle we could go to, well stocked with plenty of awesome whisky."

Erin was already on her feet. "Let's go."

CHAPTER 10

George obviously sensed their mood and managed to last the whole ten-minute journey back to the castle without trying to wind Abby up.

Erin's head pounded with tension, and although she'd accepted Abby's offer to talk, right now what she needed was solace. She needed to process the information from James and think about her next step and what it might mean.

George headed into the castle ahead of them. "Catch you later."

"Thanks, George," they said in unison, and once he'd disappeared, Abby took Erin's hand.

"So, this is a big, old castle. I know a few places we can go hide out if you still want to talk? Or if you need some distraction."

Erin did her best to smile reassuringly. "I'd love that." She looked up towards her bedroom window. "But…"

Abby stepped back. "Ah, there's always a 'but'."

"Hey, don't take it that way, Abby. Having you with me today…well…thank you. I need a little time to myself, that's all. My head's pounding with information, and this has felt like a really long day already."

Abby looked off across the castle gardens. "You say that as if it's been all bad."

Erin closed the gap between them, linking their fingers. "It most definitely has not been all bad. I've loved spending time with you. You've really no idea what it's meant having you with me today."

It felt important to let Abby know how much easier the day had been because of her. Their connection was real. Whether it was temporary or something more, Erin didn't know. What she did know was it was overriding her usual reserve. For the first time that she could remember, she had the urge to take the lead and it didn't terrify her. She knew Abby was somehow meant to play a part in her journey, and she'd never been more grateful for a stranger's kindness.

Whether it was her newfound bravery in that moment of clarity or the effect of alcohol, Erin wasn't sure. She tucked a finger under Abby's chin and raised her head, connecting their lips lightly together. It took less than a second before Abby responded, pressing harder, and Erin felt a hot tingle travel through her body. She pulled back before she found herself adrift. She already felt the weightlessness of having stepped off a cliff, and her mind wasn't ready for any more.

"Can I come find you later?" Abby was smiling again, and despite everything the day had thrown at her so far, Erin couldn't help thinking it was the sweetest to date.

She returned the smile with sincerity. "Sure."

~ ~ ~

Safely ensconced in her room again, Erin pulled out the worn notebook from under her pillow and the stack of letters from her case. The dots were connecting in her head, but she needed to get them on paper, visualise the facts, and draw the literal lines.

She sat at the dressing table with the book open and lined up her cosmetics mechanically, giving herself a moment before running through the conversation with James.

Graeme Carter had been a teacher but went by the name Eddie with his pals. He might or might not have still been living just outside the village. His wife had committed suicide or something to that effect, but his daughter was still alive in the Highlands somewhere.

Could this really be her dad? And if it was, would he be pleased to see her? What was he like now? Would Erin even recognise him? So many questions, with only one way to find out: go and knock on his door.

It seemed so simple, but her still-clammy hands and thumping heart told her otherwise. She ran a finger along the worn edges of the letters, neatening the pile and retying the ribbon that held them together. They were notes sent to her for more than a decade, almost every Christmas and birthday, until they'd stopped at her eighteenth. She had found them unopened amongst her mum's possessions and had cried for days realising they'd been withheld from her. After opening one, it had only been once the tears subsided that she had been able to gather the strength to open the rest. The contents weren't particularly inspiring—questions about school, friends, what hobbies she enjoyed, if she played any sports.

There was no doubt in her mind that cutting him off had been the right decision at the time. She trusted her mum, knew she would do anything for her, and only meant to protect her. But there were three words at the end of every letter that choked her each time she read them.

I miss you.

No matter what had gone on back then, most of which she could only guess, those words cut her deep, because the truth was, she missed him too. Not the physical person, not the man—she didn't know him. It was the notion of having a father out there but being unable to say the word "dad".

That was what she missed. The feeling of being connected to the other half of her genetic makeup. The other side that had influenced the woman she had become despite only being present for those first few years. His actions in that time had majorly dictated the course of her life from then onwards. To know that he had wanted some sort of relationship with her...that he had wanted her in his life still and hadn't forgotten her...it left an open wound filled with anger at her mother that she couldn't exorcise. She would never be able to ask her mother about it now. Never be able to get her to explain. All it could do now was fester.

She thought of her mum. What would she have said right now? Would she have tried to stop her from finding out more? Warned her away? Who knew? Amelia had gone from being adamant that Erin didn't need her dad in her life to a cryptic note saying, "Maybe it's time", left with the bundle of letters.

Her eyes burned from staring at the page. For once, hiding away alone didn't feel like the solution. There were no more answers to be found in her book or the letters; she'd exhausted them. The answers were waiting for her out in the real world.

She shoved the book back under her pillow and placed the letters neatly in the drawer of her bedside table. After pacing a few moments, her reflection caught her eye, and she sat back down at the dressing table.

With her mind emptied of everything she'd learned that day about the Carters of the village, she allowed it to revisit the previous hour when she had left Abby in the castle car park. She closed her eyes and relived it, running her fingertips across her bottom lip and savouring the brief moment of intimacy she had shared with Abby.

Go find her, you fool. She's the best thing that's happened to you in probably forever.

She pushed away the misgivings and reservations that niggled her subconscious and left the room in search of Abby.

CHAPTER 11

"Hey, George. Have you seen Abby around anywhere?" Erin caught him between the kitchen and bar and figured he was the best place to start.

"Not since I brought you both back from town. My guess is she's either in her room or the tower."

That caught Erin's interest. "The tower?"

"Aye, she hides there sometimes. Not sure what she does up there though. She's the only one with a key, and I'm strictly forbidden for fear of physical assault."

Erin laughed. "Aw, are you afraid of your short-arse sister?"

"Hey. Mock me now, but she's got a killer punch that can deaden anyone's arm."

"It's okay, George, I won't tell her." She patted him on the shoulder condescendingly, and he rolled his eyes.

"Sure you won't. Anyway, our little living space is through the door marked 'private' before you hit the second set of stairs up to your room. Otherwise the tower is that way." He pointed to a wooden door, curved with the arch it led through. "Prepare yourself for about a hundred stairs."

"Thanks." She watched him head through to the bar and then looked between the stairs to the rooms and the tower door. It felt a bit weird to go to Abby's room uninvited. Besides, the tower was too intriguing not to investigate first.

George hadn't lied about the stairs. She stopped to catch her breath as they rounded past a small window, perfectly framing the sun as it began to set. The cornfields that gave the castle its name were shimmering golden in the waning rays, and Erin wished she had her camera.

"Who's there? George, if that's you, you little shit..."

Erin leant over the banister, looking up through the middle of the staircase. Abby's head hung over at the top, her hair falling over her shoulders, shining like the fields of sun-ripened wheat.

"It's only me. George said I might find you up here."

"Oh, hey, come on up."

Abby's head disappeared and Erin continued her climb, passing a fuzzy grey cat who seemed to purposefully give her a disinterested wide berth. Eventually, the stairs led her up through an open trapdoor until she stepped directly into the curved room of the tower.

It was a small space, but Abby had made the most of it. She was sunk into the corner of an overstuffed sofa, draped with a riot of colours from various throws and cushions. On the narrow table next to her, a stack of books leant precariously, almost hiding the library lamp behind them. A window, wider than the ones she'd passed on her climb, sat deep in the thick, grey brick. Erin looked between it and the sofa. Despite their earlier moment outside, she felt nervous. The tower felt more personal. It was Abby's space, and here Erin was strolling in uninvited.

"Are you going to stand there making the place all uncomfortable or are you going to sit down?" Abby tilted her head towards the other end of the sofa. A half smile warmed her face, and Erin felt a little better. Cushions covered the windowsill, and she crossed to it instead, peering out before taking a seat in its cosy depths.

"You don't mind me coming up here?" She swung her legs, her heels tapping lightly against the wall underneath.

Abby sipped from a delicate china teacup with pink flowers and gold trim. "I'll allow it this once." She smiled again and set the cup on top of the books. Erin braced herself, waiting for them to topple, but they stood firm. "But you mustn't tell George what you saw up here. I get too much satisfaction out of keeping him wondering."

Erin pressed a finger to her lips. "They're sealed."

Abby gestured in the direction of a small fridge, on which was perched a kettle and tray with all the makings of tea and coffee. "Fancy a cuppa?"

Erin shook her head. "I'm okay, thanks. Sorry, I didn't mean to intrude or anything. I guess I didn't know where else to go."

"You're not intruding. I'd have locked the trapdoor when I heard you coming if I didn't want you up here." She winked conspiratorially and extricated herself from the comfort of the sofa. "Besides, Angus wasn't really in the mood for talking."

"The cat?" Erin thought about the aloof creature who'd just ignored her on the stairs.

"The cat," Abby confirmed. "You prefer your coffee black, right?"

Erin pulled her legs up and crossed them, fully ensconcing herself in the small space. "Go on then. Thanks."

"So why did you need somewhere to go? Is there something wrong with your room?" Abby didn't speak directly to her, and Erin studied her back, wondering where to start or if she should start at all. It would be easy to shrug off and simply enjoy some idle chat over a cuppa instead. As if sensing her stare, Abby turned, leaning back against the wall next to the now boiling kettle.

Erin fiddled with a tartan button on one of the cushions. Trying to explain her feelings and fears out loud had never been something that came easily to her, or something she had even found necessary in the past. The inclination to talk about herself or her problems wasn't something Erin struggled with in the company of others. She was too used to living in her own head, and she mostly liked it there.

Over the years, it had been enough to have her mum there for advice and company. They'd been a team; they'd worked together. When she had let the odd person into her life, it was for fun, for the random laughs and adventures. She'd never made a significant enough connection with someone to have reached beyond small talk and banter.

But Abby stood before her now, asking her a question that she couldn't possibly know had the ability to open a hundred boxes in her head. Erin had the urge to open them. Wasn't that why she'd come looking for Abby? She wanted to share the contents with her.

She met Abby's gaze. "My room felt too big."

She watched Abby's eyebrows converge in a frown. "Okay, just this once, I'm going to need more words from you here." The frown softened. "Because I'm not sure what having a large hotel room is meant to be telling me?"

Erin scrubbed her face with her hands and offered a wry smile. "I can see your problem."

Abby crossed the room and handed her the coffee but didn't return to the sofa. Instead, she plonked a cushion in front of Erin and sat, elbows on knees, chin in hand, peering up at her. "C'mon, teach, tell me what's up?"

Erin laughed out loud then. "Okay, that's truly creepy. Never call me 'teach'."

Abby laughed with her, but as she did so, she took Erin's free hand and tugged her down to floor level with her, before tucking another cushion behind Erin's back.

Only inches separated them, but instead of claustrophobia, Erin felt sheltered and safe. Abby's hand rested on one of her knees, and for a moment that was all she could think about. Then Abby reached for Erin's cup and Erin watched as she took a sip, holding Erin's gaze over the top of it before passing it back and keeping her hand to herself again. Erin missed the hand.

She took a breath. "It also felt...lonely." There was no other word to describe it.

Abby didn't comment. She merely continued to study Erin, clearly waiting for more of the words she had requested.

Erin twisted the cup in its saucer, aligning two pink flowers so they sat evenly either side of the handle. "When I was a child and things got tough, I hid. I'd find the smallest space possible—cupboards, under beds, toy chests, boxes in the attic, whatever I could find. I'd stay there until my mum came to find me, to tell me it was all okay. I know that's where my nightmares stem from."

"Makes sense."

"Earlier, after we left the pub with all that information from James, I was on the verge of freaking out. The thought that my dad might be living down the road from here, that I might have a sister...I guess the reality of what I'd been searching for kicked in. Until now, it had only been an idea. You know? It was too much." She set her cup aside. "And I figured I was too old to be hiding in the wardrobe."

Abby's hand was back, this time taking Erin's. She didn't say anything, but it was enough reassurance for Erin to continue.

"I know my next step basically involves me going and knocking on this guy's door, and that scares the crap out of me."

"How can I help?"

"Hide me up here forever?" Erin was only half joking, but Abby laughed.

"If only life were that simple."

"You're telling me." She took Abby's hand in both of hers and traced a finger down her palm to the tip of her index finger. Abby's hand flinched and then it was gone. "Sorry. I..."

Abby cut her off. "I have an idea. I still have a couple of days' holiday left. Why don't we go do something tomorrow? Away from here. Maybe head up to the Pentlands or down towards Dumfries and Galloway forest?"

Erin extricated herself from between the wall and Abby. "You don't have to do that. There's probably a million other things you'd rather be spending your time doing."

Abby held up a hand and stood with her. "My options are dreaming about adventures, reading about them, or actually going on one with a real-live human. A human I happen to like a lot." She prodded Erin's arm. "You are real, aren't you?"

Erin chuckled. "Today, nothing seems real. But I'm almost definitely sure I am."

"So, it's a plan then. See you outside after breakfast?"

Erin took in Abby's lively face, the loose locks bouncing on her shoulders as she jigged on her tiptoes, waiting for Erin's answer. *There is no need to rush.*

"Say yes, Erin. I promise only fun."

Amused, Erin nodded. Abby was too hard to resist. "Sure. Why not."

"Yay." Abby clapped her hands together. "I'll sort the picnic."

Erin moved towards the trapdoor. Her spirits lifted and her worries briefly set aside at the thought of a day in the countryside with Abby. "I'll expect great things, chef."

Abby feigned seriousness. "I won't disappoint. Promise."

Erin began her descent through the trapdoor but popped her head back up as Abby flopped back down on to the sofa. "Thanks, Abby."

Abby waved her away. "I'll allow you to visit again. But remember..."

"Don't tell George what I've seen. I know."

~ ~ ~

Abby listened as Erin's footsteps faded in the stairwell and the echo of the bottom door closing drifted up. She threw her head back against the sofa and huffed out a breath. "Crap."

Her thoughts drifted back to a few hours before and their moment on the castle steps. Since then, she'd chastised herself for expecting anything more from Erin than friendship. It felt selfish and uncomfortable given everything she was going through. If Abby were in the same position, she'd be a mess. How could she expect Erin to decipher any possible feelings towards her from the riot that must be already going on in her head?

By her third cup of tea, she had been resolute. Leave it alone, be there for her as a friend, offer comfort and understanding, and be satisfied with that.

Then she thought of those lips on hers again. Added to the tingle that had crept through her as Erin's finger traced her palm and she knew she was in trouble.

"Crap."

Maybe she was worrying too much. Overanalysing and assuming Erin's state of mind or feelings towards her. Maybe all she needed was her comfort and understanding, nothing more.

Then why kiss me?

Although able to acknowledge that it was hardly a declaration of some simmering passion that Erin was unable to contain, it still felt much more than a thank you.

Tomorrow. Sleep on it, Abby. See what tomorrow brings.

She curled up and tucked a cushion under her head, staring out at the red-streaked sky. *You offered fun and distraction, that's all she's expecting.*

It was quickly becoming clear, however, that Abby would be willing to show her more. So, much more.

CHAPTER 12

Abby was right on time the next morning. Erin leant against her car and laughed as she bounded down the steps and practically skipped Erin's way.

"You sure you don't mind driving?" Abby handed her a picnic rucksack and well-worn walking boots to add to her own in the back of the car.

"I'm sure." Erin headed to the driver's door. "It'll feel like an adventure driving on roads I don't know."

"Calm down." Abby hopped in the passenger side. "It's Dumfries, not the Dalton Highway."

"The what?" Erin paused midway to fastening her seatbelt.

Abby seemed to squirm. "Err...it's a road in Alaska. Crazy long and dangerous, with barely a sign of life."

Erin's brow furrowed at the odd reference. "Random. Have you been?"

"Not exactly." Abby didn't look her way. Instead, she started tapping digits into the satnav.

"Read about it?" Erin wasn't sure why Abby was being so cagey, but she was curious to find out. She had visions of her on a grand expedition across Alaska, trussed up in polar gear, commanding a pack of huskies as they steered her sledge across—

Abby broke through her reverie. "Okay, okay." She threw up her hands dramatically and let them slap back down on her thighs. "I watch *Ice Road Truckers*. There. Now you know. Judge me all you want, but those folks have crazy skills. I find it oddly mesmerising." She threw Erin a look that almost challenged her to take the piss.

Erin thought of her brief vision and wasn't sure whether to be disappointed or laugh. "You should never admit that to anyone else." She held her face fixed for about three seconds before crumpling under Abby's miffed glare.

"I'm kidding. I'm kidding." Erin bumped her shoulder with a fist, then started the car. "Although I am going to tell George that's what you get up to in the tower."

"Ha." Abby seemed triumphant. "Nice try. He loves that show more than me."

"Dammit. Should've known." Erin eyed the satnav screen. "So where to?"

Abby looked out of her window up at the sky, as if needing final confirmation that it was in fact still drizzling. "Definitely south towards Dumfries and Galloway. There'll be no point climbing Tinto today with the rain. It'll spoil the view."

"All right, your shout. The forest it is."

On the road, Erin turned the radio up, happy in the comfortable quiet. She would flick her gaze towards Abby occasionally, smiling as she mouthed along to the music. Every now and then, Abby would catch her and return the smile, seemingly not feeling the need to talk either.

As they pulled off the main road, Abby lowered the music and gave directions towards a car park she knew and a walk that would take them to the small beaches of Loch Dee.

"You know the area well then?" Erin had driven the motorway through Dumfries and Galloway, en route to England, but had never ventured beyond it into the countryside.

"Aye, we used to come down here as kids. Ride our bikes, fly kites, and kayak on the lochs. Even when I was older, dad would drag me along to help entertain George."

They both leant against the car, changing into boots. "So, where are your parents anyway? You said they owned the castle, but I haven't seen them."

Abby shrugged on the picnic bag and tucked a blanket under her arm. "Ah, they're retired now, hiding out in a cottage in France. They have a manager, that's Ann who's normally guarding reception. Otherwise they trust me and George to make sure things are running as they should."

Erin took the blanket from her. "Here, let me at least carry that."

They set off at a steady pace, Abby leading the way. "Isn't that a lot of responsibility though? I'm not sure my mum would have trusted me with her business."

"I guess. It's been just over two years now and I miss having them around. But most of the staff have been there for yonks and know what they're doing. They're practically part of the family. I only really have to worry about the kitchen. Oh, and keeping George out of trouble."

Erin laughed. "In a town the size of Hopetoun, I don't imagine that's hard."

"You'd be surprised. Do you know how many pretty girls come through our doors?"

Erin raised her eyebrows. "Do you manage to keep yourself out of trouble as well?"

Abby only smirked. "I'm not sure I know you well enough for that kind of conversation."

The track narrowed as the trees became thicker. Light drizzle still fell and they both pulled their hoods up. Scots pines surrounded them, tall and proud, laying a carpet of needles that muffled their heavy boots. Moss grew thick on every boulder, and Erin inhaled the damp air deeply, feeling more at ease than she had done in months. It was becoming a theme in Abby's presence.

Abby glanced back over her shoulder. "My favourite time to come here is early spring. The snowdrops completely blanket the ground, sometimes fighting with actual snow for space if we've had a late winter. It's pretty special to see. And later, once they disappear, you get bluebells."

"Sounds beautiful," Erin agreed. "I'd love to see that one day."

The trees eventually gave way to a small clearing trimmed with a stretch of sandy beach. Abby dropped the bag on a flat patch of grass backed by the thick trunk of a beech tree. "Is this okay with you?"

The water stretched before them, lapping over pebbles, and occasionally broken by jumping fish. Erin could see patches of blue sky and took down her hood now the drizzle had passed. "Perfect." She unrolled the blanket and laid it alongside the bag as Abby unpacked a flask.

"I realised after you left last night there was a question I never asked you."

Erin frowned. "I seem to remember plenty of questions."

"Ah, but this one is kind of important."

"Okay." Erin drew the word out, worried what Abby was angling at.

"Is there a boyfriend or girlfriend back wherever you've come from?"

Erin laughed then, relieved it wasn't more difficult. "No."

Abby stopped unpacking. "Seriously? All I'm getting is a 'no'? You are hard work. You know that, right?"

It was Erin's turn to smirk. "I thought we didn't know each other well enough for this kind of conversation?"

"I changed my mind."

Erin watched her unscrew the flask and produce two cups from the bag. "Is that tea?"

Abby began to pour. "Aye, I already added milk, I hope that's okay?"

"Fine with me. I'll not be drinking it."

"What? You don't like tea? What kind of person doesn't drink tea?" Abby stopped mid-pour in surprise.

"The kind of person that doesn't have a girlfriend and has never had a boyfriend."

Abby went back to pouring, and Erin didn't miss her smile. "Okay, I'll forgive the tea thing now I have a full answer to that. Here." She passed Erin a bottle of water instead.

They stretched out their legs, backs against the trunk, and took in the view. A small fishing tour boat chugged by, the captain raising a hand in greeting to them. They waved back, and Erin wondered at the kind of life it would be, working on a boat all day.

Clouds gave way to more blue skies and their coats were discarded with them.

"Hungry?" Abby pulled the bag towards her and took out a couple of salad boxes. "Chicken and halloumi, with couscous, tomato, cashew nuts, and pineapple."

"Thanks." Erin tucked in eagerly. "This is delicious. Beats a dried-up supermarket sandwich any day."

The pleasure clearly showed on Abby's face. "Glad you approve. You know, I don't remember the last time I ate someone else's food. Unless you count George's—midnight cheese toasties."

"You never let anyone cook for you?" By "anyone", it was Erin's turn to angle back towards exes. She might live in sleepy Hopetoun, but she couldn't believe someone as amazing as Abby had always been single.

"Hmm…one person. Not including my mum. But her cooking sucked."

She looked thoughtful, and Erin almost left it alone. Almost. "An ex?" There, she'd put it out there; she was officially being nosey and inviting the same questions back. She didn't care. She had nothing much of interest to tell. No tales of unrequited love or heartbreak. She'd never made it that far with anyone.

Abby put her lunch down, turning towards her. "My, aren't you suddenly full of words when the questions are reversed?" She tugged off her shoes and rolled up the hem of her jeans and then wordlessly took her cup of tea to the water's edge.

Erin followed suit and joined her. "Is it me not getting an answer this time?"

She watched as Abby sipped her tea, staring across the water over her cup. "Yes, it was an ex. And actually, her cooking didn't suck. It was awesome. That's why she ditched me and small-town Scotland. To go find fame and fortune in the bright kitchens of London."

"Ah. I'm sorry, Abby."

"No big deal." She tipped the dregs of tea away and threw the plastic cup back towards the blanket. "Let's skim stones."

With their heads down searching for thin, rounded stones, Erin felt like a kid again. Then the competition started as they took it in turns and counted each other's bounces. "Seven!" She beamed Abby's way, hands thrown up in victory. "You'll never beat that."

"Just you wait." Abby held up a particularly perfect stone that she'd obviously been saving. "This is the winner." She took aim, and as her arm came back, Erin nudged her shoulder and watched as the stone went into the water with a single splash.

"You cheat!"

Abby kicked sand her way, and Erin jumped to escape it, but Abby didn't let up. She gave chase across the narrow beach, kicking as she went until Erin had nowhere to go. She caught her breath against a tree. "All right, all right. I give up. I'll forfeit my seven and we can go back to being even on five."

Abby shook her head. "Not good enough."

She closed in, and Erin held her hands up in surrender. "Okay, you win. I'll forfeit my five as well. Please no more sand." She shook a leg to dislodge a clump from her trouser cuff.

Abby grinned and pinned Erin between her and the tree. "What's my prize?"

She didn't wait for an answer. Her lips were on Erin's. The shock only lasted a moment before Erin gave in to them. They were cold but sweet from the pineapple and stole Erin's breath away. She felt chilled fingers slide around the base of her spine, inch under her T-shirt, and pull her in tighter as the kiss became more urgent. The blood rushed from Erin's head and any semblance of control slipped as Abby's tongue found hers before it drew back and traced a light path across Erin's bottom lip.

Then her lips were cold again as Abby stepped away. With a grin, she kicked a last spray of sand at Erin before turning and heading back towards the water.

Erin stood dazed, watching her retreating back. The ache of desire was fully settled in her stomach, and she had to take some breaths to calm the thunder in her chest. The chaste kiss of thank you the day before didn't compare. In those few, precious seconds connected to Abby, she'd felt something unknown to her before. Even without knowing what it was, she knew she wanted more.

"Hey, wait." She jogged up to Abby, catching her hand. She linked their fingers and Abby kept walking, not looking her way. "Do I get a prize if I beat your five again?"

Abby's smile was mischievous as she looped Erin's arm across her shoulders and tucked herself in close under it. "I'm sure I can come up with something."

CHAPTER 13

As Erin pulled up to the castle, she heard Abby let out a long sigh. "You okay?"

Abby turned her way. "Aye. Back to reality, I guess."

"I didn't realise we'd been anywhere else?" Erin shifted in her seat to face Abby.

Abby was quiet a moment. She looked back up towards the castle. "I suppose most people would think living in a castle wasn't real life. But the shine soon wears off."

"You don't like it here?" Erin had been quick to assume living and working in such an amazing place would be wonderful.

"No, no. I do. I love it. It's my home. I suppose I'm a little frustrated, that's all. Twenty-seven, still essentially living at home and working for my parents. I always thought of myself as more independent than that. More ambitious."

Erin nodded, understanding where she was coming from. "Do you have an idea of what your life might be if you left? What's the dream?"

"That's my problem. I genuinely have no idea." She reached for Erin's hand. "All I know is today it felt as if I was in another world, and I didn't want to leave it. I haven't enjoyed a day off so much in a long time."

Erin leant in before her brain could engage and think too much about it. She cupped Abby's cheek and placed the lightest of kisses at the edge of her mouth before pressing her lips to Abby's with a strength she hoped conveyed that she felt the same. She pulled away slowly, but their lips remained only millimetres apart. "It doesn't have to end."

A slow grin spread over Abby's face, then she was on the move. Out of the car, Erin followed her progress until she was at Erin's door, throwing it open and pulling her out. "Tower. Now."

Erin allowed herself to be tugged through the front door, past a puzzled-looking Ann on reception. They stopped abruptly at the tower door, Abby fumbling with impatience to get it unlocked.

George appeared from the bar. "Oh, hey, Abby, I need…"

"Not now, George." Abby cut him off. The door was open and Erin could only shrug his way before being yanked through it. They started half running up the tower steps, taking some two at a time, breathless and laughing. As they approached the trapdoor, Abby stopped unexpectedly and Erin bundled into her. Then she was against the stone wall, immobilised by the urgency of Abby's lips. Abby's hands raked through her hair, tugging lightly when they reached the nape of her neck. Erin groaned into her mouth, which only intensified the pressure, and her lips and her hips, her everything, melded into Erin. Both their hands roamed clumsily. Erin wanted to touch every bit of her all at once. Her foot slipped and they both stumbled sideways on the stairs, tearing their lips apart. Thankfully, it was only for a moment. Erin never wanted them to leave again.

Abby began backing them up the last few steps slowly, her hands on the small of Erin's back, guiding her, until they were in the room and Abby was pulling Erin on top of her on the sofa.

Erin sat, straddling her, their gaze of intent never breaking as Abby pulled Erin's T-shirt over her head before removing her own. The world slowed around Erin as she reached out to trace fingertips along the edge of Abby's bra line until they made their way up to the straps and slowly pulled them down.

Abby reached back to unclasp Erin's bra. Once removed, Abby immediately found a nipple and closed her mouth over it gently. Erin twitched at the light contact; it wasn't enough. She was immediately impatient and wound Abby's curls around her fingers to pull her in tighter. She felt the moan of pleasure sweep through Abby and transfer itself to her. Abby's lips held the force of magnets, inexplicably pulled to every sensitive part of Erin's body. Abby reversed their position, tipping Erin on to her back while her lips continued their exploration—across her stomach, her sides, until they reached the waistband of her jeans. One button, two, three, and her jeans were sliding off, quickly followed by her underwear. Abby moved up on to her knees, between Erin's legs, and Erin took a moment to appreciate the beautiful woman before her. Then she reached out both arms, encouraging Abby back down towards her.

"Erin."

Hearing her name said with such urgency and hunger sent an intense rush of heat through her entire being. Then she was back in Abby's arms again, feverish with need. As she worked her lips over every inch of skin, her fingertips traced a slow and gentle path until they found the place she ached to touch. Abby was quick to take control and apply her own pressure, her body telling Erin exactly what she wanted from her.

Erin gave everything to the moment. Every need that passed Abby's lips, she acquiesced with pleasure. Until she heard the delicious sound of Abby's breath hitch, as her body momentarily became rigid, before it dissolved on top of her into a satiated essence of warmth and breathlessness.

~ ~ ~

Abby had tucked herself into the crook of Erin's shoulder, her arm thrown across her waist, one leg hooked around Erin's. They lay tangled amongst the throws on the sofa, clothes, and pillows scattered the floor, and the only light came from the full moon, sitting high and proud, filling the small space with its luminescent glow.

Abby's breathing was slow and deep as she slept. It soothed Erin, and she focused on its rhythm as her own eyelids began to droop. She had no idea what time it was and she didn't care. No one beyond these walls knew where she was and no one cared. Apart from the beautiful woman in her arms.

For once, that thought didn't unsettle her. She glanced down at Abby's still face, the hint of a smile flickered at the corner of her mouth, and Erin wondered what she was dreaming about. Secretly, she hoped she was there, in Abby's dreams. She lay a light patter of kisses amongst Abby's curls, and with the sweet scent of them fixed in her mind, finally gave in to sleep.

CHAPTER 14

"Erin," Abby whispered gently in her ear. She traced a finger along her cheek, let it dance lightly over her nose and lips, but still she didn't stir. "Erin," she tried again a little louder.

Erin squirmed and let out a satisfied moan as she stretched her limbs, eyes still closed, before pulling Abby close to her again. "Don't tell me we have to get up. I never want to get up."

Abby kissed her lips, her cheeks, her shoulder, her neck. Each one elicited a murmur of pleasure. "Okay, we don't have to get up. We never have to get up." She let out a yelp of surprise as Erin rolled her in one swift movement so Abby lay the length of her. Erin's arms circled around her waist, and their legs instinctively entwined.

"Phew." Erin grinned and kissed her, her eyes now open. "Although..."

"You're hungry." Abby laughed at the surprised look. "I took a wild guess because I'm starving."

"You did indeed read my mind. What would you suggest? Can anything be done that doesn't require you to leave this spot?"

Abby chuckled. "I wish. I'm afraid you might have to let me loose for a few minutes at least."

"Ah, you have a plan then?"

"I do. What if I sneak down to the kitchen and see what I can conjure? I'm pretty sure it's well after hours. There shouldn't be anyone around."

She watched Erin look off to the distance in contemplation and couldn't resist the lure of her exposed neck. She bent to nibble at it, trailing her lips lower. "If you keep doing that, I'm not going to be able to agree to your plan."

Abby placed a final kiss behind her ear before finding willpower she didn't realise she possessed and pushing herself up off Erin.

Erin tried to pull her back, "No. I don't agree. Come back."

"It'll be worth it. Promise." Abby was on her feet, yanking on her jeans and a hoodie she found draped on a chair by the trapdoor. "Ten minutes." She blew Erin a kiss and started her descent before her resolve gave way.

The castle was still, save for its usual creaks and moans as it settled down for the night. She could place them all: The wood contracting as the fires died and the rooms chilled. The ticking of the antique grandfather clock as it echoed through the reception. The underlying hum of refrigerators, doing their job in the bar. And the night-watchman, Raymond, snoring gently from behind the reception desk.

Barefoot, she made no sound as she crossed the lobby towards the dining room and kitchen beyond it. She shielded her eyes as the kitchen lit up and immediately hit a few switches again so only one light shone above the centre island. She already had an idea of what to get and headed straight for the fridge.

If wasn't long before she was back at the trapdoor, panting. The contents of the board in her hand wobbled precariously, and Erin got to her feet to help. Wrapped in a throw, she took the tray from her as Abby climbed the last two steps.

"Wow, this looks amazing. I feel as if I didn't know what I wanted, but you still somehow read my mind. Again."

Abby smiled. "You're sure this is okay?"

She flicked on a tall lamp in the corner and pulled the ottoman over in front of the sofa so Erin could put the tray down. Abby had made up a large cheese board—brie, stilton, strong cheddar, and oatcakes. She'd added grapes, sliced apple, and melon, along with a homemade caramelised onion chutney. She'd finished off the tray with a bottle of Prosecco.

"It's perfect."

Erin did the honours opening the Prosecco, and Abby realised she'd forgotten glasses. "Teacups it is." She laughed. "And here was me trying to be all sophisticated." She passed them over for filling.

Erin winked at her. "You can get more in a teacup."

They huddled close on the sofa, tucking into the various combinations the board offered. Abby felt the bubbles go quickly to her head, and by the looks of Erin's pink cheeks, she wasn't the only one feeling it.

"I'm glad the day didn't end in the car park." She leant into Erin and kissed her bare shoulder.

Erin turned and planted a melon-flavoured kiss on her lips. "Me too. I think I've managed to forget reality as well, being up here with you."

They were both quiet for a while, savouring the bubbles with each delicious bite. It was Erin who broke the silence, surprising Abby.

"You never did tell me. Did your ex find her fame and fortune?"

Abby wasn't sure why Erin had brought it up. She was here with Erin in the present, but given how their day had ended, she couldn't blame her for being curious. Abby nodded, taking a sip from her cup. "Laura. That was her name. And yes, unfortunately, she did. Have you ever watched *MasterChef*?"

"I've seen the odd episode. And why 'unfortunately'?" Erin sank back into the sofa and Abby joined her.

She turned towards Erin, pulling her legs underneath her. "Well, basically, Laura won the professionals' version a couple of years ago. Now she runs her own kitchen in some swanky place in London and from what I hear is on her way to a Michelin Star. It's unfortunate because it makes me hate her a little bit more."

Erin's eyebrows furrowed. "Hate's a strong word. Did it really end that badly?"

Abby sighed, realising she was probably giving off more of a bitter vibe than she actually felt. "No, it really didn't. In fact, although it's taken me a while, I realised she wasn't my forever girl. I guess it still stings a little bit though every time I see her on TV or mentioned in a magazine. If I'm honest, it's mostly jealousy."

"Why? Is that something you'd think about doing? Leave all this to run a kitchen in the name of accolades and TV appearances? I mean, from where I'm sitting, you're doing more than okay here."

Abby was thoughtful for a moment, swirling a pinkie through the bubbles. She stopped and sucked the liquid from her fingertip. "Not even a little bit, which makes it all the more strange." She laughed. "I love this castle and I love cooking here. I know what I said earlier, but actually, bottom line, that's the truth. I guess I'm not the first person ditched because of someone else's ambition. Still sucks though."

"Yeah, it does." Erin nodded towards Abby's cup. "Top up?"

Abby held it out as Erin poured the last of the bottle into their cups. "Have you thought much about going to see your dad? I mean, of course you have. I was wondering earlier if you'd decided whether to check out that address."

She watched Erin take a gulp before setting her cup aside. "I think I'm going to give myself a few days. Think a little on it, explore the area a bit more, and try to clear my head some. I've decided I'll definitely check the address out, but it won't hurt to wait a few more days."

"You seem sure." Abby didn't want to force her to talk about it but figured it was worth a try while she seemed in the mood.

"I am. It doesn't have to be tomorrow, but I'm doing it. I keep telling myself there's no rush. So even if I only drive by the place before turning around and coming back again, I know I'll eventually need to at least take that first step. It's time."

Abby put down her own cup and pulled Erin to her. They burrowed back down on the sofa, and Abby dragged another throw from the floor and draped it over them both. This time she tucked Erin under her arm and hugged her close. "I think you're very brave."

Erin didn't say anything; she simply squeezed Abby back in response.

"And if you want my help, you only have to ask." She kissed the top of Erin's head and stroked her fingers softly through her hair. "You don't have to feel alone."

CHAPTER 15

"Why don't you come to the pub with me tonight?" Abby stretched the length of the sofa and lay on her side, head in hand. She watched Erin dress, savouring every last moment of her nakedness.

"Is that a good idea?"

"Sure. Why not? It'll give you a chance to meet a few other folk." Abby pouted as Erin pulled her T-shirt over her head. "Tell me again why you're getting dressed?"

Erin laughed and crossed to the sofa. "I'm pretty sure it's all your fault we have to." She leant down for a kiss. "And okay. You're on for tonight."

Abby sat up then, excited. "Do you do karaoke?" She cracked up laughing at the look of dread that flooded Erin's face. "Silly me, of course you don't."

Erin stood and picked up Abby's hoodie from the floor. "On second thoughts..."

"I'm kidding, I'm kidding." Abby tugged at her leg and pulled her back down. "I think tonight is a quiz. We might have a chance with your well-schooled brain."

"Unless it involves numbers, I think you're going to be disappointed."

"Impossible." Abby grasped the back of Erin's head and showed her just how impossible it would be to disappoint her.

"Mm...okay, that's your last." Erin draped the hoodie over Abby's head, separating their lips. "Get dressed."

Abby shook it off. "You had enough of me already?" She was only half joking.

The smile Erin offered immediately put her at ease. "Of course not. There's a few things I wanted to check out today, that's all. And you've agreed to cover the lunch shift. That's why we're in this predicament in the first place, remember?"

Abby sighed. George had called up a little earlier to tell her that Michael was stuck behind an accident on one of the back roads. He was her assistant chef and covered her days off. He promised he'd be in before the dinner shift, but that hadn't made up for her disappointment at losing time with Erin.

"Aye, I suppose I should sort myself out before George starts hollering again." She put on jeans and her bra, but Erin caught her in her arms before a T-shirt could make it over her head.

"Okay, one more." Erin chuckled mischievously, and Abby made the most of it. "You know I wouldn't be going anywhere if you didn't have to work." She kept her arms fixed firmly around Abby.

"I know. Bloody Michael." She pushed her bottom lip out.

"Abby," George's voice echoed impatiently from the stairwell.

She sighed and planted one last peck on Erin. "I guess that's our cue."

~ ~ ~

The library hadn't been as fruitful as Erin had hoped. The assistant had helped her log on to a computer, and a quick search had brought up countless stories surrounding Marie Carter's disappearance. They were brief, however, lacking in any real details, and hadn't made it further than the regional press. A few days after Marie had been found, there was a short recap repeated on a number of online news sites. It had the addition of a quote from the police ruling her death an accident.

She had thought about asking to use Abby's computer, given the lack of decent phone signal, but she knew it would more than likely lead to further questions, and at this stage, she needed some time back in her own head. Besides, she didn't want to mar their time together with constant morbid reminders of Erin's past. Abby had said she would be there if Erin needed to talk, and she knew Abby's offer of help had been genuine. But there were some things she needed to figure out on her own first.

Her curiosity around Marie Carter's death had been piqued as soon as the pieces that potentially linked Marie to her father had come together. But the news stories held no more information than what she had heard in the village. All it did was give her a general timeline and tell what seemed to be the truth of the tale. There was no mention of a child, only that Marie's family were devastated and asked to be left in peace to mourn. One additional thing it did tell her, however, was where Marie Carter had been buried.

That was where Erin found herself, crossing the dampened grass of the local church cemetery. She took her time, reading names and dates, mostly old and worn. The notes of sentiment and various quotes embellished on the headstones choked her up for a moment, but she swallowed back the tears and strode on. It was the first time she'd been in these surroundings since laying her mother to rest, and she was sure it would do her no good to linger.

The older part of the grounds, close to the church, led her on to a winding path. She followed it and crossed a minor road, passing through a gate into the newer field of stones. They seemed more extravagant and still held their shine.

Flowers and trinkets adorned the majority, and a few she saw with teddy bears and framed pictures of children set the tears flowing freely again. She swiped impatiently at them and took a few breaths, looking to the sky for strength and calm.

A few rows in, she found what she was looking for.

HERE LIES MARIE CARTER. BELOVED WIFE, CARING MOTHER, CHERISHED DAUGHTER.

A lone jar filled with wildflowers sat at its base. She moved it a little, and the date it uncovered stopped her cold for a second. She almost lost her grip on the jar but caught it at the last moment.

Thirtieth of June.

Today.

It had been eight years to the day since a thirty-seven-year-old Marie had tragically taken her own life. It seemed surreal that Erin would be standing there, questioning the mysterious fate of this woman, on the day of her death. Erin brushed her fingers over the numbers, and they trailed back eventually to the freshly picked flowers.

Their presence properly registered for the first time, and she recoiled as if they had scorched her.

Who had laid the flowers? Her family? Friends? Or had he been here?

She turned in a rapid circle, investigating every inch of the field, but it appeared she was alone. She glanced back at the date and flowers. A chill ran through her. She wasn't sure if it was a sense of foreboding or a little excitement at the possibility of being closer to him than she had been in twenty years?

Was it possible? Had her father been standing on that same spot that very day?

CHAPTER 16

Eddie squinted across the field but couldn't make out any recognisable features of the tall stranger standing over his wife's grave. He stayed pressed against the tree trunk, sure she couldn't see him.

It was the only time of year he ventured into the village. He'd circumnavigate it and approach from the narrow road that came from the north, avoiding the drive through the high street and any chance of recognition.

Curiosity tugged at him, but he remained still. Marie had little family and certainly none local that he knew of. He had never in the eight years since her death met anyone he recognised in the graveyard. So, who was this woman?

He watched her stand and turn, glancing around as if she were aware of his gaze. He knew she couldn't see him, but he waited a few moments before peering out again.

Eddie searched his memory for friends or family of Marie's who would fit the description, but all he had to go on was her height and slim build and short, dark hair. She was vaguely familiar, but his memory failed, and without a face, a name wouldn't come.

Maybe a distant relative passing through? An old colleague? The date they had chosen to visit couldn't help but make him suspicious. It seemed relevant that they would appear on the anniversary of her death, that they were someone close to her.

His stomach clenched with a rush of nerves. After all this time, he had thought he was done with folk poking their irritating noses into his business. Asking incessant questions and giving him "that look", like it was his fault. Why hadn't he seen how unhappy she was? Hadn't she given you any idea she was thinking about it? Were you sure there wasn't a note? Maybe he could have stopped it?

There had been no stopping it. Marie had done it to herself, and she was the only one to blame. As far as he was concerned, she had committed suicide.

He felt no guilt over her death, but every year he laid the flowers. For their daughter. For the fact she would never know her mother. She was the only good thing to come out of their marriage, and it seemed only right to at least acknowledge the gift Marie had left him.

He watched the woman lay a hand on the headstone before bowing her head and turning back towards the road. He circled the tree to stay out of her line of vision and waited until she had rounded the corner and disappeared back into the churchyard.

His car was parked only a few yards away, but the presence of someone else nagged at him as he walked back to it. Who was she? He knew it was likely to play on his mind for some time. Should he follow her? He took a step in the direction of the church but caught himself. What if there were other folks around? He couldn't risk being seen. He hadn't changed much over the years and knew there was a chance of being recognised. Once upon a time, he had been a well-known part of the community.

Since Marie's death, his cottage in the country had remained its own place of solitude. His mail was redirected to a post office box in the city, and he took no other deliveries there. Cars passed en route to elsewhere, but he was sure they never gave his home any more than a cursory glance.

It occurred to him then that she hadn't brought flowers. Wouldn't someone visiting a lost relative normally bring a token of their esteem? That line of thinking only confused him further.

He took a few more steps and angled himself to peer around the hedged border of the church, searching for one more glimpse of her.

She was gone.

~ ~ ~

The feeling of being watched didn't leave Erin until she rounded the church and stepped out on to the village green. She was grateful to climb into her car and reached for a tissue in the glovebox.

To have ended up at Marie's graveside on the anniversary of her death had been enough of a coincidence, but she also felt an inexplicable twinge of fear that she couldn't shake off.

It mingled with sorrow for a little girl left without a mum. Since James's revelations, the question of who and where she was vied for equal attention in her search. Seeing Marie's grave had brought back all-too-fresh memories and compounded the need to find out more about her daughter. Erin's half-sister.

What was her name? Did she know Erin existed? How was she coping growing up without a mum? Erin couldn't imagine the prospect, given her own close relationship with Amelia.

She started the engine and turned the heat up high in an attempt to counter the chill that seemed to have seeped through to her bones. She closed her eyes and took a few breaths, willing her heart rate to settle.

Why was she so rattled? Was it the thought of possibly having come so close to randomly bumping into her dad?

There were a number of other people who could have visited Marie's grave that day. Erin knew nothing of her extended family or friends, and to assume it was her dad was maybe her own self-involvement.

But what if it was him? She gripped the wheel and mentally shook herself.

You're looking for shadows that aren't there, Erin.

Or was she? The feeling that she wasn't alone in the graveyard wouldn't shift. Maybe it wasn't her dad, but someone had been there. She knew that for sure. Who it was, was another question for her notebook.

CHAPTER 17

Abby tapped on Erin's door eagerly. She couldn't help but be excited about their night ahead. Okay, it might only be a few drinks in the local, but it was her local, and she was looking forward to introducing Erin to the few pals she still had left in Hopetoun.

Erin called out, "Just a second."

When the door opened, Abby was pleasantly surprised to find her still wrapped in a towel, fresh from the shower. "You don't strike me as a running-late kind of person." She couldn't help her eyes from roaming.

Erin didn't laugh and mumbled at the floor. "Sorry. I won't be long."

She turned back into the room, but Abby caught her by the wrist and spun her back. "Hey, what's wrong?" It was only then that she noticed Erin's red-rimmed eyes and strained expression.

"Nothing. Really. I fell asleep, that's all. I won't be long."

She extricated herself from Abby and headed back to the bathroom. Abby wasn't buying it. She hadn't exactly expected Erin to throw herself into Abby's arms at the sight of her, but some acknowledgement of the previous night and their morning together would have been welcome.

She closed the door and followed Erin to the bathroom where she leaned against the doorframe. "There is something wrong."

Erin gave her hair a last swipe with a towel and sighed. She perched on the edge of the bath and threw up her hands. "I'm a bit stressed, that's all."

Abby crossed her arms, waiting for more. Erin merely looked at her, so she took the lead. "Might it have something to do with whatever you were checking out in town today?"

Erin's expression said it all, and then she was crying.

Abby knelt before her, circling her arms around Erin's shoulders. She felt a little resistance before Erin gave in to it and buried her face in Abby's shoulder. She held on tight and let the tears flow. Eventually, they subsided a little and Abby pulled away, removing Erin's hands from her face gently.

Erin kept hold of one and offered a tender kiss to her palm. "Thank you. I needed that."

Abby reached for a tissue and offered it to her with a reassuring smile. "Tell me what happened?"

"I went to Marie Carter's grave."

It came out with a regrettable sigh. It was the last thing Abby had expected to hear. "Wow." She sat back on her heels. "What on earth made you do that?"

Erin shrugged and shook her head at her own lack of reason. "I'm not really sure what made me go. Morbid curiosity? I did a little research into her death and found out she was buried here, and, I don't know. Something made me want to pay my respects."

"And did you find anything?" Abby moved between her legs, rubbing the goose pimples from Erin's arms.

"I found out today is the anniversary of her death." Erin sniffed and wiped the final few tears from her cheeks.

"Okay, that's a weird coincidence, but I'm still not sure what's got you all worked up?" She slid her hands around Erin's waist and tugged her closer.

"There were flowers there. Fresh flowers. And I had this sense that someone was watching me, or had maybe only recently left them..."

She twirled one of Abby's curls around her finger absently and seemed to stare at it without seeing. Abby knew she was back at the graveside, reliving the moment, and it didn't take much to realise what those flowers might mean. "And you thought it might have been your dad," Abby finished for her. Now she fully understood. "Oh, Erin. No wonder you're so freaked out."

Erin's attention came back to her with a small smile. "You don't think I'm overreacting?"

"No, of course not." Abby squeezed her in reassurance. "Here's you being all sensible, taking your time, making sure you're ready. When today you could have stumbled upon him unaware. And the coincidence with the date. You've every right to feel weird right now. Even I feel a little weird."

Erin held her gaze and reached for her cheek. She let her thumb trail a path along her jawline before pressing it to Abby's lips. Abby obliged it with a kiss.

"Thank you." Erin followed her thumb with tentative lips.

"What for?" Abby whispered, wishing the lips had never left.

"For being here. For being you. I was going around in circles, and it was driving me nuts."

"Why didn't you come find me?" Whatever the previous night had been and whatever this night might be, every moment with her was becoming precious. The desire to be someone to Erin grew with every touch.

Erin smiled sheepishly. "I don't know. I knew you were busy with work, and I kept thinking how unromantic it was dumping this emotional crap on you. Especially after last night."

At the mention of the night before, Abby couldn't help but grin. "Always come and find me. Okay?"

"Okay." Erin kissed her again, this time without restraint, and Abby was suddenly very conscious that all that separated her from Erin's naked body was a towel. She pulled away reluctantly and stood up, tugging Erin to her feet.

"I'm going to go wait for you in the bar while you get ready."

Erin held on to her hands. "It's okay, you can wait up here."

Abby was already shaking her head. "Nope. That involves you being naked at some point. If nakedness happens, chances are we're never getting out of here tonight."

She was pleased when Erin laughed. It was genuine, and she wore a little relief on her face. A few more laughs and some drinks, and Abby was hopeful Erin could put the day behind her and enjoy herself. The late-night hours still held plenty of possibility for them.

"Well, if you're sure." Erin reached towards the knot holding the towel in place.

But Abby was already backing away in the direction of the door, hand over her eyes. "Seriously, you need to stop that. And hurry. We still need to think of our quiz team name."

CHAPTER 18

The quiz was in full swing and, as predicted, their team was woeful. Fifth place didn't sound too bad, but when there were only seven teams, it was difficult to make excuses. The obvious way to go was to blame George.

"Seriously, George. How can you mix up Ukraine with Sweden?" Erin laid into him again.

"What? At least I tried. Both their flags are yellow and blue."

"What is it with pub quizzes and Eurovision questions?" Abby chimed in. "I can't believe you watch that crap, George."

"Says the girl who watches *Ice Road Truckers*." Erin threw her a cheeky look over the top of her pint.

Abby gave her a good-natured shove. "Oi. Don't knock it till you've tried it."

"Exactly," George agreed. "And I watch *Eurovision* for this reason." He swept an arm around the pub. "There's always *Eurovision* questions in a pub quiz."

Abby wasn't letting up. "Yet you managed to get all four questions wrong."

"Hey, apart from that last one, I wasn't even alive for the others."

"It's called history, ya nugget."

Erin threw him a bone. "To be fair, *Eurovision* history is a rather niche subgenre."

"Still." Abby pointed towards the bar. "You're clearly the weakest link. Get those beers in."

George huffed but did as instructed. Erin knew it was only because it gave him an excuse to talk to the new bar girl.

She'd caught him eyeing her up earlier in the evening, and they'd watched with barely concealed amusement as he'd attempted to engage her in some chat.

Wow, that boy was bad at flirting. "You think he'd be better with girls with you for a role model."

Abby chuckled. "I'm not sure what you're getting at, but I don't think I like what you're insinuating."

Erin held up a hand innocently. "Not a thing. From what George has said, it seems more fact than insinuation."

Abby threw daggers at his back and Erin laughed.

"Calm down. I'm kidding. I'm only seeing what I can get you to admit."

"I'm saying nothing." Abby finished the last of her pint and eyed Erin mischievously.

"You certainly didn't waste any time with me."

"Listen." Abby leant closer and laid a hand on Erin's thigh, letting it drift a little higher as she talked. "I know when I see something I like. What's wrong with that? Besides, are you complaining?" She moved so her lips were almost touching Erin's—almost.

Erin gave in and kissed them before a cough snapped her back to the room.

"Enough of that, thank you very much." George was back with the drinks and nodded in the direction of Abby's hand. Erin squirmed a little, but Abby kept her hand where it was a few seconds longer in rebellion.

"Any luck?" Erin asked, nodding towards the bar girl.

"I got a name." He was clearly pleased with himself. "Emily."

Abby slow-clapped condescendingly. "Great. Another week and you might manage to find out if she's single."

He glared at her before his attention was caught by something over her shoulder. "Aw shit."

Erin and Abby turned simultaneously to follow his now-mortified stare. A petite girl, barely five foot, with masses of red hair, was scanning the room. It didn't take her long to settle on George.

Abby chuckled. "It's your lucky night."

"Who's that?" Erin whispered, even though the pub was rowdy, feeling part of a secret.

"That's the one girl George doesn't want but can't get rid of."

"Fuck," he groaned.

Erin turned to eye her again. She was pretty enough and looked to be a year or two older than George. She watched as the girl elbowed her way through the crowds, a determined scowl on her face.

"Please, please. Help me," George pleaded with them, shifting into panic mode. Erin tried not to laugh at his discomfiture. "I've tried everything. Talked to her, replied to every one of her hundred texts, even told her friends. She won't take no for an answer."

Erin figured she owed him one. Despite the annoying teenage boy in him, George had been nothing but good to her since her arrival. She slid her pint across the table and switched seats, sitting next to George. She quickly moved her chair closer and looped an arm through his as the girl reached their table.

Her face hardened on Erin for a moment before she addressed George. "Hey."

"Oh hey, Stacy." He attempted surprise and failed miserably. Erin watched Abby cover her mouth to stifle a laugh and bit her own lip to do the same.

"Who's your friend?" Her stare was back on Erin as she emphasised the word "friend".

Erin didn't give him a chance to answer. She reached out a hand. "Hey, I'm Erin. George's girlfriend. Nice to meet you."

Stacy's eyes shifted between the two of them and her mouth dropped open a little. "Girlfriend." She said it more to herself. "But you're so..."

"Yeah, I know. But age is only a number." Erin cut her off mid-insult. "It's quite new, but I'll not be letting this one go anytime soon." She feigned adoring eyes and gazed up at George, before squeezing his arm and planting a peck on his cheek.

Abby full on laughed at that.

"What's so funny?" Stacy's attention was on Abby.

"Nothing." Abby straightened her face. "I'm so happy my little brother has found someone."

The obvious relief on George's part when Abby played along was almost too much for Erin. She pressed her face into his arm to muffle a laugh.

"So, are you here with anyone?" George asked casually.

Stacy eyed them all suspiciously. "I guess not."

She spun on a heel, and the elbows came out again as she headed for the door.

Abby and Erin collapsed into laughter while George downed half his pint. "Erin, I think I love you." He hugged her so tight she squealed.

"Hey, hands off, chancer." Abby swatted at him. "That was a one-time-only deal. You'd better go find yourself someone for real."

He stood, straightening his shoulders and shirt, his gaze fixed firmly on Emily behind the bar. "I'm on it. I'm asking Emily for her number."

"Good luck," they called after him in unison before succumbing to the laughter once again.

CHAPTER 19

Eddie knocked back another shot. It was cheap whisky, not the kind meant for savouring, but it would do the job.

The ancient mobile phone he kept solely for work buzzed again on the table.

Fuck 'em.

He couldn't remember the last time he'd called in sick, and it was unlikely there'd be any major repercussions. He was a solid worker; one blemish wouldn't hurt.

He rubbed a thumb across the framed picture in his hand. Marie smiled out at him, almost glowing with the sunlight beaming behind her, a gurgling Thea in her arms. It was the last photo he'd taken of them both, before her smart mouth had tormented him one too many times.

This was the only day of the year he allowed himself to remember. To wonder at the choice he'd made that day and mourn his loss. Thea's loss. He felt the usual anger bubble up, not at his actions, but at the disappointment he always felt when he thought about the life they could have had. If only she'd lived up to be everything she'd promised to be on their wedding day. Why'd she have to push him? Needle and question him every step of the way?

She had accused him of being the one guilty of shortcomings.

Why do we never go anywhere? Why don't you want to take me out? Why can't we buy nicer things? Why are you always so serious?

She'd never understood or appreciated that his only goal had been to take care of them. To keep them safe, and make sure his family stayed together. He had worked so hard in the beginning, determined not to repeat the same mistakes a second time around.

Fool me once, shame on you; fool me twice, shame on me.

Shame on him? No. He didn't accept that.

It was them who had lied. Had tricked and misled him from day one, turning out no better than each other. There were rules to marriage, expectations to be lived up to, and he had held up his end of their vows. How many times had he warned her? Given her chance after chance to change, to learn. To show him some fucking respect. But that smart-arsed mouth of hers just didn't know when to shut up. In the end, she had left him no other choice.

His mind drifted back to his visit to Marie's graveside and the dark figure he had glimpsed. There was something about the way she'd held herself and her walk as she had stridden from the yard. He thought the whisky might loosen his memory and pull something out, but it still gnawed at him, sitting frustratingly out of reach of recognition.

Who was she?

He laid the photo aside, face down, and downed the last dregs of scathing liquid. It had done nothing to dampen the feeling of foreboding that had permeated his every thought since his near encounter that day.

The clock ticked on, drawing the day to an end. Tomorrow would come, and with it all the memories of Marie would be placed back where they belonged.

Outside of this day, nothing more existed than his world with his tiny, beautiful daughter.

She was worth his sacrifice.

~ ~ ~

"So, your place or mine?" They had reached the top step of the main entrance, but Erin was stopped from entering by Abby's hand on her wrist. A taxi had dropped them off, and George had already scuttled inside, eyes glued to his phone, waiting for Emily to reply to his eager text.

"A little presumptive, aren't we?" But Erin found herself unable to protest as Abby hooked her fingers into Erin's jeans pockets and drew her in closer.

"Nope. I merely read your mind." The glow from the lanterns touched her cheeks, and Erin couldn't resist placing a light kiss on one of them.

"Damn. I forget you have that skill."

"It's a curse most of the time." Abby's eyes shone with alcohol and mischief.

"What about this time?" Erin stepped in a little, turning Abby and pressing her against the door. She laid the full length of her body against Abby's and glided her hands under the back of her T-shirt.

"Definitely not. Right now, it's most certainly a pleasure," she murmured in Erin's ear. It was enough to spread a weakness through Erin's legs that she had found Abby could elicit with the merest touch.

"Well played."

"I try. So..." Abby trailed her lips from Erin's ear to her neck.

Erin pressed harder, and the grand door began to open with their weight. She slinked through the gap, trailing her fingers across Abby's stomach as she went.

"My place."

CHAPTER 20

It had been hard to leave Abby that morning. They'd both awakened with the sunrise and explored each other once more until exhaustion. Abby had eventually drifted back to sleep while Erin lay thinking. Ensconced in Abby's arms, she had felt safe, hidden from the darkness, and not alone. It was a new feeling. One she had wanted to hold on to as long as possible because who knew what the day ahead might bring, how it might change things.

Now, as the cottage came into view, Erin's heartbeat quickened and a pit of dread occupied her stomach. The outside of the building was worn but not untidy. Built of sturdy-looking granite, paint peeled from the window frames and moss grew in patches on the roof. But the grass was cut and the hedges trimmed, sweet williams and pansies in a cornucopia of colours lined the gravel path leading to the front door. A few outbuildings that hinted at the croft's former glory dotted the space behind and to one side of the cottage. They looked to be nothing more than a dumping ground for retired tools and machinery, a decrepit shadow looming over the humble home.

She wound down the car window, filling it with a wet, grassy scent, and she inhaled deeply in an effort to dampen her nerves. The faint sound of the river rushing nearby was only interrupted by bird chatter and the idling of her car engine.

Anyone looking out of a front window would have seen her approaching. It was too late to turn back. Or was it? *C'mon, c'mon. You can do this. Don't lose your bottle now. All you have to do is knock on the door and take it from there.*

She switched off the engine and sat a minute, staring at the green wooden door until her eyes blurred. If anyone was home, they gave her no indication she'd been spotted. A little relief seeped in. Maybe no one was home. Maybe this was a good first step, like the one she'd talked about with Abby. She could come back another day for the next one.

A shadow passed a window to the right of the door and her heart leapt. *I can't do this.*

Her fingers trembled as she fumbled with the keys, attempting to start the car again. Then the front door opened and they stilled.

She knew instantly.

It was her dad.

Thick waves of dark hair to match her own were pushed back on his head with a pair of glasses. He stood maybe an inch or two taller than her and carried some extra weight around his waist. Compared to the photo she had, his chin now sagged a little and the moustache was missing. His shoulders hunched slightly in the way hers did when she was nervous and wanted to retreat. She wondered if he was nervous. Did he know who she was?

Of course he didn't. She was merely some weirdo stranger currently sitting in his driveway staring at him. He raised a hand slowly in greeting, but she could see his forehead crease in confusion.

Get out of the car, Erin. No going back now.

She extricated herself from the car, her gaze never leaving him. She watched as he pulled the front door to and came to the top of the porch steps.

"Can I help you?"

She didn't reply, simply concentrated on putting one foot in front of the other along the path. She was halfway when he stepped back and the frown disappeared. His eyes wide open.

"Erin?"

That stopped her. Her dad had just said her name. Tears blurred her vision, and she could only nod. Then he was coming down the steps and towards her, opening his arms.

"Is that really you?"

She didn't fight it. She allowed herself to be enveloped in his arms, tucked her face into his shoulder, and couldn't help but inhale. Pears soap. It was a scent she'd carried with her but never known why she'd loved it so much.

He let go and held her at arm's length. "I don't...I can't... What are you doing here? How did you find me?"

The last question held a hint of accusation, and Erin stepped away from him, attempting to compose herself. The memories that haunted her in the night flooded to the forefront of her mind, and she tried to remind herself why she hadn't seen him in all these years.

"Sorry about that." The hug now felt strangely inappropriate to her. "It's been a while, you know. I guess we both have lots of questions."

He glanced back at the house, and it suddenly occurred to her that he might not be alone. Did he have a new wife? Other kids? And here she was barging in on them uninvited.

"Aye, I guess we do." He put a little more distance between them and looked around, as if wondering what to do next.

She tried to save them both from the awkwardness that quickly filled the space between them. "Listen, I shouldn't have turned up like this. It's okay. I'm not expecting anything. I wasn't even sure you were my dad."

At the word "dad", his attention returned to her and she watched as his eyes crinkled a little at the small smile he offered. "It's been a long time since I've heard you say that."

"Aye, well, for good reason, I'm told." She never imagined a reunion would be easy. Or if she was honest, she had never intended to make it easy on him. Her trust in her mum was absolute; there was no talking the past away, only finding out if anything had changed that meant a future was possible.

To his credit, he didn't try to deny anything, merely nodded. "Are you staying local? What are your plans?"

"I'm up at the castle. No fixed plans. I wasn't sure what I'd find down here."

He seemed in two minds about something and scratched at his head irritably and then pulled off his glasses before pushing them back up into the same position. "Erin, believe me when I say I'm so happy to see you. In fact, I can't quite believe you're in front of me right now. But..."

She knew it. There was a cosy little family inside, and he didn't want her trampling all over it with his past. She started back towards the car. "It's okay. You don't need to explain. I shouldn't have come."

"No. No." He quickly followed and grabbed her forearm as she reached for the car door. "Erin, you misunderstand."

She yanked her arm from his grasp, his touch suddenly repelling her. "It's fine. I don't need excuses."

"Will you listen?" His voice raised an octave in frustration, and she flinched.

He seemed to notice, and his features immediately softened. "Sorry. It's only that...well, I'm kicking myself here because I have to go to work. That's all. I was going to ask if you could come back tomorrow. So we can talk properly."

"Oh." She paused and looked at him. He looked genuinely sorry to be turning her away. "Yeah. Tomorrow's fine. What time?"

"Is evening okay? Give me a chance to give the house a tidy."

"You don't have to do that." An untidy house didn't concern her. What did was a whole other night and day stretching before her with nothing to fill it but anxiety and uncertainty.

"I know. But still...you leave a man living alone long enough, things slip. I was only ever good in the garden."

So, there was no one else. She wasn't sure if she was relieved or sorry for him.

"All right. I'll come after dinner."

He nodded again and smiled his thanks, then reached out and squeezed her shoulder lightly. "It really is so good to see you, Erin."

It was her turn to nod. The lump lodged in her throat was rising. She got back in the car without another word. She held her hands in front of her, took a breath, and willed them to stop shaking before she started the car and turned it back towards the lane. Her eyes never left the rear-view mirror, watching as her dad stood with his hand in the air in good-bye until she was out of sight.

CHAPTER 21

The castle came into view, and relief swept through Erin. It was quickly becoming her sanctuary, and the thought of Abby increased her eagerness to be back in its warmth.

She needed to calm down first though. The pulse of blood in her ears told her she was moments away from freaking out, and she figured she should probably be on her own for that.

She merely nodded at Ann on reception and took the stairs two at a time, practically running along the corridor to her room. She slammed the door behind her and fell back against it, where she tore off her bag and coat, which followed each other in quick succession across the room.

Calm down, Erin. You're safe. You're okay.

She paced to the nightstand and picked up her book and put it down again. Then to the bathroom. She splashed cold water on her face and pressed her fingertips tight into her eyes, so when she opened them it was only blackness and stars for a moment. Then her face appeared, staring at her from the mirror. She moved close, studying every freckle and blemish. She concentrated on them until her breathing steadied and the hands gripping the sink became still and her feet felt grounded.

"That was my dad," she whispered to the empty room. "Fuck. I don't think I'm ready for this." The words seemed to echo and wrap themselves around her, squeezing her chest. She scrubbed her face dry, bringing colour back to her pale cheeks.

"Abby." She turned and headed for the door. It was an unfamiliar feeling, the need she felt to see Abby's face in that moment, to touch her. But she had said she would be there, had told Erin to always find her, and Erin believed her.

She found herself running towards the stairs again, leaping the last four into the reception and almost landing on George.

"Whoa there, what's your rush?" He caught her by the arms and kept them both upright.

"Sorry, George." She tried a smile for his benefit. "I'm looking for Abby. Is she around?"

He shifted from one foot to the other and glanced towards the lounge. "Um, yeah. She's a little busy though. I can tell her you were looking for her."

"No, that's okay. Where is she? It'll only take a second." Erin had thought she was still off work and didn't want to interrupt, but she knew merely the sight of her would go some ways to calming her down.

"I don't mind. She said not to disturb her." He looked anywhere but at Erin, and she got the feeling this was him attempting to lie.

What he was trying to cover, she couldn't tell. Was this Abby using her little brother to give her the brush-off? It didn't seem right, but if it was, she wasn't getting away with it that easy. "George." She reached up to grip his chin, forcing his attention to her. "Where is she?"

His shoulders sagged and his face said he felt like the shittiest brother ever. "She's in the lounge. Erin, wait..."

But Erin was already heading for the lounge. She surveyed it from the doorway and recognised Abby's blonde curls in a second. What she didn't recognise though was the perfectly polished girl with auburn hair sitting close to her on the sofa.

George appeared at her shoulder and whispered by her ear. "It's not how it looks, Erin. That's Laura. She showed up out of the blue earlier. Abby couldn't exactly..."

Erin wasn't listening any more. Her focus was on the familiar way Laura's hand lay on Abby's arm and the smile that went with it. *Pull away, Abby. Please pull away.*

She didn't.

Instead, she looked up and caught Erin watching them. Then she pulled away. Abby made to get up, all the time lightly shaking her head and holding Erin's gaze. Erin watched as the hand of the other girl caught Abby's before following Abby's stare. She looked between them both quizzically, and Erin watched her lips move.

"Who's that?"

Exactly. Who was Erin? Or more importantly, who was she to Abby?

A guest. That was all she was. Someone passing through, useful for killing some time with. No more of a permanent fixture in Abby's life than Erin had ever been in anyone's. She had been foolish to consider anything else.

In her rush to leave, Erin almost bundled George over again. "Get out of my way, George." She shoved him in the chest and couldn't miss the hurt look as she pushed past him, but she didn't care.

She was out of the front door before she remembered her car keys were in her room. "Fuck." It was too late to go back. She stalked across the lawn, smacking the water in the fountain as she passed, determined not to look towards the lounge windows. A path she'd noticed from her breakfast table called to her. She climbed with it as it cut through the trees, narrow and quiet underfoot, eventually opening into the field above the castle.

The field was muddy and unenticing, so instead she followed the grassy verge, stamping out her anger on the soft turf until her legs ached and she needed a rest. The drystone wall looked safe enough, and she hopped up on to it as heavy breaths panted along behind her.

"Shit, you're fast."

"What are you doing here, George? Did Abby send you?"

"No. She doesn't know where you are. I just wanted to see if you were all right." He made to climb on to the wall next to her, but she held up a hand.

"I'm okay, George. You can go back. I want to be on my own."

He ignored her and sat down anyway. "Tough."

She picked at some moss and threw it at him. "Fine. But I hope you're not expecting me to talk."

He folded his hands in his lap and stared out at the view across the rooftop of the castle. Erin followed his gaze. Beyond it the hills rolled for miles, sprinkled with wind turbines and sheep. The lines of the river and railway cut through them, linking the villages that would otherwise be lost in the vast landscape.

"You only have to talk if you want to."

"Well, I don't want to."

"Fine."

"Fine."

To his credit, he stayed quiet, although Erin knew it was probably killing him. She also admitted that having him there wasn't the worst thing in the world. Her initial burst of anger had subsided, and for once it was the wide-open space and the company that had done it.

"So that's Laura." It was more a statement than a question.

George turned her way and nodded. "The one and only."

He didn't seem particularly happy about it either. "You're not a fan?"

Erin secretly hoped he wasn't, as unreasonable as that might be. "She's all right, I guess. But she broke Abby's heart. So, I'm not exactly thrilled to have her here."

"Why is she here?" Erin tried not to sound too interested, but she guessed after Abby's PDA in the pub, George had figured out there was more than friendship happening between her and his sister.

"I've no idea. She showed up after lunch looking for Abby, and they'd not long sat down when you got back to the castle."

"Hmm...you don't think? I mean, is she here as a friend? Like passing through. Or do you think there's more to it?"

He half-smiled her way. "You really like her a lot, don't you?"

She smacked his arm good-naturedly. "Shut up."

"Erin, I have no idea why she's here. All I'll say is, if you really do care for Abby as much as I think you do, then you need to give her some credit and have a little faith. Laura is her ex. She broke Abby's heart, and now she's sitting in our lounge. There's unfinished business, but I'm sure it's no more than that."

"Maybe." The image of Laura's hand on Abby's arm filled her vision, and it was all she could do to fight back the tears.

History. It was always getting the better of her. Despite the wonderful few days they'd enjoyed together, how could Erin ever expect that to be enough of a reason for Abby to turn Laura away?

It had never been enough in the past. She recalled all the times she was the shiny new girl, at school, at work, in the local bars of the places they moved to. Interesting for five minutes before folk got bored of her reticence and went back to their tried-and-tested circle of relationships. Eventually, she'd learnt it was better not to bother. She was as happy on her own as she was in company, so why let herself in for unnecessary heartache? She'd had plenty of that.

Erin rubbed moss between her fingers, watched it crumble and stain the tips. "In my life, George, I've been given very few reasons to have faith." She hopped down from the wall and patted his knee. "It's okay though. I'm a big girl, and I've done all right so far on my own. You and Abby don't owe me anything."

He didn't move to follow as she wandered away back towards the path. She turned and called back to him, "Thanks anyway, George. I'm sorry I took it out on you."

CHAPTER 22

Eddie scooped potato smiley faces from the baking tray and added them to the plate with fish fingers and baked beans. Thea's favourite. He normally insisted on vegetables of some variety, but this was easy to make, caused minimal mess, and he didn't have much time before Erin was due to arrive.

Erin. He still couldn't get over the fact she was here. Had been standing in front of him the day before. His mind had done circles all through his shift at the factory and long into the night. How had she found him? Why was she here? What did she want? What did she know?

He placed the plate on a tray with a glass of milk and some chocolate-chip shortbread from his work and headed down the stairs.

As he unbolted the door, he could hear Thea singing to herself, a Disney tune that couldn't help but get stuck in his head every time he heard it. She was hidden behind the easel but jumped out excitedly as he entered. "Hey, Daddy, what's for din-dins?"

He held the tray out for inspection before putting it on the toy chest and pulling up a chair for her.

"Yay, my favourite." She clapped her hands and did a little twirl before hopping into the chair and stuffing a smiley face in her mouth.

It was toddler food, but she loved it, and he couldn't deny her what she loved. "Slow down there, peanut, or you'll choke."

She gulped at the milk, leaving a crescent moon on her cheeks before it was wiped away with a sleeve. "Napkin." He was stern, and she stopped mid-chew to apologise.

"Sorry, Daddy."

He sat at the end of the bed while she ate, wondering how to explain she would have to be on her own for the night. It wasn't unusual; she had an early bedtime and sometimes he worked. But he was also going to need her to be quiet and not call on him for anything.

He thought of Erin again. Did Amelia know she was here? Does she know about Thea? He knew some of the various rumours that had circulated around the village after Marie's unfortunate departure, but none ever came close to the truth. Erin couldn't possibly know.

"Finished!" Thea jumped up, napkin in hand, and she scrubbed it across her face. "Can we play a game now, Daddy?"

He shook his head and hated how her face fell. "I have an adult coming to visit soon, and we know what that means?"

She sat back in her chair with a huff. "I have to be quiet," she recited gloomily.

He moved to kneel in front of her. "Good girl. Because what happens if the other adults know that you're here?"

She crossed her arms, understanding but still not happy about it. "They'll take me away from you."

"That's right." He took her gently by the shoulders. "And why is that bad?"

She poked out a bottom lip. "Because the upstairs is dangerous for children. And they'll take me to the upstairs."

"Exactly. So missing out on one game isn't the worst thing that could happen. Is it?"

She was still smarting, but fear had won out, as it always did. "No. I want to stay here with you, Daddy. I don't want to go upstairs." She looped her arms around his neck, and he hugged her tight.

"That's not going to happen, my little pea. Not while you've got me to look after you."

She climbed into his lap and rested her head on his chest. "Who is it, Daddy? Who do you have to hide me from?"

He sighed. He was going to have both his girls in the same house, yet they wouldn't be together. For now.

"Someone from a long time ago. Maybe one day you can meet her."

Her head looked up in surprise. "But I thought all the adults wanted to hurt me. Won't she take me away?"

He stroked her head and reassured. "That's what I'm going to find out. But I hope not."

"Do I still get a story?" Her voice was quiet but hopeful.

"Of course you do. Then we'll get you tucked up for the night."

"Am I allowed to use Tinkerbell?"

He glanced to the bedside and the button that sounded a buzzer upstairs if she needed him. "Not tonight." He reached to the end of the bed and plucked a stuffed elephant from a row of her favourites. "But Jasper here has been given strict instructions to take care of you."

She giggled. "Daddy, Jasper isn't real. I'm not five anymore, you know."

Yes, he knew. She was growing up too fast, and her curiosity was growing with it. Every film, every book, even when he thought he had vetted them sufficiently, still brought up questions he hadn't anticipated. About the upstairs. About the adults.

She was eight now. And sharp with it. He was going to have to be more careful and creative.

"Silly me. You're big enough now to take care of yourself, aren't you?"

"Yip." She still hugged Jasper to her chest.

"So, no Tinkerbell. And you get an extra story. Deal?"

"Deal." She hopped up and headed for her bookshelf. "I'll be good, Daddy."

CHAPTER 23

Erin lay on her bed, studying the intricate cornicing on the ceiling, counting leaves and swirls. It was almost time to head to her dad's, and she was attempting to stay calm, taking a few moments to try and clear her mind. To think of nothing.

It wasn't working.

A knock at the door made her jump. It could be only one of two people, and she was pretty sure George wasn't in a hurry to see her again.

She considered ignoring it but knew that was childish. Plus, it was one more thing to play on her mind, and that she could do without. She still took her time answering, with the small hope Abby would assume she wasn't there and go away.

It didn't work.

"Hey." Abby's greeting was tentative, and the look of sorrow on her face immediately began to melt Erin's resolve. But it didn't completely.

"Hey."

"Can I come in?"

Bad idea. Erin heard the desperation in Abby's voice, but she had enough going on right now. Her emotional capacity was already brimming to full. She stepped into the hallway and pulled the door to behind her. "I'm busy."

"How did it go with Eddie? Is he your dad?"

"Don't, Abby." That was the last thing she wanted to talk about with her.

Abby nodded slowly in understanding. "We're back to short answers then?" She tugged at the strings of her hoodie and was clearly uneasy, despite her attempt at humour.

Erin might be angry, but she didn't want this, didn't want Abby to feel this way around her. "There's nothing else to say. You don't need to explain."

Abby moved towards her, reached out a hand for Erin's, but Erin moved back against the door away from it. Abby sighed. "Of course I do. It's not what you think, Erin. She turned up yesterday out of nowhere, wanting to talk. You came back and saw us before I had a chance to tell you. I promise, she'd only been there about ten minutes when you came in."

"And yet it's still taken you a whole day to come and talk to me."

"I'm sorry. I wanted to come sooner, but Laura...I wanted to hear her out."

"So, it's exactly how I think then. She wants you back?" Abby dropped her gaze, which answered Erin's question. "And you're thinking about it?"

"Erin, no. There's nothing to think about. I heard her out, but I'm not interested. I've told her that."

"Where is she now? Is she staying here at the castle?"

Abby could only nod.

"Well, she obviously thinks differently. Otherwise, why would she stay?"

Abby's response was mumbled, but Erin had heard enough anyway. Protection mode kicked in just the way her mum had taught her. It was better to volunteer for the swift, sharp sting in the short term than try to survive the lightning strike further down the line. Her mum had told her that lightning would always come. It was just a matter of when, not if.

"Abby, you don't owe me anything. We spent a couple of nights together. It was fun, and I'm sure I'm not the first guest you've taken up to the tower. No big deal."

"Erin, please. You've got it all wrong." Abby reached for her again, but Erin was already opening the bedroom door behind her.

"It's all right, Abby. I'm used to being the new girl. You and Laura have history. Even if I wanted to, I can't compete with that." Erin knew she was being overly flippant and a little cruel. But the words wouldn't stop tumbling out. It was her childhood all over again. Always the new girl, always the odd one out. She was used to it, had made peace with being that girl.

She was giving Abby an easy out, and that was okay. It was better this way. Better to offer her the opportunity early and make her inevitable decision between Erin and Laura straightforward. Erin's feelings towards Abby were new and raw but still relatively unknown. They were special because no one had ever elicited this reaction in her. But special didn't necessarily translate as worth it. Erin knew she could come back from this place. This was the sting. But if she allowed herself to delve any deeper, something told her she would always be fearing the lightning.

"Abby, do what you want. Do whatever makes you happy. I won't get in the way."

She turned to leave, but Abby grasped her arm. "It's not that simple, and you know it." There was a fire in her eyes. They bore into Erin's, and despite everything, it was all Erin could do not to kiss her in that moment. Her body vibrated at a frequency she only seemed to reach in Abby's proximity. She felt her resolve begin to crumble and knew her defence had only seconds left standing before it would fall.

"That's the problem, Abby. I don't know anything, and I don't know you." She tugged her arm free gently and hoped her expression conveyed how sorry she was. "And you certainly don't know me."

She knew her words hit hard. Saw the tremble of Abby's mouth as she made to protest before Erin found her last shred of strength and closed the door.

CHAPTER 24

The drive to the old croft seemed much quicker than the last time. Too quick for Erin. As she pulled into the driveway, any second thoughts had to be pushed to the side as the front door opened before she had even turned off the engine.

Eddie raised a hand in greeting, and she nodded his way, gathering a shopping bag and her handbag from the passenger seat.

He waited for her on the porch. "I'm glad you came back. I wasn't sure... Well, I was worried you'd change your mind."

Her thoughts returned to a few moments before, to how close she had been to doing exactly that.

"Almost. But here I am." She held up the bag. "I brought liquid courage."

"Aren't you driving?" He stepped aside to let her pass through the front door.

It felt like the biggest step of her life setting foot into the cottage hallway, and she was glad of the bottle of whisky she had picked up en route. "A friend is picking me up. So long as you don't mind me leaving the car?"

He ushered her through towards the kitchen. "Not at all. At least I know you'll definitely be back." He smiled, and it unsettled her again how similar they looked.

The kitchen was dated: beige cupboards with fake wooden trim handles ran the length of two walls, broken up by an old electric cooker. It was the same model her grandmother had had, with the grill hanging from the top. She remembered her mum burning sausages on it when they'd visited once, to the extent the fire brigade had to be called and the kitchen had to be completely redecorated. The chrome sink was dulled and stacked with freshly washed dishes, and the matching beige countertops still shone from a recent wipe down.

In the centre sat an oak table that looked older than the house, scratched and watermarked, a tin of shortbread biscuits in the middle. He gestured to one of the four chairs whilst opening a cupboard. "What kind of glasses do we need?"

She plucked the bottle of single malt from the bag. "Whisky glasses."

"Ah, a girl after my own heart."

He smiled and took the seat across from her, a couple of dram squares in his hand. She offered the bottle for him to do the honours. The house was still save for a radio in the windowsill. It played barely audible classical music that vied for attention along with a dripping tap. Every drip seemed to coil her stomach tighter, and the urge to flee became almost unbearable.

He passed her a glass, and by habit she made to clink her glass with his. But what was there to toast? She still had no idea if this had all been one huge mistake. She took a gulp and coughed as the liquid took the back of her throat by surprise. Heat spread to her cheeks, and thankfully the second sip went down smoother.

"Where do you work now?" It seemed an easy place to start.

He tapped the tin in the middle of the table. "Out at the biscuit factory near Lanark. Not exactly exciting, but it pays all right and the monotony suits me."

"Oh." She felt vaguely disappointed. "I thought you were a maths teacher?"

He quirked an eyebrow. "You've been doing your homework. Is that how you found me?"

"That and a few other things. I got your letters."

He leant back and surveyed her a moment. "When?"

"After mum died."

His face seemed to harden a little at mention of her mum, but the fact she had died registered quickly. "I'm sorry, Erin. I didn't know."

"Why would you?"

"True. I'm still sorry."

She nodded. Whether he was sorry or not didn't matter. Nothing he could say would make her feel better about losing her mum. "I teach maths." It wasn't normal for her to volunteer information, but he had gone quiet and the dripping tap had started to niggle again.

He seemed surprised. "Well, isn't that a pleasant coincidence."

She didn't care for the way he said it. Almost as if he had something to do with her choice of career. "Mum encouraged it. I was always good with numbers."

He uncorked the bottle and topped up their glasses. The silence stretched again. It seemed her less-than-talkative nature was another thing she had inherited from him.

"So, Erin..."

"I wanted..."

They both spoke in unison, and the laughter that followed was stilted and awkward. "You first," he offered.

"I suppose I've been wondering what you've been doing all these years? There are no letters for the past ten years or so, and mum never talked about you."

He shifted in his chair and took a couple of sips of the whisky, clearly considering his response. "I remarried."

She waited for more, but it didn't come and she wasn't about to volunteer the information collected from the village gossip tree. "That's it? You remarried? Then what, you happened to magically forget you had another family?"

"You weren't my family any more, Erin." There was an edge to his voice. "Your mother made sure of that. The fact she never spoke about me says it all."

"And for good reason if I remember rightly, although most of what happened is vague."

His shoulders dropped and a flicker of anger appeared and then quickly left his face. "Yes. For good reason, I'm sure. You have to understand, Erin. We were young, tempestuous, and our relationship was volatile. Right from the start, even before you came along. But I never stopped loving your mother. And I think she still always loved me."

"Even when you were beating her?" She hadn't meant for the words to come out so raw.

He closed his eyes, and she wanted to do the same. Wanted to close them and be anywhere but in that kitchen. But she didn't. She watched him inhale deeply a few times before opening them again and pinning her with their stare.

"You were young. You don't know what went on, Erin. You wouldn't understand."

The silence stretched again, and she was the first to look away. She pushed back her chair and went to the sink. "Does this tap ever stop fucking dripping?" She took a dishtowel and wrapped it around the handle, putting every ouch of anger she had at that moment into tightening it.

He didn't say anything, simply watched her until she exhausted her arms and the dripping mercifully stopped.

"Erin, sit." He gestured towards the chair again and filled their glasses once more.

She did as he asked, swirling the amber liquid and avoiding his gaze. With two words, she felt like a petulant teenager about to be scolded.

"I'm sorry. You're an adult now, and I know you want answers. But you have to understand what a shock this is. Having you here, with all these questions. I never thought I'd see you again. I've never prepared for this."

"And you think I have?" She wasn't looking for an answer. "But you're right. I'm an adult now. So, try me."

He got up from the table and started to pace. It irritated her more than the leaky tap. "Like I said, our relationship was anything but perfect. It had passion. Your mother had such fire in her. She was always determined to get her own way, to do whatever she wanted, and damn the consequences. When we got married, that didn't change. And having you didn't change it either. All I wanted was to settle down and live a simple life. But she made it impossible."

She felt she knew where this was heading. Felt the excuses coming. "Please don't try to justify beating your wife." She meant the bluntness this time.

He stopped mid-pace and glared at her. Suddenly, a shadow from her dream was materialising in front of her. She knew that face, had seen it before. She had hidden from that monster many times.

A hum of fury pulsated through her. Her skin felt tight and started to itch with the heat of frustration. She bit her lip in an effort to contain every maddening thought and question that had been locked away tight all these years. The strain of holding back choked her throat until it was no longer rage building but infuriating tears.

She'd said it herself—she was an adult now. So, why was it so hard to let loose and berate him for every fucking cruel and horrific thing he had done to them?

The simple answer was: she was still scared of him. And she hated that fact with every fibre of her being.

"I don't need to justify anything. You have no idea what she did to me, Erin. No idea. How she pushed my buttons, taunted me, always forcing me to the edge until I couldn't take it any longer."

"So, leave." She raised her voice to match his. Her tears were on the brink, but she swallowed hard. Determined to at least try to overcome them. "Your fists were clearly not the answer, so why didn't you leave? Mum said..."

"Oh, I bet your mum said a whole fucking lot. Where was my chance to defend myself?"

"Are you fucking kidding?" She tried to channel her mum. To think how she would react coming face to face with her oppressor after all these years. "I mean, can you blame her? Give me one good reason why she should have stayed. Should have carried on and put up with the terror and pain."

He banged his fist on the table. Their glasses jumped with the force, and so did Erin. Her fleeting moment of bravery dissolved at the act that was the foundation on which her nightmares were built. She felt herself internally retreat, back to the safe place.

Time to go.

"Because of you, Erin." He pointed at her sharply. "You're the reason. She never gave me a chance to know you. To try to make up for everything. It might have been over with us, but I was still your dad. She hid you away from me like the selfish bitch she was and didn't even pass on my letters. She broke our family up, not me."

Erin was on her feet then, the chair falling with a loud clatter behind her. Whatever the reason, she couldn't hear him talk that way about her mum any more. "Stop. Please stop."

It was Erin's turn to point the finger, but the fight was gone. Her voice was barely a whisper. "Nothing she ever did can excuse how you hurt her. How you hurt us both. So please stop trying."

And he did. Before Erin could protest, he was wrapping his arms around her. She stood rigid for a moment but didn't move away. Her mind wanted her to fight, but her body gave in to it.

"I'm sorry, Erin. I'm so sorry," he whispered into her hair as he stroked it.

Tears came at his words, heavy and fast.

"I never thought I'd see you again. I've always blamed your mum for that. But you're here now. I don't want to ruin that. Please give me a chance."

She finally pulled away. "I have to go." She grabbed her handbag from the back of the fallen chair and took the last swallow of whisky from her glass.

"Erin, please..."

She held up a hand. "Don't. I need to go. It's too much."

Hurt crossed his face, but she wasn't about to stay to make him feel better.

"I really am sorry, Erin."

"That's not enough."

"Will I see you again?"

She stopped in the doorway but didn't turn. "I don't know."

CHAPTER 25

Erin slammed the front door and moved down the porch steps quickly. She headed past her car towards the lane as she rooted in her bag for her phone. She didn't trust her voice to make a call, so instead she sent George a text.

> Can you come and get me now? I'm heading down the lane on foot. Thanks.

She had bumped into him at reception on her way out and something had made her tell him where she was heading. As well as her idea to pick up the bottle. He'd seemed concerned, even tried to talk her out of it before suggesting she not go alone. Erin guessed she was being afforded the same brotherly protectiveness Abby received. So, when he'd offered to be her personal taxi, she'd accepted to keep him happy.

Her phone beeped, and she felt a little relief.

> Sure, I'll be there in 10 mins.

She swiped the screen to bring up the torch function and continued along the lane, determined not to look back. Thankfully, it didn't look like her dad had felt the need to come after her.

Round a corner, the shadow of a large tree stood stark against the moonlit sky, foreboding yet drawing her in. She clambered between its gnarled, sturdy roots, leant against it, and pulled her knees to her chest, waiting for George.

It wasn't long before she heard his car and headlights lit up the hedgerow. She held up a hand hoping he would see her, and the car stopped a few feet past the tree. At the sight of him the tears came again, and then he was at her side, holding her close.

"Hey, hey. What happened? Are you okay?"

She could only nod into his chest, and he squeezed her tighter.

"C'mon. Let's get you back."

She allowed herself to be led to the car. He opened the door, and she gratefully climbed inside, the sanctity of the warm space enveloping her.

He got in and rubbed a reassuring hand along her arm. "You're safe, Erin. It'll be okay."

They didn't speak on the journey back to the hotel, and eventually her silent tears subsided. Her body still trembled, and she was torn between curling up into a ball and screaming in pure frustration. It enraged her that her dad could still spark the same anxieties and dread, yet the feel of his arms around her came with comfort. The juxtaposition of feelings did nothing to help answer the one question that kept circling in her head.

Why was she doing this?

Once parked up at the castle, neither moved. "Can I get you anything? Do you want me to fetch Abby?"

She heard the worry in his voice but shook her head. "No. Don't do that. I'm okay, George."

"Are you sure? I can knock off early if you want some company?"

Erin smiled his way, grateful to have him but also desperate for him to leave her alone. *So, this is what it feels like to have a brother.* His face held concern, and she appreciated it. She could see he needed reassurance, but she didn't have more than formal niceties to console him. "I'll be all right, George. Thanks for the offer though."

"Okay, if you're sure." She could tell he wasn't satisfied, but it was all she had.

"I am. I think I'll grab something from the bar and head for a bath. See you in the morning?"

"Aye. You know where I am if you need anything."

"I do." She leant and gave him a kiss on the cheek. "Thanks again."

He covered his blush by getting out of the car, mumbling, "No problem."

They headed towards the door, but before they went in, she touched his arm lightly. He turned back to her. "Please don't tell Abby you saw me in this state."

His forehead creased. She knew it was a big ask for him to keep this from his sister. Especially when Abby was likely to ask. But he agreed. "Sure."

She watched his retreating back as he headed for the stairs to the bedrooms. She detoured to the toilets by the reception and splashed some water on her face in an effort to get rid of the blotchiness from crying.

Then the bar called.

Simon, whose name she'd finally learnt, was serving. Only a few stragglers lingered on the sofas near the fire. "Hey, Simon. Could I have one of those half decanters with whisky, please? And a glass of ice. For my room."

He nodded and set about her order. It wasn't often Erin drunk to oblivion, but tonight oblivion beckoned.

"That's a lot of whisky for one person."

The voice at Erin's side made her jump. Even before she turned to acknowledge it, she knew it would be Laura.

"The occasion calls for it." *Dammit. Why had she engaged?*

"And what occasion might that be? Out here alone in a big old castle?"

The last thing Erin wanted was to make idle chit-chat with Abby's ex, but well-drilled manners kept her frustration muted. There was nothing to be gained by causing a scene with her. "Why do you assume I'm alone?"

Laura leant on the bar, a deliberate smile spread across her face. "I couldn't help but notice you at breakfast."

Erin couldn't believe the hint of suggestion creeping into Laura's voice. *Was she flirting?*

She laid a hand lightly on Erin's arm. "And you didn't seem to be with anyone."

She was flirting.

The bitch.

Was this woman for real?

Erin wasn't sure what she was more annoyed about, that Laura was clearly hitting on her or that Erin hadn't noticed her at breakfast. But then, she had sat in her usual window seat, hiding behind a newspaper and doing anything to distract herself from the night ahead and thoughts of Abby.

Erin extricated her arm and took a deliberate step away. "Ah, right, sorry. I can't say the same." It was satisfying to see the smile slip a little, and Erin hid her own.

Simon placed the tray with her order in front of her. "Do you want me to get someone to carry that up, Erin?"

She signed the receipt. "No, it's fine. I'll manage. Thanks, Simon."

Laura hadn't moved; instead, she held out a hand. "I'm Laura. Nice to meet you, Erin."

Either she had missed Erin's obvious dismissal or she wasn't someone to give up easily. Erin picked up the tray and ignored her hand. Manners be damned. "Again, I can't say the same." She turned her back on the raging look that crossed Laura's face. "Goodnight, Simon."

She didn't look back. She was fuming again. It was the final piece to complete a really shitty day. How fucking dare she? Come here and spin some line to Abby about wanting her back. Mess up any possible chance that her and Abby's fledgling romance could have had, and then hit on the first girl she met in the bar behind Abby's back.

Hit on Erin of all people.

In Abby's home.

What the hell could Abby possibly see in her? She didn't know who to be madder at.

Furious, she stormed along the corridor, keeping an eye on the contents of her tray. From the corner of her eye she saw the "Private" door opening and barely managed to swerve it in time as Abby came through, almost colliding with her.

"Erin."

Seeing Abby's face, the anger towards her dissipated momentarily before coming back full force at the injustice of the situation. "Excuse me."

Abby looked confused for a second before realising she was blocking Erin's way. "Oh. Sorry. Listen, Erin, can we talk, please?" She surveyed the contents of Erin's tray. "Unless you're not on your own?"

Distress etched across Abby's forehead, but Erin was in no mood to mollify her. "Abby, not right now. You need to get out of my way."

Abby took an exaggerated step to the side. "Okay, no need to be that way. What's your problem? Why won't you give me a chance to explain?"

Erin moved past her. She hated to see the hurt and defeat in Abby's voice. Her instinct was to reach out and take back every negative word she'd ever sent Abby's way. But between her dad and Laura, she'd hit her limit and just didn't have it in her. One moment longer, and she was going to tell Abby exactly what, or who, was her problem, and there was only damage to come from that.

She softened her tone but didn't look back. "I can't do this right now, Abby."

"Then when?" She heard Abby sigh, heard the crack in her voice. "Please don't push me away."

Erin continued up the stairs, ready to walk away without another word.

"Erin?"

She could feel Abby's gaze and willed herself not to turn. She failed. She glanced back down towards her and was surprised to see the shine of tears in Abby's eyes. Shame only allowed Erin to hold her gaze for a moment.

"Abby, go. Please." It was a plea rather than an instruction, but Abby didn't move. Exhausted, Erin could only muster a weary half-smile, and she turned again towards her room. She threw a final deterrent in the hope Abby wouldn't follow her. "The charming Laura is waiting for you in the bar."

CHAPTER 26

One glass flew across the kitchen, followed in quick succession by the other. Eddie grabbed the bottle and swigged straight from it. He considered sending it in the same direction as the glasses, but it was quality whisky and he had other plans for it. If it meant drinking alone, well, what was new?

It had been her.

At the graveside a few days before. He should have known the moment he laid eyes on her, but caught up in the emotion of seeing her after all these years, the mystery of the stranger had disappeared from his mind. But he knew now it was definitely her. She may have his colouring, but the long stride, the way her head had tilted slightly as she had regarded the grave, it was every bit her mother. It had hit him as he'd watched her tear out of the house.

There was an ulterior motive for her visit—there had to be. It had always been that way with her mother, and there was no reason to think she was any different. Any time Amelia had paid him real attention, cooked his favourite dinner, bought in a bottle of his favourite single malt, there had always been a sting waiting. A question.

She wanted to go visit a friend, alone. Erin needed something new and expensive. There was a sale on in her favourite clothes shop. Could they book a holiday?

She was never fucking satisfied with what they had.

The way Erin had defended her mother riled him. After twenty years, he was still the bad guy, and who knew what that sanctimonious bitch had filled Erin's head with in all that time. As always, there was only Amelia's side of the story. No one wanted his. He might have been physical, but she had tortured him mentally.

He had thought he could swallow any attack Erin might direct his way, had expected some difficult questions, but she had laid into him almost immediately. Barely a question of what he had been doing since her mother had stolen Erin away? How had he been? Where had he been? Even when he had mentioned remarrying, she'd shown no interest. Although the lack of questions about Marie was probably for the best.

Instead, the past had been thrown like a grenade with no thought as to whether he was wearing armour. Was it any wonder he hadn't been able to maintain his temper? It was painful for him too. He had lost his wife and daughter.

If only she would listen. Maybe he could talk her around and help her gain a little perspective on how things had been back then, why he had reacted the way he did.

That's all it was. All it had ever been. A reaction. Amelia had been no saint.

Youth was no excuse. She had flirted with every guy who'd paid her the slightest bit of attention, right under his nose. Sure, she claimed it was all in good fun, she was sociable, having a laugh, and it was harmless. She was going home with him, wasn't that all that mattered?

But he knew better.

When he was at work all day, he could only imagine what she was getting up to. And no doubt she would be laughing about it behind his back, making him a fool. He was her husband. He had deserved her respect. And if she wasn't willing to show him it, then he had been prepared to dole out the consequences.

The buzzer sounded, snapping him out of his reverie.

"What the..."

He thumped the bottle on the table and tore open the cellar door, taking the stairs at speed. The bolts slid back and he shoved it open, letting it swing back and bounce against the wall behind.

"What did I tell you? Hey? What did I say?"

He watched Thea scarper to the end of her bed and pull the duvet with her. She peered doe-eyed over the top of it at him.

No. Not this time. That wouldn't work.

"What if the other adult was still upstairs?" He was shouting now. "I told you not to buzz. What did we talk about?"

"I'm sorry, Daddy. I'm sorry," she squealed from behind the covers.

"Not fucking good enough. Do you know how stupid that was?"

She was crying now and had pulled the cover over her head. He could hear her repeating how sorry she was, and the words finally penetrated.

She was scared and it was his fault. That wasn't how things were meant to be.

"Hey. Shush." He sat on the edge of the bed and drew the covers from her head gently. She glared at him, eyes shining with fright and tears. "I'm sorry, peanut. You scared me, that's all."

She still didn't say anything, and he moved closer. She flinched as he reached to smooth her hair, and an unbearable feeling of sorrow washed over him. "I'm so sorry," he whispered and tried again to reach out. She allowed him this time. "I'm so, so sorry," he repeated, cupping her cheek in his hand.

She took his hand and moved across the bed into his lap. "Daddy, don't cry." She wrapped her arms around his waist and spoke into his chest, "I'm sorry too, Daddy. It's all right. We're still safe down here."

"Yes, we are, sweetheart."

Safe. That's all he'd ever wanted for his daughter. For his daughters. It was the answer.

No one out there could care for his girls in the way he could. Thea understood that, how he protected her and made sacrifices for her. He had had Thea's whole life to create their perfect world, and she loved him for it.

Now he had an opportunity to do the same for Erin, to reunite his family and make things better. For her. For them. The savageness of the world had clearly taken its toll on Erin. But he could sooth her pain and show her a life free of worry.

It would take time, but he would prove himself, show her what she had missed, what he was prepared to do to make up for lost time. He could be a good father. He could make things right. Wasn't that why she had come looking for him? To discover if what she had lost could be found again?

He hugged Thea close. Both his girls needed their dad, whether they knew it or not.

CHAPTER 27

Habit took Abby towards the kitchen, but as she crossed the bar entrance, Laura's laughter drifted her way. She paused a moment, caught in two minds. Then Erin's hostile words echoed in her mind. She shrugged them off, the anger far from dissipating at how she had spoken to Abby. All she had asked for was a moment to explain.

The laughter got louder as she entered the room. Laura sat on a sofa by the fire, holding court with a couple of newly arrived guests. She spotted Abby and waved her over to join them.

Laura made the introductions as Abby avoided the seat next to her and, instead, took an armchair. "Abby, this is Jaako and Malaki. They're visiting from Finland. Guys, this is Abby, the castle's chef."

The flames from the fire heightened their alcohol glow, and they seemed well on their way to being pissed. Abby shook their proffered hands and smiled a greeting.

Typical Laura. She had never been any good at being alone and made a habit of picking up strangers wherever they went. From holidays to a quiet drink in the pub, she was a magnet for strays. In the early days of their relationship, when they were still figuring each other out, Abby had taken quiet pleasure in Laura's social abilities. She had been proud to be introduced as Laura's girlfriend, with her "hang loose" attitude and flamboyant charm. It was inevitably going to attract people.

It had quickly become tiresome.

Laura's problem was she had no concept of boundaries and tended to give off a little more than friendship vibes. At first, Abby had thought it innocent enough, and the men and women who thought it to be anything more were merely presumptuous. However, it hadn't taken long to realise that Laura knew exactly what she was doing, and she revelled in the attention and drama that sometimes came with it.

On reflection, Abby realised her behaviour was no more than a ploy to try and make Abby jealous. To evoke a reaction and confirm to herself that Abby was still there, still cared, still wanted her. Towards the end of their relationship, Abby had reacted less. She became practised at shrugging it off, extricating Laura from the situation, and setting the incident aside in the box marked "boredom". Whether from weariness or something more, she didn't know at the time. It became something she accepted as par for the course in their relationship.

But in the months after their breakup, as Abby nursed her heart and dissected every modicum of their relationship, she had realised that her blasé attitude had more than likely influenced Laura's decision to eventually choose her career over Abby.

Abby sat back in her seat and surveyed the scene before her, waiting for it to play out.

"So, you are both chefs?" It was Malaki. Even though he referred to both of them, clearly he only had eyes for Laura.

Abby nodded. "Aye. And we're both very gay."

"Yes, yes. Laura told us."

Abby raised an eyebrow in Laura's direction. That made a change.

"We do not believe it though," Jaako weighed in. "We think Laura is only letting us down gently."

Abby rolled her eyes. "And you think we're too pretty to be lesbians, right?" She stood and shot a mental dagger at Laura. "I need a drink." That had to be a record for the time it took for her to be done with the situation.

She'd made a mistake. Already wound up by Erin and her earlier dismissal, it was idiotic thinking on her part that Laura might somehow make her feel better. Even if only as a friend. She reached the bar and glanced back over as Malaki roared at something Laura said and placed a possessive arm across the back of the sofa behind her.

"What's up, Abby?"

She turned to Simon's friendly face behind the bar. "Ah, nothing new, Simon. Women. You know?"

He chuckled. "Oh yeah, I know. I have a wife, remember."

Abby blew out a consolatory breath. "More fool you, mate."

"You say that now, but it'll be you one day. Drink?"

"Don't bet on it. And please. I'll just have a coke." Abby turned her attention back to Laura while he poured. If she thought this was somehow going to work on Abby, she was wrong. Simon passed her the drink, and she stayed put at the bar. There was no telling how sharp her tongue might become if one of the guys came out with another tired old stereotype. They were guests, she reminded herself. Best to play nice.

Besides, she had Erin to figure out. Something told her it wasn't all Abby that had stirred up such a reaction in her. But then how well did Abby really know her? It gnawed at her, the possibility that she had misjudged not only the type of person Erin was, but that their time together had possibly meant so little to Erin. Was Abby merely a distraction from all the heavy stuff Erin was dealing with? Was she so easy to dismiss?

On the other hand, Erin was simply passing through. On a journey that Abby was only playing a bit part in. What indication had she given Abby that she was anything more than an escape when things got rough?

She watched Laura excuse herself and head in Abby's direction. She braced herself. Abby could recognise the look in Laura's eye even from across the room.

"Why are you stood all the way over here, alone, when you could be having fun with me?" She sidled up close to Abby.

"Why do you do that?" Abby was in no mood for games, and it was about time she called bullshit.

"What?" Laura feigned innocence.

"You know what. You're leading those guys on. Malaki has clearly taken a shine to you, and you are letting him think there's more to it."

"So what? I can't have a conversation with a guy without him expecting to sleep with me?" She attempted an indignant pout, but Abby didn't buy it.

"I don't mean it like that and you know it. There's having a conversation and then there's what you do."

Laura leant away from her. "What I do?"

"Yes. The touching, the fake laugh at their jokes, the innuendo. That's not friendly banter, Laura. It's flirting. Can you blame them for wondering if a little more is on offer?"

"Are you jealous?"

Abby signed. Here it was. "No, Laura, I'm bored of it."

Laura paid no attention. "Come and have fun with me. Have a drink and enjoy it. Why do you have to be so serious all the time?" She trailed a finger down Abby's arm and took her hand.

She had always had the ability to make Abby second-guess herself. She manipulated her self-doubt, and it enabled her to talk Abby into almost anything. But this time the doubt was fleeting, the shine had finally worn off. "I don't think I'm up for your kind of fun anymore."

Abby tried to pull her hand away, but Laura held on tight and leant in closer, holding her hostage between the bar and the door. "Are you sure?" she whispered it on to Abby's lips, her breath hot and scented with peppery red wine. She held Abby's eye. Another few seconds and she knew Laura would kiss her.

Abby slid sideways against the bar, disengaging herself before making a mammoth mistake. "I'm sure."

Laura shrugged. "You say that now, Abby. But I know you, I know what makes you tick." She bent down close to her ear. "I know exactly how you like it."

At her words, a passing wave of memories flew warp-speed through her mind. Had she been too quick to dismiss Laura? There had been plenty of good to go with the bad. Her mind eventually settled on the tower. But the face she saw there with her wasn't Laura's.

Abby sighed and shook off the minor effect Laura could still bring out in her. "Not any more, Laura."

"Ladies." Malaki waved in their direction, gesturing for them to re-join him.

Abby moved towards the door. "I have an early start tomorrow. Your audience awaits."

CHAPTER 28

Erin set the tray on her nightstand and dropped onto the bed where she shrugged off her jacket and bag. She kicked off her boots and threw them against the wardrobe. *Fuck.*

She manoeuvred to the centre of the bed and crossed her legs, pulling the tray towards her. Her hands shook as she poured a generous measure of whisky, adding a couple of cubes of ice. The ice was there merely to slow down the drinking.

One tumbler down, and her heartbeat finally started to slow, her hands steadied, and her breathing returned to normal.

A knock came at the door as she poured another.

"Go away," she called out, not caring who stood at the other side.

"Erin, it's me, George. Are you okay?"

She huffed out a breath. How could she turn him away after how he'd helped her earlier that night? She unfolded herself and stomped to the door then threw it open and retreated to the bed without a word.

He edged towards her and sat tentatively on the end of the bed. "You can tell me to piss off if you want."

She took a large swallow. "Piss off." He laughed, and she joined him. Maybe having him around right now wasn't such a bad idea. "But if you stay, you'd better grab a glass and help me out with this."

He eyed the decanter. She guessed whisky wasn't his drink of choice. At nineteen, that wasn't surprising. But he leant over to the sideboard and took a glass nevertheless, pouring a reserved measure for himself and adding a handful of ice cubes.

"Wuss," she teased.

"Hey, I'm still an amateur. Give a guy a chance."

She clinked her glass to his. "At least you're trying."

He took a sip and choked much the same as she had earlier that night. She couldn't help but laugh. "The second sip'll be smoother."

"I bloody hope so." He held the glass out and eyed it with distaste. "Anyway, what's going on? I heard you and Abby in the hall. Thought I'd check in."

The whisky had loosened her tongue, and suddenly talking about it didn't seem all that bad. But not about Abby. "I'm not talking to you about your sister. It wouldn't be fair."

He nodded as if she had given him the right answer, but she could tell he was still disappointed. "I could use an ear after what happened with my dad though."

He shifted on the bed. "Uh. Sure. Although maybe that's something you would rather talk to Abby about?"

"Not right now. Stop fishing."

He smirked. "Sorry. I'll quit. What happened with your dad?"

"Apart from the painful awkwardness and shouting, not much." Not surprisingly, George looked confused, so she elaborated. "It was nothing how I imagined, George. I mean, I don't even know what I did imagine. But I'm pretty sure that wasn't it."

"Shouting? Did he hurt you?"

Erin was taken aback by the vehemence in his voice. "No. Why would you think he hurt me? What's Abby said to you?"

"I...I don't know. Abby hasn't said anything." He shifted again and stared out of the window. The curtains were still open, but there wasn't much to see, save for a sprinkling of stars and the shadows of trees.

"We exchanged words. It was intense, that's all. And disappointing. I guess I imagined we'd have this instant connection. That it would feel as if there'd been no time since I last saw him, you know? He'd look at me, and know me, and there would be no need to explain anything. It was childish to think that way."

"I don't think so." George turned back to her. "I suppose it's the child in you that's missed him. That wants him to make it all better."

She tipped her glass to him. "Two sips of the hard stuff and he's a philosopher." He frowned, and she felt bad for making fun of him. "But you're right. I'm sorry. I suppose I didn't expect to feel so removed from him, from his life. It was as if I wasn't his daughter."

"You're not. You haven't been for a long time, and it'll be hard to ever get that feeling back, I imagine."

She nodded. "I suppose I didn't expect him to be so closed off. As soon as I mentioned the past, or my mum, he totally flipped. Blaming everything on her. I left none the wiser as to the person he is now. All I saw in him was bad memories and nightmares."

"They say you can never really know someone."

"I don't buy that. I mean, of course people keep a part of themselves private, a part that's only for them. And that's okay. But it felt as if he was hiding things. He went straight on the defensive, blaming her for taking me away from him and for breaking up our family. He basically said she asked for it."

"So, you flipped back?" George took another sip, and Erin smiled inwardly as his jaw flinched. She topped up both their glasses anyway.

"Damn right I did. I may have been young back then, but I'm not anymore. I couldn't listen to him trying to justify what happened."

"Are you going to see him again?"

She clinked the ice cubes around her glass and thought a moment. "He's still my dad, George."

He laid a hand on her knee and squeezed. "That doesn't make him worth your time, Erin. That doesn't make him a good person."

"I guess." Erin eyed what was left of the decanter. The whisky was starting to hit hard, and she knew she should stop. But fuck it. She couldn't face a night of dreaming. She swallowed it back and didn't stop, even as the ice hit her teeth.

"Maybe you should slow down a little."

She knew it only came from concern but couldn't help the retort. "Okay, now you can piss off." No sooner had she said it than she wanted to take it back. "I'm sorry. I didn't mean that. Don't go."

Then she burst into tears.

"Hey, hey. C'mon. Don't do that. He's obviously not worth your tears." George shifted next to her on the bed and draped a gangly arm across her shoulders.

"It's not that." She reached to the nightstand and plucked a tissue from its box. "I can't believe she's so blind, George. I mean, what the hell does she see in her? And that smug grin, I mean, what the fuck is that?" She knew she was rambling but couldn't stop. She mimicked her earlier encounter at the bar,

"*I couldn't help notice you at breakfast.* Oh, please. Give. Me. A. Break. She's so phony. How can she be so oblivious?"

She looked up at George, expecting an answer. His eyebrows were raised. "We're talking about Abby and Laura now?"

"No. Yes." She hung her head. "Laura tried it on with me in the bar earlier."

"Oh shit."

"Exactly. I mean, I can't tell Abby, because either Laura will say I made it up because I want Abby for myself, or she'll deny it, or say it was the other way around, and then Abby will have to decide who to believe. Or Abby will think I'm making it up to hurt her. But on the other hand, if I don't tell Abby, and she finds out, she'll be hurt I didn't tell her. Or she'll think I didn't care enough to tell her. What should I do George? What?" She slapped his leg in frustration.

"Whoa, take a breath." He took her glass and shifted the tray back to the nightstand. "You have definitely had enough of that."

She glared at him, but he didn't budge. She flopped back on the bed with a growl.

"So you want Abby for yourself? Why not tell her that? Otherwise how does she know how you feel? She's working with half the facts right now. Especially after the crap you threw her way earlier."

The pillow she threw missed him, and he laughed. Even when she followed it with her jacket and bag. "Okay, now you really can piss off."

He picked up her things and didn't argue, heading for the door instead. "Good talk, Erin. I hope that head is not too sore in the morning."

CHAPTER 29

Abby threw her dirty whites into the washing machine and slammed the door. She was attempting distraction and avoiding the bar with some late-night chores, but so far everything had failed. It was time to give up and give in to the inevitable period of wallowing. The tower called.

Right on time, Angus appeared at the utility room door. "Hey, where have you been hiding, cat? I thought you'd abandoned me for that pit George calls a bedroom?" She headed back to the twice-cleaned kitchen with only one thought on her mind.

Wine.

Angus dutifully followed, and she rewarded him with a few drops of fishy cat treats. Clearly the new brand wasn't to his liking, and he pushed them around the floor fussily with his nose before sauntering towards the door again.

"Little bugger," Abby muttered.

Bottle and glass in hand, she made to follow until George appeared, blocking her way. He gestured towards the wine. "Pour me one, will you?" Then he pushed past her into the kitchen and took a stool.

"Okay." She drew the word out in confusion but took a second glass from the cupboard. As she poured, George fidgeted on the stool, rocking it back and forth. "To what do I owe the pleasure?" She handed him a glass.

He gulped the wine back and held the glass out for a refill. "More wine first. You should have one too."

His eyes were a little glassy, and she recognised the pinkness in his cheeks and over the bridge of his nose. "You've been drinking already." It was a statement and it couldn't help but come out accusatorily, but only because George rarely drank.

"I'm allowed, you know," he snapped at her, and that was when she knew something was wrong.

She did as he asked and refilled his glass, then took a healthy swig of her own.

"Out with it."

He took a more measured mouthful and looked anywhere but at her. Angus had taken a seat on the carpet on the other side of the door and slow-blinked at her in lazy impatience.

She felt her own patience wearing. "George, what's going on?"

He spun the glass by the stem between both hands. "I've been upstairs with Erin. She's in a bit of a state."

Abby's instinct told her that wasn't a suggestion she should go to her. And although every part of her fought it, her legs began to engage of their own accord when George stopped her.

"Wait." He stood and came towards her. "I don't think it's a good idea if you go up. She's kind of angry."

"At me? Yeah, I know. But if she's really upset..."

He cut her off. "She's not only angry at you."

"What have you done?" It was automatic, because she knew her little brother and was all too familiar with the damage his size fourteens could do.

"Oh, cheers."

She didn't apologise, only glared at him.

He sighed and plonked down on the stool again. "It wasn't me, or you. Okay, maybe it was you a little, but right now it's her dad. And Laura."

"Laura?" Abby's voice went up a notch in confusion. "Why? Have they met? What's she done?"

"Of course, they've met. It was bound to happen sooner or later. There's only so many places in the castle to go. In fact, while we're on it, why the hell haven't you told her to fuck off yet?"

Abby leant back in surprise. George rarely swore and certainly not with such vehemence. The alcohol was obviously making him brave.

She immediately went on the defensive. It seemed to be a habit when it came to Laura. "I'm not sure that's your business. Who the hell do you think you're talking to?"

"That's where you're wrong. It is my business. When I'm caught in the middle between an angry, sobbing Erin and my miserable sister. That's when I deserve some answers."

"She was crying?"

"Of course, she was fucking crying." It was George's turn to raise his voice, and she saw Angus scarper from the impending drama. "Have you any idea how it must feel to be in her shoes right now?"

"How the hell can I?" Abby matched his volume. "When she won't bloody speak to me?"

"And do you blame her? She's miles from home, grieving the loss of her mum. You've come and strolled into her life at probably her lowest point, with who knows what going on with her dad. And now you're trampling all over her feelings by letting that bitch, Laura, hang around."

That George was defending someone else over her spoke volumes and made Abby bite back any pointless retort she might have otherwise spat at him. He was right.

She stepped towards him and he flinched, probably expecting a smack around the head. Instead, she pulled up the stool next to him. "When did you get so wise?"

He sighed and took a moment to top up his glass. "Not wise. I happen to have my eyes open, that's all. Plus, I probably have a little more info than you." He fidgeted again, then the words came out in a rush, "Laura hit on Erin."

Abby closed her eyes and counted to five, drawing in a long, slow breath.

"Don't go mental." George's tone was pleading.

"I won't." She opened her eyes and laid them on his worried face. "You did the right thing telling me."

"Really?" His shoulders dropped in clear relief. "Because I'm only telling you for purely selfish reasons, you know? I've never liked her. I think she's manipulative and patronising and treats you as nothing more than a toy. Someone she can pick up when she's bored and put down for the same reason. You've got to break the tie once and for all, Abby."

Abby didn't say anything. She picked up her now-empty glass and held it out in front of her before purposefully releasing her grip and letting it fall. She closed her eyes again at the satisfying tinkle as the delicate glass shattered.

George chuckled beside her. "Better?"

She offered him a half smile. "Aye."

"So, was the glass because you're upset that Laura tried it on with someone else, or jealousy over the fact it was Erin she tried it on with?"

"A little of both, I guess. Did Erin say anything else?"

George held up his hands. "That's all you're getting. She'd kill me if she knew I'd told you this. But you're my sister, and you needed to know about Laura before she had a chance to hurt you anymore. Plus, Erin was all in knots wondering how you'd react or who you'd believe if she told you. I thought I'd do her a favour. You know she's telling the truth, right?"

Abby leant in and squeezed him into a hug. "Erin will understand. And yes, I'm sure it's the truth," she murmured into his chest. He held her tight and didn't let go until she released him.

"I hope so. I can tell you this—she needs someone right now, even if it's purely as a friend." He got up and teetered around the glass on his way towards the door. "You need to get your house in order, big sis. Figure out what, or rather who, it is that you want before it's too late."

She nodded at his words, disappearing into her thoughts as he made his escape.

CHAPTER 30

Erin's head was more than sore. It throbbed the moment she tried lifting it from the pillow, inducing a low moan of regret and outright physical pain.

The events of the previous day flooded back to her in a tidal wave of emotion that her hung-over brain wasn't ready for. She lifted a spare pillow and smothered her face under it. She wasn't ready to be awake, wasn't ready to deal with it all.

The pillow eventually joined the one she had thrown at George on the floor.

George.

Erin cringed, remembering her behaviour around him the night before. What the hell had she been thinking, drinking that way? Alcohol had never suited her. Then she remembered her dad, Abby, Laura. That was right—she hadn't been thinking. She had only wanted to forget everything the day had thrown at her.

Abby's face stuck at the forefront of her mind. She tried to imagine how she would react if Erin told her about Laura's not-to-subtle come-on in the bar. Tried to imagine how she would feel in the same position.

Then her dad's twisted face took Abby's place. Telling her she didn't know the truth, telling her it was all her mum's fault. He was wrong, she knew that, but it didn't stop her subconscious trying to make excuses for him. Didn't stop her wanting to see him again. If only to put things straight and put him in his place.

Today she knew there were things she needed to put right. Hangover or not. If she could fix things in her own mind, that would be a start. Then everyone could worry about themselves, and Erin would simply have to wait and see how the pieces fell.

She sat up and looked across the room to the mirror. Her hair was no more dishevelled than usual, but the bags hung darker under her eyes and there wasn't a hint of colour in her cheeks.

Okay, one step at a time, Erin. First, get out of bed and drink some water.

Water and toothpaste did little to counter the sour whisky taste at the back of her throat, but she persisted with mouthwash and a second brushing.

Right, shower, then get dressed.

Her stomach objected when she considered breakfast, so, bottle of water in hand, her next objective was to slip out of the castle, preferably unseen. She didn't know where to start with dealing with everyone else, but a walk to town, coffee, and fresh air felt like the first step to figuring it out. Her car would have to wait.

The sun shone, which lifted her mood a little as she crossed the car park towards the winding drive. Her escape had gone well; even Ann had been missing from her usual post at the desk. She stopped at a familiar sight, parked in the shade under trees. Her car. She approached it almost with suspicion and noticed an envelope tucked under the wiper.

I stole your keys last night. Thought I'd save your hangover the trouble. G x

He was a cheeky little shit, but in that moment, she loved him. Erin jumped in, grateful to be able to drive instead of walking the few miles to town.

Hopetoun's mood seemed to have lifted with the sun as well. People drove with their windows down, the flowers stood vibrant, and children skipped and chased each other, decked out in shorts and T-shirts.

Coffee.

Erin queued behind some workers in the café, a mesh of helmets, high-vis and dusty trousers, waiting for their bacon and sausage rolls. Finally, a large, steaming cup was placed in her hands, and she could have kissed the guy that handed it to her.

She took it to go and followed the same path she and Abby had taken on their trip to the village together. Their bench was empty by the war memorial, and she sat down gratefully, tilting her head to the sun and savouring the first few sips of heaven in a cup. Life was returning to her already, but she couldn't quite fully shake the maudlin mood she had woken up with.

All around her people smiled, stopped to chat, called to each other in greeting. Kids screeched with glee, passing car radios threw out the chipper words of morning DJs, and even the dogs seemed to be walking with an added spring in their step.

Am I the only miserable person in Hopetoun this morning?

Probably not. The lasting effects of the alcohol were clearly continuing to play with her emotions, bringing with them the usual paranoia and irrational fear.

A vaguely familiar form caught her eye and drew her attention to the flower shop. She watched as Laura fondled rose petals and sunflowers, a wistful smile playing on her face as she moved from bouquet to bouquet.

Bitch.

Erin wasn't sure if the shitty feeling at the sight of Laura was because of what had happened the night before or because she was clearly buying flowers for Abby. Something Erin had never had the chance to do. They were over before they had really begun.

Does it have to be?

At last the reasonable part of her brain was fighting its way through the fog, becoming a little clearer with each sip of coffee. Maybe Laura's history with Abby didn't have to count against her. In fact, it might be the opposite, considering how Laura had treated Abby in the past. And if her behaviour last night was anything to go by, surely Abby was wise to it by now? Was it finally okay to be the new and unknown person? Maybe what Abby had learnt about Erin was already enough for her. Enough to make her count.

They had something. Erin could pretend all she wanted, but she knew in her heart and head that for her, it wasn't a passing fling. She had known that first night when Abby had joined her for coffee that she was a game changer. Erin had never made it easy on the few people who'd shown an interest in her over the years, had never been compelled to give them a chance to show her what a relationship could be. She was convinced that she operated best alone—her mum had shown her how.

She had never allowed anyone to love her. If they had, she had been oblivious.

Now here she was, despite her best efforts, unable to dismiss Abby from her life and unable to think of anyone else she'd rather have next to her in that moment.

She sat straighter on the bench, resolute.

Maybe this was the time that Erin needed to stick around to find out what came next. To see if it was worth it. Instead of conceding defeat in the first round and quietly slipping into the background.

She had time to figure out her next step with her dad, but watching Laura walk out of the shop with what seemed to be their full stock of roses, she knew time was precious when it came to Abby.

She thought back to what George had said about half-facts and her confrontation with Abby in the hall. He was right; Erin had given Abby no reason to think she meant anything more to her than a couple of sexual liaisons. She shook her head and chastised herself. "Aw crap, why was I was such a bitch last night?"

An elderly lady passed by. "What was that, dear?"

Erin put up a hand. "Never mind. Have a nice day."

She drained the last of her coffee and headed for the post office. Thankfully, Mary wasn't there to hold her up with chat. She was in and out in a few minutes with writing paper and a fancy pen under her arm, along with the directions to a nearby park.

She went via the café again, this time for pastries to go with her second large coffee. She added a blanket from the car to her supplies and set off on foot for the park.

CHAPTER 31

With breakfast over, Abby knew her next mission: find Laura and tell her to go.

She reached the reception as Laura swept through the front doors, breathless, with her arms filled with roses.

Internally, Abby groaned. She'd forgotten just how predictable Laura could be. Whether it was a special occasion or there was an apology required, it was always roses that appeared. Laura also seemed to think the more there were, the more romantic. After what had happened the night before, Abby wondered which reason they were being presented for this time—romance or apology.

"What's all this?" She did her best to offer an ounce of surprise as Laura bundled them into her arms and planted a kiss on her cheek.

"Oh, nothing." Laura was positively breezy. "I felt like spoiling you."

"Okay." Given their last conversation, Abby couldn't help but be confused. She had expected Laura to stay for maybe another day before her long drive back south, but here she was still, bringing Abby flowers. "We need to talk."

"Yes, I think we do. Fancy taking me to the tower?"

The hint of suggestion in Laura's voice made Abby cringe. She thought of Erin again, of the last time she was in the tower. The idea of somehow tainting it with Laura's presence spoke volumes to her, and it was the last shred of motivation she needed. She was doing the right thing.

"No, let's head through here." Abby didn't wait for an answer. She started towards the staff lounge, bumping the door open with her backside. She headed to the kitchenette and was relieved to empty her arms of the flowers.

Laura wrinkled her nose and scanned the space. "I'd forgotten how old-fashioned some parts of this place still are. You know there's tons you could do with this whole castle, to really put it on the map, attract the more extravagant visitor with real money to spend."

Abby sighed. She'd heard the same spiel so many times. "The staff feel at home in here. It's cosy and it's theirs. And the place is doing absolutely fine, thanks. We prefer to welcome anyone, no matter their wallet size." She took a bucket from under the sink, added some water, and dumped the bouquet in it, telling Laura exactly what she thought of her ideas.

"Seriously, Abby. Who crapped in your pillow case? I was only making a suggestion. You know I think your talent is wasted here. Is it really so wrong of me to want more for you?"

"It is when you equate 'more' to money or success that I have a problem. 'More' never meant that to me. Somehow you still haven't figured that out."

"Now you're talking nonsense. I know you better than you think, Abby." Her voice went up an octave with her need to make Abby believe it. "I know you were upset the other night, but I thought that it was only because you were shocked to see me. And despite the way you were, I still stuck around, didn't I? I came all this way for you, I apologised, offered you the world, and you still treat me like this? I—"

"Stop. You need to stop talking." Abby slapped an irritated palm on the worktop. "It's all you've done since you got here. You haven't listened to a word I've said."

Laura took a few steps towards her, but Abby moved, putting a worn brown sofa between them. "You left, Laura. You left me behind and any future we might have had the day you chose your career over us."

"You could have come with me. I begged you to." Laura's tone was sullen. Always playing the martyr and never able to admit her part when something went wrong. She hadn't changed a bit.

"You know that's not true. Deep down, I know you didn't really want me to come, and I wish you would just admit it. But that's okay, I'm over it. I've forgiven you because I realise now it was the right decision. We never had a future, not the forever kind. I would never have been enough for you."

"You're wrong, Abby. Why do you think I came back?" A tear slipped free, and Abby gripped the back of the sofa cushions, ignoring her compulsion to go to Laura, to comfort her.

"I really have no idea. All I can see is that you're not happy, and maybe nostalgia brought you back here to a time when you were."

"That's what I'm saying, Abby. We can have that again, we can be happy. I can move back here, or maybe you would think about coming with me this time. It could work. We can make it work."

Abby shook her head. "I will never be enough for you. That's what ended us back then, and nothing has changed now. You'll still always be looking for the next exciting thing to do or person to be around, and I'm not the girl to satisfy that need. But I'm sure there's someone else out there who will."

"Don't you love me at all anymore?" Laura was almost pleading for validation, and Abby refused to give it to her. She'd come this far, to a point where only honesty would do.

"I'm not sure I ever did, Laura. And I can't be sure you ever really loved me. That's why I know this is over."

Laura was silent. She didn't try to argue or object to Abby's final words.

"Your silence says it all. I think it's best for both of us if you leave. Today."

Laura's shoulders dropped in defeat. "I guess so." She rounded the sofa and Abby didn't move. "Take care of yourself, Abby."

Three years on and history repeated itself as Laura kissed her on the cheek and left the room without a backward glance.

CHAPTER 32

Erin descended the castle stairs when a voice stopped her. Eddie. She listened as he asked for her at reception.

"I'm her dad. Can you call to see if she's here?"

"Certainly, Mr Carter." Ann was courteous, but Erin heard the suspicion in her voice. "If you head through to the lounge, I'll let you know when I reach her."

She pressed herself against the wall before the final turn down to the lobby and waited as his footsteps passed. She peered around the wall at his back as George came from the kitchen, heading in the same direction. His stride faltered at the sight of Eddie, and she watched the colour drain from his face. "Mr Carter." George offered a small nod.

"Do I know you?" Eddie had stopped and sized up the lanky teenager before him.

She remembered her car, and wondered how George had managed to get it without speaking to him.

"Erm..." He did the nervous flick of his hair that Erin had come to recognise. "No, I remember your picture. At the rugby club. Are you here for Erin?"

That seemed to satisfy Eddie, but Erin couldn't help thinking George was lying.

"Aye, the woman on reception was going to call up for her. Is the lounge this way?"

George nodded again. "Aye, after you, sir."

She watched Eddie head through to the lounge, but George hung back a moment. He scrubbed at his face, frowning, and she swore his hands were shaking. George watched as Eddie disappeared into the room before heading back in the direction he had come from.

An uneasy feeling settled over her, and she filed the encounter away as something to ask George about later.

Ann appeared, catching her hovering on the bottom step. "Ah, Erin. I didn't think you were here. You have a visitor." She gestured towards the lounge. "Says he's your dad?"

"Aye, he is."

Ann squinted at her in the way a nosey auntie would, waiting for the full story. "Do you want to see him? I can say you're not here?"

Erin shook her head. "No, it's okay, Ann. Thanks though. I'll head through."

Ann didn't seem convinced but didn't argue. "All right, well, you know where I am."

Erin smiled at her retreating back. She might have only been there a week or so, but the sense of protectiveness she felt was comforting. As if the folk here at the castle were in her corner.

Eddie was sat on a sofa by the window. He looked genuinely please to see her and half-rose as she approached. "Hi."

"Hey." She stayed on her feet, and he stood up. For a moment, she thought he was going to try and hug her but clearly thought better of it.

"Will you sit with me a minute? I owe you an apology."

She was glad to have him here, on her turf. The castle around her seemed to give her strength. It was beginning to feel like home, and for once, she wasn't the outsider.

She took the armchair opposite and waited, saying nothing.

"Firstly, I need you to understand something." He fidgeted with his hands, clearly looking for the right words. She wasn't going to help him. "I want you to try and understand the frustration and anger I've had pent up all these years. Trying to live with, and deal with, the fact that my daughter was taken away from me. That she probably wouldn't even remember me anymore."

She couldn't hold her tongue. "For good reason. I wasn't taken from you. You lost me."

"I know, I know." He held up his hands in acquiescence. "I'm not making excuses for my actions back then. I shouldn't have tried to the other night. I know the consequences were my fault. I guess that only made it harder to reconcile."

"Good. I won't have you badmouth my mum. She did the best for me, never left me, never hurt me. She loved you once, and you threw it away. Not her."

"I realise that now. I also realise the second chance I've been given, and I'm hoping I haven't ruined that. I can never make up for the past, Erin, but can I at least try? Will you let me? I want to show you how I've changed. Can we start again?"

Erin took in his features, eyebrows knitted in a frown, his eyes shining with emotion behind tortoiseshell frames. He held his hands open towards her, pleading.

Is this real? Does he mean it? Has he changed?

She was struggling to shake off the memory of the anger that had oozed from him only a day earlier. But was she ready to turn him away? Was she ready to give up on him?

"You get one more chance."

His shoulders dropped in relief, and he sighed back into the sofa. "You've no idea how happy I am to hear you say that."

"I'm serious. What happened last night can't happen again. I won't listen to it."

He sat forward again in his seat and reached for her hands. She didn't retreat as he clasped them within his own. "I promise. All I want is to get to know you, Erin. And for you to know me as I am now. Maybe we should leave the past where it is for a while? Catch up on what you've been up to since instead?"

"Maybe."

Simon appeared beside her with two pints. Wordlessly, he set them down in front of Erin and Eddie. "We didn't order these, Simon."

He merely pointed behind her. "On the house."

She turned to look over her shoulder. Abby stood behind the bar looking sheepish. It was the first time Erin had seen her since their encounter in the hallway. Her smile somehow had the ability to instantly fill Erin with strength and hope, and she wondered if Abby had read her note.

Erin returned her smile and mouthed a thank you before turning her attention back to Eddie. One thing at a time. She could think about Abby later.

"Who's that?" he asked, taking a swig of beer.

"Abby. Her family own the place."

"Ah yes. I remember her as a kid. Didn't realise the Millers still had this place. Are you friends?"

It hit Erin then how little her dad knew about her. There was a twenty-year gap to fill him in on. And it worked both ways. Maybe he was right that they should leave what went before untouched for a while. "Aye. I hope so."

She watched him scan the room and settle back in the sofa, pint in hand with a small smile. "I'll admit this feels very surreal right now. I never thought I'd see the day I got to have a pint with my daughter."

She raised her glass to his and joined him in a drink. "That makes two of us."

~ ~ ~

Abby swiped the half bottle of wine left over from the night before and headed for the tower stairs, puffball Angus in tow. After the clattering din of the kitchen, the silence was welcome as she cocooned herself in a blanket and Angus took his rightful place smothering her feet.

Twenty-four hours of freedom stretched before her, and it felt heavenly. Wine in hand, carefully she unfolded the note Erin had tucked under her door that afternoon.

Abby, I don't know your past, and I can't tell you the future. All I know is waking up next to you meant something to me. Erin x

She read it twice more before pressing it to her chest, eyes closed, picturing Erin saying the words aloud. The note was almost as good. She considered everything that Erin had going on in her life, and how throwing the drama of her and Laura into the mix could easily evoke the reaction she'd received the night before.

Abby didn't blame her. The easy option was to tell Abby where to shove it and cut herself loose. Well, it was easy enough if Erin didn't really care. But the note said she did. Erin had reached out despite it all to tell Abby that the connection wasn't one-sided. What that meant for them both was a whole other conversation.

She thought about her earlier confrontation with Laura. Her showing up had been unwelcome and unsettling. She was angry at Laura's ability to suck her in so quickly but laid some blame at her own door for allowing it to happen. She also couldn't help feeling frustrated at her timing, at the trouble it had caused with Erin. But she had felt something for Laura once and owed her a last chance, if only to reconcile what Abby already knew to be true, that they weren't meant to be together.

She slipped the note inside a copy of Willa Cather's *My Antonio*, which never left the side table, and reached for Angus's ears. His eyes screwed up in satisfaction as she scratched behind them, and he burrowed deeper into the blanket.

That was how she had felt when Erin had walked in on her and Laura. She had wanted to crawl into the nearest small space and hide under a blanket. That it bothered Abby so much was the first sign that their time together was meant to be more than those two nights. The second had been when George had told her about Laura's behaviour in the bar. The searing pang of jealousy that had shot through her had taken Abby by surprise, particularly when she realised it wasn't because of Laura. After George had left, she admitted to herself that anyone could have hit on Erin and she would have felt the same.

Then seeing Erin in the bar with her dad, the tension that surrounded her, it had made Abby's heart ache. Any lingering anger she'd still felt towards Erin after being dismissed with such callous words had disappeared in an instant.

The strained expression etched across Erin's face had brought out feelings of inadequacy and exasperation, all in one moment. All she wanted was to reach out, to sooth it away, and make it all better. But how? Despite Erin's note, Abby was still sure she had thrown away the potential for something great.

Then Erin had turned and smiled. And the promise in that smile had made Abby's heart sing again.

Now it was Abby's turn to find the words. Or was there something more? Something that would show Erin she didn't need to feel alone. That Abby was there for her, in whatever capacity that might be.

Abby jumped from the sofa, eliciting a hiss of dissatisfaction from Angus. He leapt away from her in disgust at being disturbed. But Abby wasn't paying attention. One by one, she tugged out the drawers of her antique apothecary cabinet. In her impatience to find her prize, it somehow felt as if every bit of crap she had accumulated in her entire life was in those drawers.

"Aha!" She beamed at Angus, triumphant. He didn't look impressed. "What do you know anyway, cat?"

She rubbed at the metal object in her hand, traced the intricate pattern at one end, and checked it for damage. Plenty of small scratches had marred it over the years, but it still felt solid and had held its shape. A little polish would tidy it up lovely.

"Perfect, Angus." She headed towards the trapdoor, picking up a blanket as she passed. She dropped it on top of him knowing it would annoy him. "There you go, grump. You'll have to keep yourself cosy. I've got a plan to make."

CHAPTER 33

Erin let out a satisfied groan, stretching her fingertips to the top of the headboard and her toes to the carved wooden foot of the bed. She'd slept well and felt renewed, cheerful at waking with the morning sun. Optimism for the day filled her, and she planned to make the most of it.

The previous night had gone much better than expected with her dad. They had enjoyed a couple of pints, a little random chat—hobbies, the places Erin had lived. Girls.

He'd reacted less to learning about that part of her than he had when she'd declared she preferred football to rugby. Apparently, no daughter of his should enjoy football. But appreciating women he could understand; he liked them, too.

Erin kept the subject away from the pressure point that was her mum. But he had asked about other family, what was waiting for her back in Glasgow apart from a job, and she had answered him honestly—no one. Erin had felt herself clamming up at that point and didn't want to spoil the fledgling bond by veering into those memories and reasons why she now found herself alone.

So, she'd asked him for a few days to think things over, and with a pledge of honesty from them both, she had watched his retreating back as he'd left the castle, a glimmer of a smile on her face.

That smile was back as she thought of Abby. At the very cute, sheepish look she had given Erin as she sent the pints over and the grin it had elicited in return. Erin could only assume Abby had received her note. Erin had never sent a note of that kind to anyone before. Had never had reason or inclination to open herself up in that way. She cringed a little, wondering how it had been received.

Why did I send a note? Why not bloody speak to her? At least then you can see her reaction.

Coward.

Or was it romantic?

Neither of the two were descriptions she would normally associate with herself.

She pondered if Laura was still in the castle and thought back to her smug face in the bar that night.

Nope.

Erin threw back the covers and hopped out of bed. *I'm not heading down that track again. Today will be a good day and that's it. No room for doubts. The note is sent.*

She stood naked, hands on hips, and looked about the room defiantly. *It's up to Abby now.*

The sun beckoned her to the window, and she pulled a curtain across her nude body and peered out at the day before her. It was a day for a climb. Tinto Hill was waiting.

Her optimism began to sour again when a familiar figure strode purposefully from the castle entrance across the car park. *Laura.*

Erin watched her throw a bag into the boot and then pause with the driver's door open. It was as if she sensed Erin watching, and she stepped back from sight quickly so as not to be seen. She risked another quick peek, Laura was now in her car and the wheels spun unceremoniously as she skidded on the gravel towards the drive.

Erin couldn't help but grin. What it meant for her and Abby, who could guess, but at least it was one question answered.

A knock at the door made her jump, and she became acutely aware of her nudity. "Hang on." She scurried through to the bathroom for her robe and pulled the belt tight before opening the door. "Abby."

"Hey. Did I wake you?"

She was clearly nervous, and Erin hated that she made her feel that way. "No, I've been up a little while."

"Good. Erm..."

Erin decided to help her out. "We need to talk."

Abby raised her eyes to Erin's. "Aye. I got your note. I really want to explain."

Erin had to agree. "I think we both have some explaining to do. Can you walk and talk at the same time?"

Abby looked rightly confused. "Yeah. I like to think I'm multi-talented in that way."

Erin grinned, glad to hear the cheekiness back in Abby's voice. "Great. You, me, and Tinto? I take it as you're not in the kitchen for breakfast, you're free?"

She watched mild surprise cross Abby's face at the invitation, but her eyes told Erin she was delighted. "Perfect. Half an hour? I can pack some breakfast things rather than eating here?"

"Coffee?"

Abby laughed. "Of course. I wouldn't make that mistake again."

She held Erin's eye, and a moment passed, the tea a reminder of their first real kiss on the beach. Erin wondered if Abby was thinking about the same thing and struggled with the urge to grab her and drag her into the room. To forget the past few days and go back to where they had left things before Laura had shown up.

She felt her hand reach for Abby's when George called up the stairs, "Hey, sis. Supplier on the phone says he has a problem with tomorrow's fish order."

Abby sighed, and Erin stuffed her hand in her robe pocket.

"Shall we make that an hour?"

"Probably best. I'll see you later."

Erin watched her descend the stairs. *Look back. Please look back.*

She did, and Erin's insides did a small victory dance. "See you later, Abby."

CHAPTER 34

Pieces of newspaper stuck to Eddie's fingers. He picked at them and watched Thea paste another strip on to her balloon. They both sat cross-legged on the large sheet of plastic he insisted on when papier-mâché was involved. Paint palettes and paste brushes littered the space around them, and he took care standing up to go wash his hands in the bathroom.

"Are you finished helping, Daddy?" His little girl looked up sadly, and he hated having to leave her alone for another afternoon.

"I'm sorry, sweetheart. I need to head to Glasgow for a few things. But I promise it will be worth it."

She dunked her brush back in the paste and slapped it on the balloon with a carelessness that gave away her disappointment.

He squatted down beside her again. "Hey, don't be grumpy with me. I have to go get some things if I'm going to be able to surprise you."

Her brush stopped moving at the word. "What kind of surprise?"

"The best one ever. So, are you going to behave?"

She nodded vigorously. "Can you give me a wee clue?"

He stroked his chin in thought, and she jiggled on the spot waiting for him to answer. "Well, it's a big surprise."

"Big?" She held her arms outstretched as wide as they would go. "This big?"

He stood again and put a hand up to the level of his eyes. "More like this big. Or should I say, this tall." He had already considered that making it a surprise might not be the right way to go. It was going to be a shock for Thea and some reassurance beforehand might be better. Seeing the look of confusion on her face now helped make his final decision.

"How would you feel about sharing your room?"

The brush was completely forgotten now, and she was on her feet. "My room? Someone in my room? To play with? A friend?"

He took her by the hand and led her to sit on the bed with him. "Yes, someone to play with and share with. What do you think?"

"But who, Daddy?"

He pulled her into his lap. "Your sister, Thea. Your big sister. She's coming home."

She disentangled herself from him and scooted to the other end of the bed. Her favourite spot when she was upset. He let her go and didn't say anything as she cast a suspicious eye over him. "My sister?" It was a whisper, and he couldn't read the emotions fleeting across her face.

"Yes, Thea, your sister. Isn't it wonderful?" He kept his tone light, making it seem as if it was no big deal. He needed her to see the positive, to see how happy it was making him in the hope she would feel the same.

Her nose crinkled and her eyes darkened. She pulled a teddy close to her chest and pressed herself into the corner of the bed against the wall. "But how do I have a sister? And she's big? You said she's big, Daddy. Is she an adult? Shouldn't she stay in the upstairs? I don't understand? Did they take her away the same as they might do to me?"

The volume of her voice increased with each question. It became shrill, and he knew she was nearing panic level. He shouted to snap her out of it. "Stop, Thea. Stop it." He thumped his fist into the mattress, and she stilled.

Eddie made to move closer to her, but she cowered and hugged the stupid teddy closer. Then the tears came.

He stood. Everything he had done for her, yet she was determined to ruin what should have been a joyous moment. Why didn't she understand?

"I told you to stop. I will not have tears. I will not have this ruined. She's your sister, and she's coming home. Now stop being a silly girl and quit that crying."

He glowered down at her until the tears became merely a whimper. He hated being rough with her, but it was necessary sometimes. She had to toe the line. Any childish ideas, and who knew what trouble she could cause for them. It was bad enough losing one daughter—he couldn't risk another.

"You want her to like you, don't you?" He lowered his tone and moved to sit near her on the bed again. She didn't answer. Simply stared at him over the head of her bear through watery eyes.

"She was taken away, Thea. I didn't know how to protect her the way I protect you now, and the bad ones took her. So, you see, that's why you have to behave and do as you're told."

She lowered the bear a little and wiped at her eyes. "How did you get her back?"

He glanced at the rows of books for inspiration, taking a moment to think how best to make her understand. He needed a story she could relate to. "She escaped. She was brave and ran away and came to find me. Just like all those princesses in your books. And now she needs me to protect her the way I protect you. She isn't safe in the upstairs either."

Thea nodded slowly, digesting the words. Her fairy stories told similar tales, and her interest was taking over the resentment at being shouted at. "What's her name?"

He moved to tuck her under his arm again and she didn't resist. "Erin."

"That's pretty."

"It is," he agreed. "And she's also pretty, almost as much as her little sister." That won her around fully, and she grinned up at him.

"Do we look the same?"

"Well, she has hair as dark as yours is light, the same as mine. But you both have the same nose and an equally lovely smile."

She showed him her smile. "I think it will be okay, Daddy."

"What will, peanut?"

"Sharing my room. I think she'll have fun here."

He hugged her close, glad the tantrum was over. Now he could focus on preparing for Erin's next visit without worrying about Thea. "I think she will too."

CHAPTER 35

The well-trodden path snaked through the landscape before them. It taunted Erin's weary legs, the end nowhere near in sight. She looked back, scanning the vista sprawled before her, and noticed the double-ring formation of the Roman fort remains that Abby had pointed out at the start of their climb. It felt almost a lifetime ago.

They had since passed the cairn marking the ridge of Totherin Hill, which Abby informed her was around two-thirds of the way. Erin suspected she was lying.

She stopped, hands on hips, and gulped in some air. "I thought you said this was an easy hill."

Abby's laughter caught in the wind and drifted down to her. She turned and took a few steps back towards Erin. "You clearly spend too much time stuck in a classroom. Here." She reached out a hand. "Do you need me to pull you up?"

Erin swatted it away. "Cheeky. I'm not quite there yet."

Abby laughed again. "Okay, well I do piggybacks as well. For a fee."

"Why do I get the feeling I won't want to pay your price?" Erin arched an eyebrow and started to move again, but Abby stood firm, blocking her way.

"I guess that depends on whether you've forgiven me or not?"

Erin stopped before her, the hill putting them level in height. They hadn't spoken yet about Laura, about anything. Erin's burning thighs told her now was as good a time as any.

"Did you pack coffee?"

Abby nodded. "Black. There's granola bars, fruit, and chocolate, too."

Erin stepped off the track, away from her, towards a patch of boulders. Abby followed and watched as Erin shook her arms out of her coat and laid it over a relatively flat rock.

"Sit." She climbed up, and Abby did as she was told, joining her on the rock. "You talk while I eat, drink, and learn to breathe properly again."

Abby chuckled. "Am I allowed to drink as well?"

"I guess." Erin rubbed her hands together in anticipation of the coffee. As ever in Scotland, the weather was unpredictable, and at this height the breeze was still cool and bit into her fingers. Abby poured and handed her a cup.

Erin heard a sigh as she sat back against a higher boulder. "Are you all right?"

"Aye, wondering where to start."

Erin leant back with her. Their thighs and shoulders connected, and the warmth radiated through Erin. "The beginning?"

Abby nudged at her. "Smart-arse."

Silence wrapped around them, and Erin didn't interrupt it. Abby would talk in her own time.

When she did, her voice was small. "I'm sorry."

Erin kept her eyes on the view. "I know."

"She'd only been there ten minutes when you saw us. I thought I'd get a chance to speak to you before you realised who she was. I didn't know she was coming."

"Hey, you've barely known me ten minutes. You don't owe me anything."

"We both know that's not true. I owe you an explanation."

Erin looked her way expectantly. "So, explain."

Abby dropped her gaze first and rubbed absentmindedly at a patch of moss on the rock. "She said she still loved me. I thought for so long that hearing those words from her were all I wanted. I used to dream about her coming back for me. Then I finally heard them and I felt cold. They meant nothing. I realised Laura only wants what she can't have. She's never been able to commit to anything other than serving her own self-interests, and it was pure nostalgia that made her take the trip to the castle."

"So not even a little bit of you considered taking her back?"

"Of course. I can't lie. For a moment, the nostalgia got me as well. I heard all her promises. She reminded me of the good times when we were younger and impetuous. Still free of responsibility and ties. I had to think about it. I at least owed myself that."

Erin couldn't believe what she was about to ask but couldn't help herself. "Did you sleep with her?"

"No!" Abby's response was instant and fervent. "She tried but...after the tower...with you...and then that night in the pub, and your room. I wanted so badly to talk to you." Abby stopped and blew out a frustrated breath.

"We had sex a few times. It doesn't have to mean any more than that. We're both grown-ups, and you didn't need my permission. I'm merely a guest in your hotel, and who knows how long I'll even be around."

Erin returned her gaze to the view. A feeling of dread had begun to seep in as the truth of her own words registered. She knew she was placing the first few bricks between them, building her own fort in anticipation of Abby's response. It was reflex to go on the defensive. The courageous words she'd uttered to herself the day before began to quickly fade along with her bravado. If Abby regretted the nights they'd spent together, that was fine. Erin would get over it. And the fact she would have to leave eventually was also true.

The note she had slipped under Abby's door suddenly seemed a very bad idea. What had she been thinking, forcing Abby to consider them anything more than a fling? And in the process turning away a potential future with someone else. Albeit a complete arsehole, but that wasn't for Erin to decide.

"So why put that note under my door?"

Erin heard the hurt in Abby's voice and couldn't blame her. Maybe Erin was the arsehole. "I'm asking myself the same question."

"So what was it? Were you mad about Laura and thought you'd mess with us? I know she hit on you."

Erin wasn't surprised she knew. If she had been in George's shoes, she probably would have told her. It was unfair for him to be expected to keep it from his sister, especially if he thought there was a chance she would take Laura back. His dislike of her had been obvious to Erin. "No. I'm not mad, Abby."

Abby continued, her anger evident. "Because you know I had already made my decision about Laura. When George told me what had happened, that only made it easier to tell her to leave."

"Abby, listen." Erin threw up a hand and let it smack back down on to her thigh. "I'm not mad. I don't know what I am. I'm...all over the place." It was vague, but the best she could do.

"Did I misread the note? Am I nothing more than a fling? A distraction from all the other crap you've got going on? Because that was a really shitty thing to do if it was purely to get one up on Laura."

"No." It was Erin's turn for vehemence. "It wasn't that at all. I don't want you to think that."

Cold fingertips rested on her wrist and squeezed gently. Abby's tone softened. "Because it meant something to me too, Erin."

Erin didn't flinch; she accepted them and turned her palm upwards until Abby's fingers were held between her own. With that small gesture, her entire body seemed to relax and she no longer felt the need to explain. She felt the security of Abby pressed against her, and although it was unfamiliar, it felt wonderful. History hadn't won. She studied their entwined fingers and realised every step with Abby was new for her. It was as if she had to learn how to do this, to hold someone's hand, to know when to offer a kiss, to learn to be with them, and not question every motive.

Abby leant into her shoulder. "I wish you'd told me about Laura, instead of hearing it from George."

Erin shrugged. "I wasn't sure you'd believe me. You hardly know me. It would have been too easy for Laura to twist."

"Well, I'm sorry she put you in that position. And you should know, your word already means more to me than Laura's ever did. I've heard too many lies from her not to know when she's doing it."

"You don't need to apologise for her." Erin traced an invisible pattern on her trousers, taking a moment, knowing her own bad behaviour needed to be addressed. "I'm sorry too, Abby. For the way I talked to you that night."

Abby squeezed her hand a little tighter. "You were upset. I get it. It's all right."

"No, it isn't. You didn't deserve that. You were an easy target at the end of a really crappy day, and I'm ashamed to have treated you that way."

She heard Abby let out a small sigh and braced herself for recrimination. "I won't lie, Erin. It hurt. A lot. Even though I told myself it wasn't all about me and Laura, that you had other heavy stuff going on, it was still hard to take."

"I know. I should have just allowed you to explain. I'm really so sorry, Abby. Will you forgive me?" Erin braved eye contact, and it only took a mere moment to know that Abby had already forgiven her.

It was Abby who closed the gap between their lips. The kiss was tentative at first, then firm. Both tender and reassuring. It was all Erin needed to know that everything between them was okay.

"Of course," Abby whispered against Erin's lips. "But don't do it again."

Erin laughed with her and felt immediately relieved. To be back in a good place with Abby, she realised, was the one piece of genuine happiness in her life.

Erin skimmed her hand over the top of the purple heather surrounding them before stopping to pluck a sprig and offer it Abby's way. "Not exactly roses, but they say it's lucky."

Abby smiled at the gesture. "Does this mean I'm forgiven too?"

Erin turned to look at the steep incline ahead of them. She lifted Abby's hand and planted a brief kiss on it before jumping off the rock and gathering up their things. "Almost. A piggyback to the top should do it."

Abby made a fine attempt, but Erin's lanky legs were too long and kept scuffing the dirt as the gradient steepened, causing them to fall in a tangle of arms, legs, and dirt. The laughter continued to the top, which came surprisingly sooner than Erin had anticipated.

The view from the summit was stunning and worth the tired muscles. The day was mostly clear, with only a few streaks of white across bright blue. "It's rare to get such a fine day up here. Look." Abby pointed north. "You can make out the Trossachs."

Erin's arms met no resistance as she slid them around Abby's waist and rested her chin on a shoulder. "It's beautiful."

She didn't let go as Abby turned them towards the south. Keeping her finger in Erin's line of vision, she traced an invisible line on the horizon. "And that's the English border."

"Cool." Erin grinned and squeezed her closer, laying a feather-light kiss behind Abby's ear. She felt the faint shudder it elicited in Abby, and the sensation only compounded how happy she was to have Abby with her on the climb. She was also relieved at how easily they'd talked. It felt good to have things out in the open. It was unusual for Erin, all this candidness and communication, but then everything about the situation she now found herself in was unusual for her.

They swayed a little together in the breeze. Abby seemed as unwilling to let go as Erin was. Eventually, other walkers reached the summit, and the moment was broken. They sat overlooking the Valley of the River Clyde and drank the remaining coffee, shaking their heads at the craziness of two paragliders as they launched themselves over the edge.

"How are things going with your dad?" Abby popped a square of chocolate in her mouth and offered a piece to Erin.

Erin took it and let it melt a little in her mouth before answering. "Weird."

"That's it? Weird?" Abby helped herself to another piece of chocolate. "Have you used up all your words for the day already?"

Erin couldn't help but smile at the notion that Abby already knew these little things about her. It was momentary, and she stored the feeling away for safekeeping before her thoughts turned back to Eddie. "I'm trying not to think too hard about it. I think maybe my situation has similarities to how you felt about Laura. I'm not sure what side of him is real. That's probably the best way to describe it."

Abby frowned and sucked chocolate from a fingertip. "What's he done to make you think that way?"

Erin told her about Eddie losing his temper. The way he had spoken about her mum with such hatred and anger. "He assures me it was only because he was taken by surprise, what with me turning up out of the blue like that. He says he's changed, that's not him anymore, and he wants a chance to make amends. To get to know me."

"And are you giving him the chance?"

"I guess. I suppose only time will tell if he's telling the truth. I've told him it's his last though. No matter what it means for me to walk away from him, I will."

"Wow. Intense."

"Aye." Erin pinched the last square of chocolate and sniggered mischievously at Abby's disappointed face. "C'mon. After what I just told you, don't begrudge me the last piece."

Abby still pouted. "Aye, all right."

The sun had dipped lower and the cairn cast a shadow across them. "Time to head back?"

Abby pushed herself up and held out her hands to pull Erin to her feet. "Probably best."

"Oh, before I forget." Erin remembered the previous night in reception. "Does George know Eddie?"

Abby frowned, giving Erin her answer before she spoke. "Not that I know of? Why?"

Erin threw the picnic bag over her shoulder. "He seemed to recognise him when he came by yesterday. When Eddie asked if they'd met, George told him he recognised him from pictures at the rugby club. His reaction seemed odd, that's all."

"That is a little odd. I'd say George has only been to the club a couple of times to watch the big Scotland matches. He's not really a fan. He only goes because his pals are into it."

"That's probably how then. I may just be a little sensitive right now when it comes to Eddie." She gave Abby a wry smile. "Or anyone for that matter."

Abby zipped her jacket and gave Erin a shove in the direction of the path home. "No comment. Let's go."

CHAPTER 36

The descent was relatively quick, and the easiness returned between them as Abby poked fun at Erin's lack of fitness on the drive back to the castle.

They both stopped on the entrance steps, away from Ann's prying gaze. It was quickly becoming a well-known spot to them. Abby took the picnic bag from Erin. "I'm going to hit the shower. Do you maybe want to have a drink later? Or dinner?"

Her tone was shy and Erin quickly put her out of her misery. "I'd love to. Let's do both. Call my room when you're ready?"

Abby beamed and bounced up the last step. "Perfect. See you later."

Erin watched her go and shook her head to herself as the solid door swung closed. It had been less than two weeks, but Abby had quickly become the sunny day in what had been only grey clouds and rain over the past few months. She scanned the gardens of the castle, so familiar to her now, and tried to imagine life beyond her stay there. She couldn't quite conjure it. Her life in Glasgow felt a distant memory, filled with emptiness and dark rooms, devoid of peace.

That was what she felt, in that moment. Peace.

She took one last look before letting her moment go, pushing through the heavy door towards the hot shower waiting for her.

~ ~ ~

Between the climb and the shower, Erin felt rejuvenated. The difficult part of her conversation with Abby washed itself away with the steaming water. All that remained in her memory was the pleasure of her touch, the heat of their legs pressed together, and Abby's fingers entwined with her own. She thought of the smile meant only for Erin.

She scrubbed at her hair with a towel and crossed the room to close the curtains. A yellow slip of paper caught her eye near the door. Abby had returned her note.

Come to the tower when you're ready. A x

She didn't even bother to dry her hair, such was the urgency she felt to have Abby back within her reach. Her legs protested as she took the tower stairs two at a time but were forgotten when the sound of a guitar being strummed floated down to her. The lyrics of a song she loved, one that never failed to fill her heart, followed the notes from the guitar.

"Caledonia."

It was Abby's voice of course. She recognised it from her first night at the hotel. She slowed her climb until she reached the window she'd stopped at that first time in the tower. She sat and let the music drift over her.

The lyrics spoke of being far from everything a person knows, of losing people and finding others, and how you change along the way. It was a love song for finding home. For the inexplicable pull of a place that beckons you to return because it's part of you. It makes you who you are. Never had the song spoken more clearly to her.

The feeling of calm that came with it was welcome. It was worth the few extra minutes before seeing Abby, her voice already having the effect that Erin craved. As the final lyrics came to a beautiful and sweet crescendo, she continued her climb.

Abby strummed the final few notes before she noticed Erin, halfway up through the trapdoor. She didn't show any surprise; instead, she set her guitar aside and patted the space beside her in the window seat. "Hey."

Erin crossed the room and squeezed on to the ledge with her. "Hey." Feet swinging, heels tapping automatically against the brick of the old tower wall, neither said anything for a moment.

"You have a habit of catching me singing."

Erin glanced sideways and gave her a half-smile. "Sorry, I couldn't help it. It's one of my favourite songs and I wanted to enjoy it without you feeling self-conscious."

Abby returned her smile. "You know now every time I play, I'll wonder if you're on the stairs."

Erin laughed. "Would it make a difference? Would you mind if I was?"

Abby ran her fingers across the strings of the guitar. "I wouldn't mind at all." She stood then and went to the small fridge. "Beer?"

"Sure, sounds good." Erin looked out of the window at the sun beginning its descent, casting red and orange beams of warmth through the trees. "I think we've earned it."

A hand laid itself on her arm as Abby manoeuvred herself back into the seat beside her. Erin was glad of the beer. She took a long drink to cool the heat spreading within at having Abby so close.

"I wanted to ask you something." Abby broke the silence again. "I know you might not have an answer, but I have to ask you anyway."

"Okay." Erin drew the word out, wondering what was coming.

"How long are you staying?"

The bluntness took Erin by surprise, but she understood why Abby was asking. The question had crossed her own mind a number of times that day. "I really don't know." She would have preferred to offer something more concrete but simply couldn't.

"Hmm…" Abby took a swig and looked out of the window. She had clearly been hoping for something more.

"I'm sorry, Abby. Until I see my dad again, get a clearer grasp on where that might go, I honestly can't say. My only fixed date is the start of the new school term."

Abby turned from the window and pinned her with blue eyes, darkened in the enclosed space. "What about where this might go?"

Erin cursed her eyebrows as they shot towards the ceiling, giving away her surprise at the question. Directness was clearly on Abby's agenda, and suddenly the window seat felt too small, even for Erin.

She freed herself from it and Abby's stare, pacing away and taking another long drink of beer. "Where did that come from?"

Abby merely shrugged. "Call me brave, call me stupid. I know we're good after earlier, and I also know there's something happening between us. Something unique—that I don't think either of us is denying. At least I don't want to deny it. So, I'd say it's a question that eventually needs an answer."

"Does it need to be answered now?" Erin was hopeful of escaping it. She thought back to only an hour before, the peace that had enveloped her standing on the castle steps. It had been the first time in a long while she had felt in the moment, with nowhere to be, no decisions to be made. Then she thought of the song lyrics, of "home", and with her mum gone wondered where that was now.

Abby took a swig of beer and set the bottle aside. "No. As long as it's something you're thinking about."

Erin offered her a small smile. "It is. I can assure you."

"Good." Abby seemed satisfied and hopped off the sill. "Then I have something for you." She crossed to the worn apothecary cabinet and picked up a blue velvet box. Erin watched her open it and remove something, but she didn't offer it Erin's way. Instead, she palmed it and crossed to where Erin stood. "Give me that." She took the bottle from Erin's hand and set it on the side table.

Abby moved around behind her, and Erin tried to turn to see what she was doing. She stilled as gentle fingertips brushed their way along her collarbone to the back of her neck. A moment later, she felt the weight of her mother's necklace disappear as Abby undid the clasp, then watched as a slightly tarnished silver key slid down the chain and fell against her chest.

Her eyes closed involuntarily at a delicate touch behind her ear when she realised it was Abby's lips.

Abby moved to face her again, and Erin lifted the key. "What's this for?"

Abby covered Erin's hands with her own, squeezing the key tightly between them. "It's a key to the tower. I want you to know you always have a safe space here."

Erin was overwhelmed. Between the moment she'd opened the door to Abby that morning, to where she stood now in the tower, something had shifted within her. And Abby was right; it was unique. She felt a lump rise in her throat at what it meant for Abby to share this place. Her quiet time, her escape.

That Abby knew it was what Erin looked for, wherever she went, whoever she was with, meant more than Erin could find the words to describe.

A few tears broke free, and Abby brushed them away. "Hey, enough of that. It's not such a big deal."

Erin shook her head, the "Caledonia" lyrics played again in her mind, Abby singing about coming home. "You have no idea, Abby."

Promises accumulated on the tip of her tongue, ones she was sure would satisfy every question Abby had, but had the potential to make her a liar. She was on the verge. Fear and uncertainty were no longer winning, but they still gripped tight enough to hold the words back.

Instead, Erin pulled her in for a hug and squeezed tight for a couple of seconds before letting go and holding Abby at arm's length. "You really don't have any idea."

Abby smiled and fingered the key against Erin's chest. "I wanted you to know it matters that you're here. And it will matter when you go."

It mattered to Erin as well. She answered her own question from only a few moments before. There was no doubt in her mind that right now this felt like home. She wiped at her face and took a steadying breath. Then it was taken from her as Abby's lips met her own.

CHAPTER 37

A soft hum came from Erin as Abby shifted against her back and slipped her hand across Erin's stomach. She let her palm slide across the smooth skin, make its way over her hip, and trail as far as she could reach from thigh to the back of her knee, before making the return journey and starting again. Erin pressed back into her, closing any minute gap that may have existed between their bodies.

Abby peppered the back of her neck with kisses before tucking her face into the crook of it. "It's still early," she whispered against the lobe of Erin's ear. "Sleep some more."

Erin's hand found hers and stopped its movement. Lacing their fingers together, she pulled it around her waist. "Then you're going to have to stop doing that."

Abby dropped another kiss on her neck. "Spoilsport." She heard the change in Erin's breathing as she dozed again, and Abby closed her eyes, listening to its rhythm.

Her mind wandered from the delicious thoughts she had woken to, to memories of the hours spent the night before, locked together in a game of discovery and luscious satisfaction. The new day was approaching them too soon, and for once it unsettled Abby that she had no idea what it might bring.

If she was being truthful, she hadn't expected an answer to her question about Erin's plans. She knew it was too soon. But her own impatience had forced the words from her lips, and now the lack of an answer troubled her. It tried to unpick the positives from her mind with its uncertainty.

She tried to picture Erin's life in Glasgow and realised how little she knew. What was her home like? Did she have pets? Plants? Who was feeding or watering them in her absence? Did she have someone important enough in her life that she allowed them into her home, alone?

Of course, she could ask Erin. But that part of her seemed so closed off. Or maybe it was Abby who had shut it out, placed Erin's real life in a box and stored it away. Instead, all that existed of Erin were the last couple of weeks they had spent together. She couldn't imagine her anywhere but the castle.

They were sequestered here in this idyllic place. Still with problems and day-to-day life to deal with, but for Abby nothing insurmountable that couldn't be talked over and solved from the predictability of her fortress. The same couldn't be said for Erin.

She was understanding a little why her parents had decided to leave. They had tried to explain their need to experience the world outside of the isolated bubble they'd created. But at the time, all Abby could focus on was the fact that it had felt as if they were abandoning her and George.

Since then she had chastised herself more than once for the feeling of resentment that occasionally reared its ugly head and tried to set up camp in her psyche. Then irritation would quickly take over. She would wonder about her own future and question when her chance to explore would come. Inevitably, she would then come full circle, telling herself how lucky she and George were, to live and work in an amazing castle that they would one day inherit.

Even if it squeezed and suffocated her with its responsibility.

She also had to admit that if leaving was really what she wanted, her parents would manage, would replace her, no problem. It wouldn't provide the same peace of mind, but then maybe that wasn't Abby's concern.

The truth was, neither Abby nor George had found a reason to leave. The insulated and certain world that running the castle offered was hard to let go of, no matter how much they complained about it. And anyway, what was wrong with safe and unsurprising? Was she really upset about a life lacking drama and worry?

She thought again about Erin and her life in Glasgow. Imagined her living in an old tenement flat with original features, simply decorated but cosy, although not in a cluttered way. She envisaged things placed very particularly, in a way that would come effortlessly to Erin, but in others would seem contrived.

Abby tried to envisage them lying in Erin's bed. What colour were the sheets? More importantly, what side did Erin prefer to sleep on?

She gave herself a mental reprimand. *You are not one of those women, Abby. Why on earth are you thinking about this stuff?*

Her mind wasn't shy in its response. *Maybe because Erin could finally be a reason to leave the castle.*

She squeezed her eyes tight until small white spots swam in front of them and the thought of them in Erin's imaginary bed was gone.

It didn't last long.

She was back there again, only now she was sitting on a stool at a breakfast bar made for two. She wondered what Erin's routine was in the morning and knew for sure there would be a coffee pot involved. It wouldn't be fancy, maybe an old-fashioned percolator that she would swear never made a bad cup.

Did she listen to the radio? Sing in the shower? Was she always looking for her keys?

Abby pictured Erin tugging on her jacket, swigging back coffee that was still too hot, piece of toast hanging out of her mouth as she lifted cushions and rifled pockets in search of her keys.

She snickered to herself. *No. That definitely wasn't Erin.*

"What's so funny?"

Abby nuzzled in. "You."

"Oh God, was I talking in my sleep or something?"

"Nope. Can I ask you a random question?"

"Only if it's whether I want coffee or not."

Abby chuckled. "What if I make that my second question?"

Erin slid around in her embrace, bringing their noses together. She kept her eyes closed and landed a kiss on Abby's waiting lips. "Deal."

"Who's watering your plants?"

Erin opened one eye and moved her head back a little in an effort to focus. "My plants?"

"Yeah." Abby slid her fingers along Erin's spine, walking them up the vertebrae in her neck before threading them through unruly hair. "Who's watering them while you're away?"

The eye closed and Erin moved back in again, tracing kisses across Abby's collarbone before burrowing down and laying her head on a breast. "I don't have any."

Abby's fingers stilled their twirling of hair. "Pets?"

"Nope. And that question was meant to be about coffee."

A seed of sorrow planted itself in Abby's heart and grew through her chest to form a lump in her throat. "It really is only you?"

Erin looked up at her, both eyes now open and pinned on Abby's. "Right now it isn't."

Before Abby could respond, Erin was kissing her, luxuriously slow, her tongue finding Abby's lazily and taking its time in its exploration. Then the tip of Erin's ran across Abby's bottom lip before she nipped it with her teeth and whispered against it. "Coffee."

Abby laughed loudly and pinched Erin's side, eliciting a squeal. "Yeah, yeah. I'm going."

CHAPTER 38

Erin pressed one last kiss to Abby's lips before reluctantly making the descent from the tower. She smiled down every one of the steps, humming "Caledonia", which had wormed its way into her head the moment she had woken.

She had left with promises of dinner together that evening and hopefully a real conversation about what came next. But before then another trip to Eddie's loomed, and a small pit of dread replaced her stomach.

After their last meeting, Erin had felt positive. Optimistic that he was someone she would come to want in her life, even need. However, the anticipation of seeing him again seemed to bring with it more worry than want, and her mum's voice became louder in her head with warning.

She pulled up to the old croft and sat a minute. It looked the same as the first day she had visited, with no obvious sign someone was home. No light or warmth to invite her in, and the trepidation of making this journey, of seeking him out, came back full force as it had that first time she had seen him on the front step.

He appeared there again and raised a hand in greeting. Unable to put it off any longer, she grabbed her handbag and took a moment longer than necessary to lock the door. *He's a stranger, Erin, but he's still your dad. Don't forget that.*

She matched his smile as she approached, and when he held out an awkward arm, she allowed herself to be pulled into the hug.

"Hey, how's my girl?"

At the words, a little comfort crept in and pushed against the doubt. *My girl.* She'd never heard those words from him before.

"Um, great. Thanks. How are you?"

"All the better for having you here. C'mon in. I've got the kettle on."

She followed him through to the kitchen and took the same seat at the table as before. He busied himself making the tea, and she didn't have the heart to tell him she hated it. The radio played, and she recognised the DJ. "You listen to Radio 6?"

He set the pot and mugs on the table in front of her. "Almost always. I enjoy the variety, and it's a good station for discovering new bands. Are you a fan?"

She nodded and took a piece of shortbread when he offered the tin bearing the brand of the company he worked for. "My only stipulation when I bought my new car was that it had digital radio so I could get that station. I love music and driving, and it's my first choice."

He positively beamed, and she couldn't help her own smile. They had the same taste in music; it was another small victory in building their budding relationship.

"So, what have you been up to?" He dunked a biscuit and settled back expectantly.

Her mind immediately thought of Abby. *No. Not something she was willing to discuss with him yet.* "Mostly exploring, checking out the area. I climbed Tinto yesterday, and I checked out one of the local pubs last weekend."

"The Rose?"

"Aye, that's actually how I ended up finding you."

He quirked an eyebrow. "James Carter still runs it then?"

"He does. With all his exuberant charm."

Eddie laughed. "Aye, sounds like the same old James I knew."

It occurred to her then the ties he had to the village, and her interest was once again piqued at the reasons why he had cut himself off from them suddenly. She knew about his wife, about a possible daughter being sent away, but that didn't explain why he had stayed. Only to shut himself away rather than head somewhere new for a fresh start.

Maybe that was her mum's way of thinking that made her consider it the obvious thing to do. She had the same constant unsettling feeling no matter where she lived. Her mum's answer? Move on.

She thought again about the potential that she had a half-sister somewhere. It itched at her consciousness, and the question sat perennially on her lips. Was it too soon to ask? They had agreed not to discuss her mum and the events before Amelia had taken them both from his life, but Marie had been a big part of his life since then. Despite her death, surely it was a part she should know about.

"So, why do you never head into the village? From what I hear, most folk think you moved away."

He shifted in his seat and his eyes strayed to his half-full cup. A finger traced the rim of it. "What else do 'most folk' think?"

She didn't miss the edge to his voice, and it confirmed that the question was too soon. But the opening was there and she couldn't help herself. "A lot of different things that, if I'm honest, have left me with an awful lot of questions. I can't help wondering what's true and what isn't."

"Fucking busybodies." He spoke through his teeth, making Erin sit up a little straighter. "I can imagine the crap they've filled your head with."

It didn't surprise her that his immediate mode was defensive. If half of what she had heard was true, then he had a sorry story hidden away inside with enough tragedy to make anyone angry. "Why don't you put me straight?"

The sound of his chair scraping back abruptly made her flinch, and she gripped both hands around her untouched mug of tea. Its warmth offered a little comfort as she watched him pace to the sink with the kettle, refill it, bang it down on the counter along with the teapot, get the milk, slam the fridge door, and finally clatter the used teaspoon into the sink.

She didn't speak. Didn't move. She let him have his few moments of angry tea making to consider her question. As each one ticked by, an old fear crept its icy fingers up her back and around her neck.

He stood over her and glanced down at her full mug. "Is there something wrong with your tea?"

She was five years old again, looking up at him wide-eyed, afraid that any answer that came from her lips would never be the right one. No matter how inane the question, his tone, his stony expression, they were the same. "I...I don't like tea."

He snatched it from her and tepid liquid sloshed over her hand and sleeve. He paid it no attention, simply poured the rest away and dropped the mug with a thud into the sink. "Why the fuck didn't you say?"

The emphasis on "fuck" penetrated those dark places she only went to in her nightmares, bringing them to the fore, to the kitchen, as vivid as twenty years ago. It was as if no time had passed. The lost years weren't lost. She realised in that moment that they would have only been a repeat of the ones gone before. He hadn't changed; the cycle hadn't been broken. Her questions didn't need answered, because it didn't matter anymore. Her mum was right; he didn't matter.

James Carter's words about the baby being alive and well pushed their way through the fear that was threatening to immobilise her. There was only one question that mattered to her. One that needed to be asked, and something told her this might be her last opportunity.

She rose from the table, flicking tea from her hand before pulling a tea towel from a rail to dry herself off.

"Do I have a sister?"

CHAPTER 39

"So, big sis, how goes it with the lovely Erin?" George took another stool down from the bar, stood it upright, and threw her a mischievous grin.

"It goes like this, little bro." She mimicked his endearment. "None of your damn business." She poked her tongue out and continued stocking the wine fridge.

"Och, c'mon. Throw me a bone. Wasn't that her I saw sneaking out of the tower this morning?"

Abby kept her back to him and shrugged. "Maybe."

She heard him chuckle before moving around behind the bar with her. "I knew it. It goes well then? You've sorted things out?"

She gave him a withering look but couldn't help the smile that came with thinking about Erin. "Aye, it goes well. I think."

"You only think? What's up?"

He leant back against the bar and crossed his arms, obviously settling in for a conversation she wasn't about to have with him.

"As I said, none of your damn business. I'm fine."

"But..." He clearly wasn't giving up that easily.

"But nothing. We have things to talk about, of course. She's a guest. And generally, guests leave." She tried at nonchalance, but she could tell he wasn't buying it.

"And that would upset you?"

She gave in and pulled up a stool. "Well, duh. I mean, at first it was cool, a little fun, you know?"

His eyebrows rose and he nodded. "Oh yeah, I know all about your 'fun' with guests."

She jabbed his arm. "Do you want to talk or not?"

"Ouch." He rubbed at his barely visible bicep. "Not if it's going to hurt."

"Sorry." She gave him her best sheepish look. "I don't want to joke about this one, all right?"

"Aye, all right." He pushed off the bar and stooped to the fridge. After relieving it of two bottles of beer, he waggled them in her direction.

"Go on then. I'm off tonight."

"Me too." He popped the tops. "So, at first it was fun, but now it's..." He rolled his hand, gesturing for her to finish his sentence.

"Now it's more than that." She took a sip of the beer and savoured the coolness, letting the bubbles roll around her tongue. "She's...different."

"You want her to stay then?"

"I didn't say that. It's not about her staying or me going. It's about the in-between. What happens before we get to that stage? If, or how, we get to that stage. I know Glasgow isn't that far, but with my odd shift patterns, and she'll be back teaching soon. I don't know, it doesn't make for easy dating."

She watched him chew at his lip in thought and almost told him off, then remembered she did the same thing. "You're right. It isn't that far. You could make it work. I don't think that's the issue here. C'mon, what's really bothering you?"

She sighed and bought a little time with another mouthful of beer. When Erin had left that morning, her reassurance had left with her. Now the doubts were tenfold and the fear of putting herself out there only to be knocked back down was intimidating. No matter how she felt, no matter how Erin made her feel, with her lips, her safe arms, her steady gaze, Abby couldn't shake the unsettling feeling that when Erin left, it was over.

She plunged on, the need to voice her fears overwhelming. "What if she doesn't want it to work?"

"Ah...now we're getting somewhere. Although I'm surprised. Is this really my have-some-fun-and-see-you-later sister having a crisis of confidence?"

She swiped at him again. "Fuck off, George. I'm not that bloody bad."

He chuckled and put his beer down. "I know, and to be honest, I don't blame you for swerving any more than that after the way Laura treated you. You know I'm only jealous, right? That my sister gets more girls than me?"

"You are woefully bad at it. I do wonder sometimes if we're related."

He should have swiped her back, but instead he came around to her side of the bar and wrapped his rangy arms around her, resting his chin on top of her head. "I'm going to take that because you're clearly upset. And I'll have you know, me and Emily have been getting on very well, thank you very much."

She accepted his arms and lay her head on his bony chest. "I'm glad. Any advice then? Even something from you is better than nothing."

"Don't be too impatient."

She pulled away then, looking up at him. "Impatient?"

"Yes. Have you not met Erin? The girl barely gives a word away, never mind her feelings. She's got a lot going on with her dad, and you need to respect that. You might not be her priority, and that's okay right now. It's not even been a couple of weeks yet. When and if she's ready, you'll know."

"You think?" Abby wasn't wholly convinced, but it made sense. It seemed her little brother was more observant and sensitive than she gave him credit for.

"I'm sure of it. I've seen how she looks at you, Abby. Curb your impatience and she'll come to you."

Abby thought back to the previous times Erin had climbed the stairs to the tower to see her, not always invited. She thought about the brief first kiss Erin had offered in the castle car park, her invitation after their day on the beach, the note she'd put under Abby's door, and the invite to climb Tinto. George was right; when Erin wanted to open the door, she let it be known. She was brave. So, why should Abby doubt the same wouldn't happen if she wanted more?

"I hate to say it..." Abby picked her beer back up and clinked it to George's. "But I think you might be right."

He feigned shock before laughing with her. "See that wasn't so hard?"

"Aye, all right. Don't get used to it though."

"Wouldn't dare. So, what are you doing with your night off?"

She thought about her plan for dinner with Erin and glanced through the doorway towards the restaurant. No, that wouldn't do. It would feel too much like work. Should she take her out? The local Indian restaurant with all its nosey patrons came to mind, and the same went for The Rose and the Italian. She wanted Erin to herself, no prying eyes, no small talk with every new person that came through the door who recognised her.

She pointed her bottle at him. "I have a plan. And I need your help."

"Sounds ominous."

"It's not, but you might not be happy with all of it?"

"Aw c'mon, Abby. Surely, I just earned some major bro points there. What are you going to make me do?"

She laughed and drained the last of her beer. "I'm meant to have dinner with Erin tonight. Will you help me set up in our wee lounge upstairs, so I can cook for her there away from all this?" She swept her arms out indicating the place they both worked.

"Oh, sure. But..."

"I know, I know. It's your night off too, and I'm sure you have a date with a video game." She reached underneath the bar and grabbed her purse, then pulled out notes and emptied the change pouch. "I'll give you twenty-seven pounds and forty-nine pence if you make yourself scarce tonight. Take Emily to the pub or for a meal, play your games at a friend's house, whatever."

He narrowed his eyes and looked over the cash, pretending to consider it. "Make it an even thirty quid and you've got yourself a deal."

She jumped off the stool and flung her arms up around his neck, bouncing up to surprise him with a kiss on the cheek. "Deal."

CHAPTER 40

"You've been lying to me, haven't you?" Eddie sneered.

Erin couldn't help noticing the clenched fists at his side, but she was determined to stand her ground, keeping the table between them. "What? No. I think it's you that's been lying and hiding things."

Eddie took a few steps in closer to the table, and she stepped back automatically. "Me? I knew it. I knew you were exactly like your mother. That fucking holier-than-thou attitude. Automatically thinking the worst of me." He slammed a fist on the worktop. "Do you know what happens when you think the worst?"

All she could do was shake her head, wondering where he was going with the question. She was convinced that anything she could say right now would only make things worse.

"You get the worst."

He was quick, but she was quicker. The table still providing an obstacle, she was ready when he moved around towards her. She sidestepped until they'd changed positions, putting himself between her and the front door. Mistake. A big mistake, she realised. She should have gone for the door as soon as his fist hit the table.

She knew there were two other doors to her left. Both closed. The kitchen was the only part of the house she had seen. She hadn't even used the bathroom. *Which door, Erin, which door?*

Out of habit, her fingers found the pendant and key around her neck, and she rubbed them as if calling for guidance. From her mum, from Abby, from anyone who might help her end this nerve-shredding game of picking doors. What was the prize on the other side? Freedom or more of his fury?

She watched his glare fall on her hand, and for some reason it made her quickly drop the pendant.

"That's your mother's." It was a statement, not a question. "Is she even fucking dead, Erin? Did she send you here?"

He was screaming, and with every word she recoiled.

"What do you want from me? Isn't she happy that she ruined me all those years ago? Are you here to do it again?"

She took what she hoped was a small, inconspicuous step in the direction of the doors, but it didn't go unnoticed.

"Don't even think about it. There's no way out through there. I want fucking answers, Erin. I might have been stupid enough to fall for that fake charm your mother practised so well, but I'm on to you now. Why the fuck are you here?"

It took everything she had to hold his glare. She still couldn't say anything, but she was determined not to give in to the fear. The incongruous sound of the radio filled the silence until she finally found her voice.

"I'm leaving now." Internally, she cursed the shaky tone that came out and tried again. "I don't want anything from you. This was a bad idea. I'm leaving."

His voice came low, each word punctuating the air in angry determination. "You. Are. Not. Going. Anywhere."

It wasn't simple fear any more. Panic crept through her insides, and it was almost a reflex that made her glance towards the two doors once more. The one closest was the obvious choice.

She lunged and yanked down the handle, halfway through it before she realised it opened to stairs. Her foot stepped on to nothing and then she fell, shoulders, head, back, and knees all taking a pounding before it was over.

A groan escaped her, telling her she'd survived the fall but not without pain. It was dark. She raised an arm, and her hand pressed against what seemed to be the door that ended her fall. She used it to manoeuvre herself around and then leant against it until she was facing back up the stairs.

He stood there. Watching her. Barely more than a shadow with the grey light of a cloudy day behind him. She couldn't see his face, but she could see what he was holding in his hand.

When he spoke, the raw anger seemed to be gone. It was somehow even more disconcerting. It offered no relief. Nothing about him did. Instead, there was a kind of calm resignation, disappointment even, but it did nothing to reassure her. She felt the anxiety grow up through her chest and join the fear, wondering what he planned to do next.

"I told you there was no way out, Erin. You shouldn't have opened the door. It wasn't time."

She licked her lip and tasted blood. She could feel a small lump already forming on one side where she'd bitten it. Her fingers found another lump on her head, but no other limbs give off a signal they were anything but bruised.

"Time for what?" She was grateful to find that her voice was yet to desert her.

She watched as he descended the top step, then another. "You need to come back upstairs."

"Time for what?" she repeated. Her hands fumbled behind her, trying to gain traction in the small space. *Was the door behind her unlocked? Was it a cellar? Maybe there's another way out.* She found a bolt a couple of inches off the ground and glanced up to see the outline of two more at the top and middle.

She slid the bottom one back and his progress halted.

"Stop." His tone was measured, soft, as if coaxing a cornered animal back to safety. "Come back upstairs and I'll explain everything."

She didn't believe him and took a breath before bracing her knees on the bottom step and pushing herself upright against the door. Her gaze never left his right hand.

"I'm sorry, Erin." His tone had softened further, though it was anything but genuine. "Leave the door alone and come up here so I can check you're okay. I'm not going to hurt you."

"Then why is there a knife in your hand?"

As he looked down at his hand, she reached up and slid the top bolt open.

He didn't miss it. "Erin. I'm only going to ask once more."

"And then what?" she challenged. One more bolt and she could at least put some space between them. Maybe find a weapon, an escape. All she knew was she wouldn't be trapped against a door, defenceless.

Her hand was on the middle bolt, and he only had six more steps. She knew as soon as she pulled it back it would be like pulling a trigger. He was going to come for her. And it was probably going to hurt. She could see his eyes clearly now, staring at her. Daring her to defy him. There was no song from the radio anymore, only their shallow breaths and pounding in her head.

"Hello."

She felt her own eyes widen in tandem with his. The word, spoken so tentatively, came from the other side of the door. The pieces clicked into place, like a Meccano set on Christmas day, when the marble finally made it all the way to the bottom.

She had her answer.

She had a sister, and she was locked on the other side of the door.

As quickly as she realised, she threw back the final lock and burst through the door. The girl on the other side obviously wasn't expecting it, as she was knocked back with the force into the middle of the floor.

In two strides, Erin was crouched beside her, but she flinched and scurried back on all fours away from her, crouching by a toy chest. Erin scanned the room, taking it all in. Beds, drawers, pictures, toys, books. He hadn't sent her away. He'd locked her up and hidden her from the world.

She could only watch as his figure filled the doorway, and he leant against the frame, blocking her way. His arms were folded, but she could still see the glint of metal poking out at the side of his chest.

"I warned you, Erin. I wanted a chance to talk to you, to explain, before I brought you down here. I wanted you to understand first."

"Understand what?" She pointed at the diminutive girl now peering out from behind an easel. "Why you've kept your daughter locked up in a cellar all these years?"

"Exactly." He didn't seem to comprehend her incredulousness and continued as if she had given him the obvious answer. "It was the only way, Erin. After what happened with your mother, and then when Marie died, well…what else was I supposed to do? I couldn't risk them taking her away from me. Of losing another daughter."

"Why would they do that?" Erin was far from understanding. "You're her father. You have a home, you work, you provide for her. Why would they take her away from you?"

"I could feel it. All the questions, the police, the fucking locals spreading their lies and innuendo. Questioning what really happened to Marie. Why would she kill herself? Why the river? Why was there no note? I knew they were pointing fingers at me. I couldn't risk it."

"But if you had done nothing wrong, then you had nothing to worry about? Did you?"

His eyes glazed and the muscles in his cheeks twitched as he worked his jaw. It was as if he was physically stifling a lie he was sick of telling. He didn't need to answer her.

"You killed her."

"Shut the fuck up." It came out in a roar in tandem with a heavy hand that cracked across her cheek. Erin resisted the urge to raise her hand to where the heat scorched her face. Instead, it lashed out and connected with his face in retaliation.

She heard the little girl let out a squeal of surprise and start to whimper behind her.

He must have heard it too because as quick as his temper flared and he had stepped towards Erin, fist raised and ready to strike again, it dampened and brought him down to a crouch in the doorway.

"Shush, Thea. It's okay. Daddy isn't mad at you."

Thea. It was a beautiful name. Erin rolled it around in her head, silently saying it. She had a sister called Thea.

"I don't want to go away, Daddy. Don't let her hurt me." It was the first words from the girl since she'd said hello. She moved from behind Erin towards her dad. Erin reached a hand out to stop her, but Eddie glared at her and she dropped it.

"It's okay, peanut. You're not going anywhere." He took Thea's hand and brought her closer.

"Then why are you fighting?"

"Shush, look we're not any more. It's all right now. Daddy's sorry for scaring you."

"Who is she?" Thea whispered, looking suspiciously at Erin.

"Remember what we talked about, sweetheart? Well, this is Erin, your big sister. She's come to stay."

That was when his plan hit Erin, and she glanced around the room in alarm. The only other door opened into a bathroom, and she could clearly see there weren't even any windows in there. There were no obvious weapons, and then she noticed—two beds.

"You aren't serious? You think you can keep me here too?" She swept an arm around the room. "So, what? We can all live here as one big happy family, locked in the cellar because you're a fucking paranoid psycho murderer?" She heard her voice rise but didn't stop it. The gravity of the situation was taking over, and despite her words, she knew reason wasn't going to save her. Her face burned not only from the blow but also anger at the insanity of the situation.

"You're fucking mental. I can't believe I thought anything different. You made me question my mum when she was right about you all these years. You bastard."

"Now, now. You need to calm down. I know you're confused right now, but you'll see. We'll be happy, Erin. A real family again. Isn't that what you were looking for when you came to find me? A family?"

She spoke under her breath. "If this is what a family looks like to you, you can keep it." She stepped towards him, but he waved the knife at his side and took aim in Thea's direction. She knew exactly what he meant by the gesture.

But the threat felt hollow. The way he spoke, the lengths he had gone to all these years to hide and protect her in his own twisted way, would he really hurt Thea to keep Erin there? It was more likely the other way around.

"You wouldn't," she challenged, and hoped to fuck she was right.

"I think I've proved there's nothing I won't do to protect Thea and you from danger, Erin. Nothing."

His eyes held steel, and she believed him. He'd killed his second wife, she was convinced of it, so who knew the lengths he would go to if he thought Erin might bring the rest of his family crumbling down. With his back against the wall, would he take her and Thea down with him? Was he really crazy enough to do that? The mere fact he was brandishing a knife in the presence of his daughters was enough to make her realise that he was. He was capable of, and willing to do, anything.

She couldn't risk calling his bluff. Besides, apart from charging at him and hoping for the best, he had the upper hand. He had the only weapon. He was between her and a way out.

She would have to find another way.

"You won't keep me here forever. That's a promise."

He merely shook his head and looked at her as if she was some misguided fool, unable to be reasoned with. "Take a bath, have a nap. There's fresh pyjamas and clothes in those drawers. I think I got your size about right. We'll talk some more later." He let go of Thea's hand and nudged her back into the room, seemingly satisfied that Erin no longer posed a threat. "I'm sorry, peanut, don't be scared. I'll be back later with dinner."

As the bolts fell into place, Erin sank to her knees. The throbbing in her head intensified. The shouting and the slap had started the blood flowing afresh from her lip. She wiped at it with a tea stained sleeve.

"Why are you upset with Daddy?" Thea had moved back behind the easel and gripped one of its legs.

Erin offered her a small smile of reassurance. She hated to see her scared. She was just a little kid after all, and this was all she'd ever known. He was all she'd ever known. "That's what daddies and daughters do sometimes. Especially when they get older. It's all right though." She offered her hand to the pale-faced girl, but she didn't let go of the easel. Erin let it drop and fell back against one of the beds, pulling her knees to her chest she rested her forehead against them.

She pressed her fingertips in to her eyes and dragged them down her face in frustration before cursing in to her hands. "For fucking fuck sake." The vision of her bag still hanging on a chair in the kitchen, her phone tucked away inside, taunted her. A lot of bloody use it would do her there.

Think, Erin, think. How the fuck are you getting out of this hell hole?

She thought of Abby then, of their dinner plans for that night. Would she worry if Erin didn't turn up? Enough to come and look for her?

She stifled a wave of nausea at what Abby might think if Erin failed to show up for dinner. Would Abby think she'd run away? Stood her up? Been scared off by the possibility of what they had? Who would blame her? Erin had given her no reason to think otherwise.

If only Erin had answered her question the night before. Why had she held back? It had been on the tip of her tongue. Why hadn't she been able to tell Abby that her heart ached at the thought of leaving, not only the castle, but more importantly Abby?

The notion of Abby believing Erin had just pissed off without even saying good-bye tied the knots in her stomach tighter. Even if it was momentary doubt. Eventually, Abby would check her room, find her bags, and know from Ann that she hadn't checked out. But still, the vision of Abby's face and the hurt she could imagine was unbearable.

And how long before Abby checked her room? Would she know where to start looking? Would it be too late?

Then she imagined Abby turning up at her dad's. What his reaction might be. Her stomach lurched at the thought of Abby getting hurt because of her. Would he do that? Or simply make up a story and send her on her way, deny she was ever there? Would Abby believe it?

Her body ached with exhaustion and resignation.

So many questions and not an answer in sight. She couldn't rely on the unknown. She needed her own plan. As always, it was going to come down to her alone. So, what was new?

A sob tried to escape, but she swallowed it back. There was no time for that. She had to get the fuck out of there. She had to find Abby. Erin knew now that Abby was the one to change everything she had ever believed about herself, and what her life could be.

She felt a tentative hand on her shoulder, but she didn't look up. She didn't want to scare the little girl away. Then a small body pressed itself against hers as the arm snaked its way around her neck and squeezed.

"He's a good daddy, Erin. And now he has his girls back together it'll be even better. I'm so lucky now I have a big sister too."

Okay, new plan.

She had to get herself and Thea the hell out of there.

CHAPTER 41

The second hand had only moved thirty-four seconds, thirty-five, thirty-six... Abby sighed and pulled her sleeve back down over the watch. Then the clock above the mantel teased her, eliciting a growl from her. Erin wasn't simply late—she was past late. Ten thirty-two pm. Two hours and thirty-two minutes late.

Abby flopped back on the sofa and picked up her phone again, willing it to ring, beep, or buzz, whatever. She wanted it to do something more than remind her that Erin was now two hours and thirty-three minutes late.

The delicious scents she'd conjured in the kitchen were long gone, and with them most of the contents of a bottle of wine. All that remained were floppy veg and a stone-cold risotto.

So far, she'd only managed to send Erin two enquiring texts. One more, Abby decided, then she was calling it a night. She picked the phone up again, longing for it to react in her hand.

Nothing.

A little worry crept in, but Abby shook herself. They were in backwater Hopetoun, there were a number of reasons that Erin could be late but safe, with no way to contact Abby. Crappy signal was top of her list. She typed off the third text anyway.

> Hey, I wanted to say goodnight. Not sure what's happened, maybe I had my wires crossed about tonight. Hope to see you in the morning. Abby x

There. It was easy-going and not too needy. Erin had missed dinner; it wasn't as though she knew Abby had anything special planned. She thought back to George's words, and they actually soothed her a little. Who'd have thought it from her annoying little brother? He was right, however, that Erin had other priorities, and it wasn't fair for Abby to expect so much this soon.

She wondered what George was up to and scrolled to his name, hitting dial. Background noise assaulted her before his hello.

"Where are you?"

"Abby? Hang on."

The noise muted slightly and she guessed he'd moved. "Are you in the pub?"

"Aye. We've got a pool tournament going and it's getting...boisterous."

"That's a big word for this time a night and how many pints in?"

He laughed. "Only a couple. Emily's here, so I don't want to be making a fool of myself. Anyway, why the call? I thought I got kicked out so you could have sexy time with Erin?"

"Ew...don't call it that, you creep. And it was. But she hasn't shown up." She tried to hide the disappointment, but he obviously caught it.

"Aw, Abs. That's a bit shitty. Have you heard from her?"

"Nah, I tried a couple of texts but no reply. I was wondering if you'd heard from her. I guess I'm clutching at straws and trying not to worry."

"Nope. But then why would she contact me?"

"I don't know. As I said, straws. It crossed my mind she might have headed to the pub with her dad, but obviously not if you haven't seen her."

"Sorry, sis. Can't help. Is that where she was then? At her dad's?"

"Aye." Abby confirmed. "Why?"

He was quiet a moment, and Abby thought he'd lost signal. "George?"

"I'm here. Just wondering if it's worth going to check out Eddie's place? Make sure she's okay?"

His tone had shifted from excitable to anxious and did little to allay Abby's fears. "Do you think? I mean, maybe they're still talking? She hasn't realised the time, or her phone's dead, whatever. I don't want to be that crazy girl who shows up at her dad's because she missed dinner. You know?"

"Aye I suppose." George didn't sound convinced. "He wouldn't hurt her, would he?"

"Hurt her? Why would you think Eddie would hurt her? George, you're meant to be making me feel better, not worse."

"Erm...forget about it. I'm being dramatic, that's all. It's the booze talking."

"Okay." She wasn't convinced. But him being half-pissed in a busy pub probably wasn't the time to get in to it.

"Like you said, there's a ton of reasons why she might have forgotten or lost track of time. Try not to worry."

"Yeah, cheers. Or you know, she could have simply stood me up."

He laughed then, and Abby felt a little better for hearing it. "There's that too. Do you want to come down here and join us? Drown your stood-up sorrows?"

She chuckled at his attempt to console her. "Thanks for the offer, but I'll leave you to it. I'm not sure being a third wheel is what I need right now."

"All right. And if she's not around in the morning, then we'll worry together. Deal?"

"Is it going to cost me?" she teased.

"Ha. Funny. No, worrying with you is a freebie. Goodnight, Abby."

"Night, George. And be good to that girl."

"Yeah, yeah."

She swiped the red button to hang up and felt a little better. It only lasted as long as it took for her to check there was no indication of a new message. She sighed and rested her head back on the sofa, surprised when the puffball appeared out of nowhere and stretched across her lap.

"Hey, mister. I'm glad someone wants to see me tonight." She reached for her wine and settled back with the warmth of Angus on her lap, thinking dreams of Erin would have to do.

CHAPTER 42

Okay, now she was allowed to worry. George had joined her as promised, despite his hangover.

"Stop being a baby and think."

"Oi, I'm not hardened to the drink like you. At least let me get a coffee down my neck."

"Here." She practically threw the cup at him with impatience. "Drink and think."

"You checked her room?"

"Yes. Ann said she hadn't checked out so I knocked, but got no answer. Then thought I'd better check inside in case she was hurt or something. Her stuff was still there but no sign of her."

"And the tower?"

She failed to hide her exasperation. "Yes, George. I've searched the castle high and low, and she isn't here. And neither is her car."

"You don't think..."

"What?" Abby knew the same question that had crossed her mind in the early hours had probably just occurred to George. Had Erin simply left? Without saying good-bye? She had spent the night, wondering and doubting, because for Abby, it was the worst imaginable reason for why Erin couldn't be found. The relief at seeing Erin's stuff still in her room had been a welcome salve to the torment but had lasted mere moments. All other possibilities now needed to be exhausted.

"Never mind."

"It's okay. I know what you're thinking because I thought about it last night too. But who just leaves without their stuff?"

"Fair point. Have you asked..."

She cut off another obvious question. "I've asked Ann, all the kitchen staff, Simon, Raymond—no one has seen her since she left for her dad's yesterday lunchtime. No one came looking for her, no one called."

"Shit." He gulped at the coffee.

"Exactly."

"I suppose we could go to her dad's?"

He didn't seem keen, but it was an obvious place to start. She ruffled his hair. "Now you're thinking. Only, I don't know where he lives. I think James Carter does though."

"It's okay, I know."

"You do?" She quirked an enquiring brow. "How?"

"Long story. I had to bring her car back from his house one morning. He'd upset her, and I didn't think she'd want to go back there in a hurry."

"She came to you?"

He shifted, clearly uncomfortable at her questioning and detecting the note of hurt in her voice. "Not exactly. Listen, it was no big deal. I happened to be in the right place at the right time to help, and you two weren't on the best of terms. Don't worry about it."

She frowned at him a moment longer, wondering at the circumstances where Erin would go to George for help over her. Was she jealous? A little. But she also felt gratitude towards her brother that he would do that. And a little pride that he was the kind of guy someone could go to for help.

"Okay. Lead the way, little brother." She looked him up and down. Shirt crinkled as if he'd slept in it, jeans that hadn't seen a washing machine in weeks, and hair that could rival Angus's. It was a good job he had personality and a handsome face, otherwise she was unsure what Emily might see in him. "I'll drive."

He nodded, topped off his mug, and carried it with him to the front door. She turned to say something, but he had stopped to sit on the front steps. "Hey, c'mon. What are you doing?"

He attempted to tame his hair before rubbing a hand over his face, scratching at the stubble. "What if she is there?"

"Well, that's good. At least we'll know."

"What if she's in trouble?"

He was confusing her, and she could tell he was hiding something. He'd flicked his hair at least eight times in the past thirty seconds.

"Why would you say that, George? You asked more or less the same thing last night."

He took a breath as if to answer, then shook his head. "It's nothing. My hangover's just giving me the fear."

She eyed him a moment longer, but let it drop. "Okay. Well what are you waiting for? Get your arse up and let's go."

~ ~ ~

"I'm sorry you had to miss dinner, girls. I thought it was best to give everyone some time to calm down."

Erin watched from the single bed as Eddie placed a tray on the wooden toy chest. Thea skipped over and drew up a plastic seat to one side of it. "That's okay, Daddy. I wasn't very hungry."

Eddie looked around, hands on hips, before bringing his attention to Erin. She glared at him and remained in place, back against the headboard, knees drawn up to her chin. She'd spent most of the night in the same position.

He smiled anyway. "Now that won't do. I'll be right back with a chair for you."

She flinched as the three bolts hammered back home. Bastard.

"Erin, don't you want breakfast?"

Thea was already chewing on a piece of toast after dipping it in her glass of milk. Erin allowed her face to soften and smiled her sister's way. "Maybe later."

She shrugged and carried on eating, alternating toast with apple slices.

The lights had come on a half hour before, scything through her eyelids and awakening the headache that had finally dulled after her head had clashed with the stairs. Since then she had scoured every part of the room from her vantage point, looking for weakness, weapons, or a chink of daylight that might alleviate the claustrophobia threatening to get the better of her.

Nothing.

From what she could see, apart from Thea's plastic easel and chair, the furniture was bolted down, the window was fake, and she didn't think a stuffed animal would make a very effective weapon.

She tried counting bricks again in an effort to stay focused and calm. Turned out there was a difference between choosing to hide in the smallest space you could find and being forcibly locked inside of one. This wasn't a safe space. This was a coffin. No one was going to appear at the door to fold her into their arms and smooth her hair until it was all better.

The bolts slid back, and she fixed her gaze on one of the many giraffe pictures pinned to the wall. From the corner of her eye, she watched him place one of the kitchen chairs at the end of the trunk opposite to Thea.

"There. That'll do for now." He swept an arm around the room. "We're obviously set up for an eight-year-old here, but I'll soon fix that. In time, I know you'll make this your home."

She refused to meet his eyes, didn't blink despite the giraffe blurring in her vision. He came closer, stood at the side of the bed. She gritted her teeth, stifling the urge to recoil as he leant down towards her. He wouldn't see her fear. She wouldn't let him take that from her too.

"You're mine to keep now, Erin," he whispered close to her ear. "No one is going to take you away from me again."

CHAPTER 43

The house looked dark despite the morning sunshine.

"It doesn't exactly give off a happy-family vibe." Abby grimaced. George was quiet beside her in the car, fidgeting with his empty mug. She snatched it from his hands, tossing it on to the back seat. "What the hell is wrong with you?"

"Nothing. Let's get this over with."

He was already unfolding himself from the car before she could reply. She huffed out an irritable breath and followed suit, catching up to him as he headed along the path.

"I don't see her car."

George nodded. "I'm not sure if that's a good thing or a bad thing."

She slapped his arm. "Way to make me feel better."

They climbed the few steps to the door, and George made to knock before hesitating. Impatient, Abby rapped the green wood herself. They waited.

"There's no one here, Abby. Maybe they went for a drive, or into town?"

She knocked again. "Maybe."

George took her elbow. "C'mon, this place gives me the creeps. Let's take a drive through town, see if we can spot her car."

The tension in her shoulders gave way for a moment and she dropped them in defeat as George led her to the steps. The distinctive sound of a latch clicking stopped them, and they turned in unison to look back at the now open door.

Eddie Carter peered out at them. "Can I help you?" His eyes stayed on George. "We've met?"

"Uh, yeah. I work at the hotel."

"Right, right." His stare shifted to Abby. "You're friends of Erin's?"

"Aye." Abby took the lead. "The thing is, we've not seen her since last night, since she came here. Is she still here?"

He crossed his arms, and the door creaked open a little wider behind him. "No. She left around dinner time. Said she had things to do."

Abby felt George's fingertips squeeze her elbow. She felt as if they were sending a message and resisted the urge to pull away from the sharp pain and draw attention to it.

"Oh. Did she say what?" she asked. George remained silent beside her and didn't loosen his grip.

"No. And I didn't ask. She mentioned something about Glasgow, but that's it. I'm sure she's fine though."

"Aye. I'm sure." Eddie Carter didn't seem too concerned to Abby, considering she was telling him his daughter hadn't come home the night before. And Glasgow? Would she really go back there without telling Abby? Without her stuff? Her earlier fear nagged at the back of her mind but again was overridden by more palatable and likely scenarios. It could simply have been an emergency? But if it was, who was it that needed her? The questions around Erin's life away from the castle circled again. Something wasn't making sense. Maybe it was Abby. Was her worry irrational?

"Do you know if she had her phone with her?"

He seemed to ponder this, tapping a finger against his lip. "You know, I do remember her saying the battery was dead."

A little relief seeped into Abby's chest, but it was short-lived. Erin wasn't ignoring her—she had a dead battery. However, it still didn't explain her whereabouts, and the idea of an emergency in Glasgow went out of the window. How could someone have got hold of her if her battery had died whilst at her dad's? How else would they have contacted her? The list of possibilities was growing shorter by the moment, and Abby didn't like it one bit. As she stood on the step of Eddie's house, "the creeps" that George had mentioned were getting to her too.

It felt wrong. And not because she was potentially in denial about the reason for Erin's absence. Abby knew herself, trusted her own intuition, and believed if something felt wrong, it probably was. It was now a case of figuring out exactly what was rankling.

"All right, well, thanks. If you hear from her, will you let us know? You can call up to the castle."

"Will do. Nice to meet you both again." Eddie stepped back inside and closed the door with a muted click.

Abby yanked her elbow from George's grasp. "Seriously, George. You need to spit it out now. You've been weird since we left the castle. And what was that all about?"

He took her arm again and began marching her back towards the car, hissing at her in an exaggerated whisper. "Did you not see? In the hallway?"

"See what? I'm half the height of you, remember."

He spun her around to face him. "Erin's bag. It was hanging on the coat stand."

Abby looked back towards the closed front door as if expecting to somehow see through it. The hairs on her arms prickled, and the feeling of disquiet set in firmly. "You're sure? Well, let's go ask him about it. Maybe she forgot it."

"No." George kept hold of her. "Think about it, Abby. If she forgot her bag, how did she drive the car without keys?"

Abby shrugged. "They were in her pocket?"

"This is Erin, sis. Orderly, precise, Erin. The girl who lines up her toiletries in order of height, straightens her place mat and cutlery as soon as she sits for breakfast every single morning, and cuts her food into equal pieces. Her keys always go in the front pocket of that bag. I've seen her do it multiple times."

"Okay, now it's you that's creeping me out." She gave him a look that she knew conveyed the question of how on earth he would notice those things. Abby had witnessed a few of Erin's unusual, albeit cute, habits. Clearly, she wasn't the only one paying attention.

"A girl in my class used to do the same kind of things when she was stressed or anxious. Erin probably doesn't even notice it herself." He waved his hands in exasperation. "And I only remember about the keys because I had to find them so I could pick up her car that day I told you about. She threw her bag at me, and I went into the front pocket without thinking." He was rambling now. "Listen, shut up about that anyway, it doesn't matter. We need to talk."

Abby watched him hurry back to the car but stayed where she was. She had never seen her brother in a state that was anything other than genial and warm. Well, apart from when the subject was Laura—for good reason, as she'd already found out. It was disconcerting, and she didn't like it.

He gestured for her to hurry, and the unsettling feeling it gave her propelled her into action. If George was troubled, it was probably a good idea to take note.

CHAPTER 44

The toast was cold and the milk warm, but Erin ate it anyway. It would do her no good to starve. She would need her strength to find a way out of here.

Then she waited.

She remained in the chair, and as expected, he returned a half hour or so later and wordlessly collected the tray. Thea attempted to engage him in some play, but he seemed distracted and waved her off. "Daddy has grown-up things to do, peanut. I'm sure Erin will play."

He'd looked at Erin pointedly, and she merely nodded, turning her attention to Thea. "Of course, I will."

Now he was gone, and she searched the room more thoroughly, with something specific on her mind. "Do you want to show me your crafting tools, Thea?"

She felt a little guilty as Thea clapped her hands excitedly and began unpacking various art paraphernalia from the chest. "...and there's glitter, look, four different colours. Bendy pipes, and balloons, and card in all the rainbow colours, and paint..." Erin had no intention of playing.

Finally, she spotted something that could work. A pair of green plastic safety scissors. She surreptitiously pushed them up her sleeve and continued to murmur her enthusiasm. "This is great. Why don't you come up with an idea for something to make while I use the bathroom?"

Thea grinned, displaying a gap where one of her baby teeth used to be. It triggered something in Erin's chest, and the fact she had a little sister sitting right across from her, finally registered. She reached out and smoothed her golden hair before cupping her cheek. "I have a sister."

For a moment, Thea didn't move, then she was on her feet and throwing her arms around Erin's neck, squeezing her with might. "We're going to be the best of friends, and Daddy will take good care of us."

At mention of Eddie, Erin untangled herself and held Thea at arm's length. "I'm going to take care of you too, Thea. But I need you to be good and do as I say."

Thea nodded furiously, clearly willing to do anything to make her happy. Erin held up a hand for a high five, but Thea merely looked at it in confusion. "Do you know what a high five is?"

She shook her head, and the gravity of what Eddie had done to this innocent child pressed further on to Erin's shoulders. She held up her hand again, took Thea's, and slapped them together. "It's kind of a way of agreeing to something that's cool, or to celebrate."

"I still don't understand. Daddy doesn't high-five."

She said "high five" tentatively, as if she was afraid to get it wrong and embarrass herself in front of Erin.

"Okay, come here. I'll show you." Erin got up and headed to the wall of pictures. She pointed to a penguin. "So, I'd say, 'Nice picture, Thea. It's really great', and hold up my hand." Erin did as she said. "Then you would say 'Thanks' and give me a high five for a job well done. Get it?"

Thea's eyebrows still furrowed and she glanced at Erin's hand suspiciously before smiling and slapping it for all she was worth. "I think so. You can keep teaching me."

"No problem, we'll work on it later. In the meantime, get to work on that project and I'll be back in a minute."

With the door safely closed, Erin shook the scissors from her sleeve. The plastic was thicker than she had hoped, but the blade safely encased in it would work. She prised the two sides apart then began bending the plastic, a little at a time, until it eventually cracked and she could break it apart to free the blade. With it palmed out of sight, she headed back to the bedroom.

She joined Thea on the floor and pulled the dining chair towards her, turning it upside down and angling it so her body shielded it from the door. She had scoured the place and was sure there were no cameras but was still afraid he might suddenly appear. Then she set to work.

"What are you doing?" Thea looked up from the beginnings of a drawing.

"The leg is loose. I'm trying to help daddy by fixing it."

"Oh, he has tools, you know. We can buzz and ask for them?"

"No, no." Erin caught her wrist as she made for the buzzer by the door. Thea had pointed it out the night before. Erin felt sick at the thought of that becoming her life. "He's busy, we can fix it."

Thea hesitated but sat back down, and Erin continued to work on the thick screws. "And when I finish it, you get to tell me what a good job I did and we can high-five."

That got a smile, and Thea carried on with her drawing, leaving Erin to her task.

The blade cut into her fingers, and she quickly sucked at the blood, afraid to scare her miniature accomplice. The first screw was stubborn but finally gave. The second was a little easier. Then it only took a minute to separate the leg from the rest of the chair.

"I thought you were fixing it?" Thea eyed her suspiciously.

Erin balanced the chair against the chest and lay the leg close to her side. "Sometimes you have to take something apart before you can put it back together."

If Thea was confused, she hid it well and carried on with her colouring. *You and me both, kid.* Although in Erin's case it felt more akin to falling apart.

She had no idea if he was still in the house. Only the sound of felt pen scratching card broke the silence. Her watch said it was almost noon—would he bring them lunch? It was a waiting game now. She would be ready.

Taking up sentry next to the door, her grip never loosened on the chair leg. She fielded Thea's questions and gave her artist's opinion and multiple high fives when required, keeping her occupied. There were only three stages to Erin's plan: hit him, grab Thea, and run.

After that, all she had was a hope and a prayer.

~ ~ ~

Abby grabbed George's hands and stilled them. "George, seriously. You need to tell me what the hell is going on. Is Erin in danger?"

"She might be." It was the first words he'd uttered since they had retreated down the lane and parked up at the gate to a field, which now separated them from the Carter croft.

"For fuck's sake, do I need to punch it out of you?"

His head fell back against the headrest, and Abby watched his eyes close. She mentally counted to five. She knew it must be serious, but her impatience at finding Erin was wearing her nerves thin.

"George?"

"All right," he growled. "This isn't easy, Abby."

This time she grabbed one hand a little more tenderly and squeezed. "It's only me remember. What's going on?"

"Remember that time, I was about ten or eleven, when I came home with my lip all busted up? Dad had to stop you going and beating on Craig Lawrie when you found out it was him who'd hit me?"

"Yeah. That little arsewipe." Abby wondered where on earth he was going with this.

"Well, we were down at the river when he'd started on me. I wouldn't cross that old hiker's rope bridge—the river was high, and I was scared I'd fall in."

"And that's why he hit you?"

George rubbed at his nose absently. "He called me a baby, and we traded insults. He wasn't used to kids giving it back. The other lads laughed at him, so he hit me. It's how he operated. Most of my pals had a thump from him at some point."

"Didn't he end up in jail?" Abby squinted, trying to picture him.

"Aye, robbery. He's out again now, living up in Glasgow."

Abby waved her hands and brought herself back to the point of the conversation. "Anyway, what's that got to do with Eddie Carter and Erin? Get to it, George."

"Sorry, right. Well, I headed home, following the river, and it brought me here." He hooked a thumb towards the lane and the direction they had come. "I heard shouting. It was a man, and then I heard a woman crying. I hid in the trees and spied, I didn't realise what was happening..." He trailed away as his voice cracked.

Abby's imagination was working overtime now. "It was Erin's dad shouting?"

He nodded and cleared his throat. "It had all become a bit of a blur over the years. I guess I wanted to forget it. But as soon as I saw Eddie in the hotel asking for Erin, I knew it was him I'd seen that day. And every moment came back to me like it had only just happened."

"Who was he shouting at?" Abby could guess but wanted to hear it from him.

"His wife. Marie. The next thing I remember was him dragging her to the river, cursing and shouting. She was screaming and crying, and I didn't know what to do, Abby. So, I hid."

Abby's heart thumped, and although she could predict his next words, she still needed to hear them, to believe what he was saying. "What did he do, George?"

His eyes glazed as he stared across the field. "I couldn't see properly at first, but I could hear splashing and him shouting some more. Like pure rage. I've never heard anything like it. That's when I knew something was really wrong. I guess curiosity compelled me to try and get closer. Fuck, I wish I hadn't. He was holding her under. She was fighting, but he was too strong. When I realised what was happening...I...I peed my pants." A sob broke free, and he swiped angrily at the tears. "I was just a kid, Abby. I..."

"Shh...take a breath." She rubbed her hand up and down his back, just like when they were kids and something would upset him. "What happened next?"

He clamped his eyes shut, and she imagined him back in the moment. His face twisted like it hurt to remember. "I was panicking. I was caught in this dilemma of fear and not knowing what to do, but wishing I could be brave, wishing I could save her. I was so scared, Abby. Scared he might do the same to me. Then before I could decide, the splashing stopped. It was quiet. The last thing I saw was him walking back up towards the house. Alone."

"Did you go to the river? Did you see her again?"

He tugged his hair and shook his head furiously. It was clear the memory had tortured him from that day onwards. "I think deep down at the time I knew what had happened but didn't want it to be true. I heard voices in the distance and panicked that it was Craig catching up to me. All I could think about was him seeing that I'd pissed myself and giving me shit for it."

"What did you do?"

"That's the point." He thumped his fists on his thighs. "I didn't fucking do anything. I crawled away like a coward, and when I hit the road, I ran. I told myself I had imagined it, over and over again until I believed it. And now here we are. Erin is missing, and it's all my fault."

The tears flowed freely, and Abby's heart broke for her little brother. For the young boy who had witnessed such a horrifying act and then shamed himself into hiding it. And for the man now wracked with the guilt that his actions may have put someone they both cared about in jeopardy.

She leant in and lifted his chin, forcing him to meet her eye. "George, you were a kid. You can't blame yourself for this. You did nothing wrong."

He jerked his head away. "Of course, it's my fault. If I'd spoken up. Even told you—"

She cut him off. "Like I'd have listened back then. I'd have told you to bugger off and stop telling stories. You're not the bad guy here, George. And what-ifs and maybes aren't going to help us find Erin."

"He killed her, didn't he?" he whispered. There was terror in his eyes, and Abby wished she could answer no.

Instead, she drew him into a hug. "I'm sorry, George."

He pulled away but kept hold of her hands. "I mean, we all heard the stories. And I knew I should say something. But I didn't see clearly everything that happened. I never saw her after, but that didn't mean she wasn't okay. Then the police didn't arrest him, and I heard she had killed herself and he had moved away. You know how it goes around here. You never know what to believe. I kept questioning myself. Had I imagined it? Made it up? In the end, I didn't know. You can convince yourself of anything if you want to bad enough, Abby. Anything."

"I know." She held him tighter, rubbing soothing circles on his back.

"I didn't know what to do." He was pleading for her understanding, and he had it. She couldn't profess that she would have been able to handle it any differently. "Then when Erin came looking for him. I had no idea he was still here. I'd convinced myself he had moved away and she'd never find him." He dropped her hands and covered his face. "If anything happens to her because of me..."

Abby felt a sense of eerie calm come over her. Her mind was jigging, slotting, putting the pieces in place, then rearranging them another way. Whatever picture she came up with, the result was the same. Erin was more than likely in trouble.

"George, I need you to get a grip. If you're right, then Erin is probably still here, and she needs us. We know he had a temper, and from the little Erin's said, that hasn't changed. What if she starts asking the wrong questions? This is your chance to make things right, George. You have to help me."

He sat a little straighter, giving her his full attention. "Anything. What's the plan? Tell me what to do, and I'll do it. I need to make this right."

"Have you got your phone?"

He dug into his pocket. "Right here. The signal isn't bad."

"Okay, keep it handy. We're going back. We need to find out if she's there." Abby was out of the car and climbing the five-bar gate into the field.

George followed suit, pocketing his phone and catching up to her. "How are we going to know?"

She didn't look his way. Instead, her gaze was trained on the rooftop of the Carter's crumbling barn. "I have no idea."

CHAPTER 45

That was definitely a door closing upstairs.

Erin pressed her ear to their prison door and strained to hear any other movements. Her leg jiggled with impatience and nerves, and her hand began to cramp. She switched the stick of wood to her other hand and flexed her fingers a moment, drawing a curious look from Thea. She had stopped asking questions a while ago, and when Erin had offered no further explanation, she had simply gone quiet and returned to her drawing.

Click.

Was that the door at the top of the stairs opening? She glanced at her watch. One fifteen. She heard slow, deliberate steps begin their descent.

This was it.

"Thea, come here." She reached out her free hand, and the girl only hesitated a moment before hopping up and taking it. Erin crouched to her level. "I need you to stand very still beside me and do everything I say."

Her bright blue eyes widened, and Erin could sense the questions there.

"Daddy's going to be angry, but I promise, I'm going to take care of you, sweetheart. But I need you to be brave for me."

"But..."

"Shush..." Erin held a finger to her lips. He was only a few steps away. "We're going to get out of here, Thea. Together," she whispered.

Erin didn't expect the alarm that crossed her face. It only occurred to her in that moment that leaving the cellar might not be what Thea wanted. That there were reasons Eddie had managed to keep her quiet down there for so long. It was too late for any more reassurance. She would have to hope Eddie would show his true colours, and it would be enough for Thea to trust and follow her. Fear might be their saviour.

She held tight to the little girl's hand as the bolts began to slide back.

One.

Two.

Three.

~ ~ ~

With George's help, Abby landed safely on the other side of the wall separating them from the gardens of the croft. They stayed crouched low, skirting an outbuilding before finding a rotting shed for cover. Abby peered around the corner, looking for any sign of life.

A flash of pale blue metal caught her eye, and she tugged George's arm, directing him to look towards the side of the barn. It was shiny, peeking out from under a tarp, conspicuous amongst the rusting machinery surrounding it.

Erin's car.

"That's hers, isn't it?" Her heart hadn't stopped hammering since George's confession, but she felt it skip at the sight of the car.

He blew out a shaky breath. "Yes."

She continued to grip his arm. "Right, now it's time to call the police."

George didn't argue. He reeled off the basic details to the operator, finishing with their location. "Yes, I know it's only been twenty-four hours, but we know where she is..." He began to pace. "No, that's the point. We think she's maybe being held against her will. Of course, we tried, but he told us she wasn't here, but then we found her car hidden out the back…"

"Tell them what you saw at the river," Abby hissed.

His eyebrows furrowed, and he shook his head. "Of course, we've tried her phone. No, we're not relatives. She doesn't have any."

Abby made to grab the phone from him, but he held her off. "Well, who the hell else is going to report it?" He slumped against the shed. "You're right, I'm sorry. We're really worried though. Please, send someone. We think she's in trouble."

A scream pierced the air, and they froze.

Abby saw her own wide eyes mirrored in George's. "Tell them to hurry!"

CHAPTER 46

As soon as he came into her sights, Erin's arm descended. The target was his head, but he must have sensed the movement and ducked instinctively. The wooden leg glanced harmlessly off his shoulder. She raised her arm again, undeterred, as he roared in surprise and spun around towards them.

Thea screamed, yanked her hand from Erin's, and ran to the opposite wall before Erin could stop her. His arm shot up, taking the second blow, before a glint of steel stilled her third attempt.

She hadn't expected the knife again.

Erin had nowhere to go. The wall pinned her back, and the open door barricaded her between it and the bed to her right. The only way out was through him.

He rolled his head, and she cringed as his neck cracked. "You need to let us go, Eddie."

He snorted. "You're as stupid as your fucking mother. I meant what I said last night, Erin. This can be hard or it can be easy. It's up to you. But you're mine now. You're my daughter. You belong here with your family, and I'm willing to do whatever it takes to make you realise that." He reached a hand behind him, but continued to hold Erin's stare. "Thea, sweetheart. Come here please."

"Thea, don't." Erin's words stopped her as she moved towards her dad. "Remember what I said about looking after you? About doing what I say?"

Eddie laughed. "You really think she's going to listen to you?" He wiggled his fingers again in Thea's direction. "Come here, peanut."

It broke Erin's heart to see the tears forming in her innocent eyes. Thea looked between them both but didn't move.

"Thea." He raised his voice a little and her tears fell. "I won't tell you again. This woman has come to take you away. To send you upstairs. But I'm not going to let her."

Thea was looking at Erin now. She wiped at her nose and the tears still fell, but there was something else in her eyes. Hurt. "You said you were going to take care of me?" The question was aimed at Erin.

"I am, sweetheart. I am. Exactly how big sisters are meant to."

"Then why are you trying to send me to the upstairs? You know it's bad up there. There's nasty people that want to hurt us. To hurt Daddy."

So that was it. He'd brainwashed her. Conditioned her to believe anything outside of this room was bad. How simple it must have been. He had a captive, impressionable child, who would do anything he said. She felt stupid for not considering it before. For not thinking what it must have been like for Thea in that room. This room was her world. He was her only contact, her only company, the only person she'd ever known. From what she'd seen, he hadn't hurt her in any way that Thea would be able to comprehend. Erin could. The rest of the world could. But not Thea. She was a child being protected by her daddy from the world that scared her outside this very room. It made perfect sense. But she'd been so caught up in effecting their escape, she'd ignored the reality she was facing. That Thea not only wouldn't want to leave this room and her daddy, but that she would be terrified to do so.

She wanted to weep for the damage that had been done to the little girl. To her sweet, innocent baby sister. How much could one man fuck up their lives? She'd hidden in terror from him all her life. Now Thea hid in terror with him. Tears stung her eyes, and she knew this was a battle she couldn't win. Not right now. His grip on the child was too strong. But she had to try. She had to. She had no idea when she'd get another chance. Or even *if* she'd get another chance.

"Thea, I know you won't believe me, but it's not true. It's wonderful upstairs. All those things in your books? All those friends and adventures, all the animals you draw. They're all upstairs. All of them. There's no one up there who wants to hurt you."

"You need to be quiet now." Eddie's back shielded the knife from Thea's view, but it was very much in Erin's. He held it out closer towards her. "You also need to drop that." He pointed with the blade to her makeshift club. "Now."

There was no way she was relinquishing her only fragment of power. "You'll have to take it from me."

He smirked.

She never had a chance to raise her arm again before it was pinned against the wall and the blade sat pointed under her chin. His nose brushed hers, his breath hot on her face. "Drop it."

She had no choice. None.

"Why the fuck did you have to come here?" He spat the words in her face, and she was right in thinking he didn't want an answer. "I only wanted to love you, Erin. I wanted to look after you and make up for all those lost years. I wanted us to be a family. Now you've spoilt it."

"You're wrong," Erin spat back. "Once again, you're blaming anyone but yourself. You spoilt this the moment you raised a hand to my mother and then to me. The moment you forced me into those dark places, to hide from someone who should have loved and protected us both. You did this."

"You're lost, Erin." He shook his head, and sadness crossed his face. "She brainwashed you. You're no different from your mother. Never will be."

"Good." She held his eye. "I'm proud to be like her, because the thought of being anything like you makes me sick."

He merely offered her a disappointed smile. "It breaks my heart, Erin. But I see that you can never be my daughter again. It's too late for you."

He turned to smile at Thea before loosening his grip on Erin and stepping away a little. "But Thea and I still have a chance. I'm sorry."

She frowned. The apology confused her, but not for long.

"Just remember, you forced me into this, Erin. You. I never imagined I'd have to do this. Never."

She heard the thud of impact before the fiery pain hit her, soaring through her body mixed with shock and wretched terror. Her knees buckled, but he held her in place.

"You have to believe I never wanted to hurt you."

She gaped at him. Her lips moved but the words wouldn't form.

"But I need to slow you down."

As he released her, searing heat tore through her side once again as the blade left her body and the blood began to flow. Erin slid to the floor, with Eddie towering over her.

"You ruined this, Erin. Not me."

Her fingers found the wound and she clamped her hand across it instinctively, to little avail. Thea had inched closer, her eyes wild, they went from the rapidly forming pool of blood to Erin's.

She screamed.

It tore through Erin's last shred of consciousness. "Thea." She found her voice. "Run."

Thea looked up at her dad, and for a split second, Erin was sure she had lost.

Then the little girl ran.

~ ~ ~

Abby didn't wait for George to finish the call, she was running. Across the sodden grass, around the side of the house, towards the front door. It was locked, but not for long. George's long leg appeared.

Kick.

Kick.

Bang.

The door burst open, and they jostled through at the same time. A charge of footsteps came from a door to the left and a young girl appeared, quickly followed by Eddie Carter. The girl ran to them, and George impulsively put himself between her and the man holding the bloody knife.

"You need to step away from my daughter." He jabbed the knife along with his words in George's direction.

Abby's mind whirled. *Daughter?* Was this Erin's sister? The girl they'd heard so many stories about over the years, the one who any number of things had happened to according to the village tittle-tattle. Had she been here all along?

"You need to put the knife down." Abby was sure she sounded even less brave than she felt. The blood on the knife held her attention. There was only one person missing from the room, and none of them were bleeding.

"Or what?" He pointed the knife back and forth between her and George. "I said step away. I wouldn't want you to end up like Erin."

Abby's breath left her, and she heard the child whimper. She squatted to her level beside George. "What's your name?"

"Don't talk to her, Thea," Eddie barked. "She's here to hurt you as well."

The child stepped cautiously away from Abby, backing towards the open front door. Her eyes darted around the room, squinting high and low. Abby could see she was physically shaking.

"Thea." Abby reached out a hand. "I won't harm you. I promise. I'm a friend of Erin's, and I need you to tell me if she's hurt?"

Silent tears fell, and the girl nodded her head furiously. "I don't want to be in the upstairs. Bad things happen," she whispered.

Abby carefully inched towards her. "They won't if you stay with us."

"Thea, she's lying." Eddie's tone had softened as he addressed his frightened daughter. "Remember all the times we talked about this. What would happen if people came for you? If you had to come upstairs. I'm your daddy. I'm the only one who will stop the bad things, Thea. Do you remember?"

She nodded again, peering out from behind George's legs. "Yes, Daddy."

"And you're a good girl, aren't you? You do as your daddy says."

"Yes." She put a little more distance between herself and Abby.

"Abby, we need to get to Erin." It was the first words George had uttered. His glare remained glued to Eddie and the knife.

"I know," Abby hissed. "But we can't just let them go."

George turned and looked down at her. "We have no choice."

"He's right." Eddie interrupted their whispers. "You have no choice. Follow me, and Erin probably dies. Stand between me and my daughter, and one of you might join her."

"How could you do this? To your own daughters?" Abby couldn't contain her disbelief.

"Erin did it to herself."

Thea hiccupped. She never stopped scanning the room through her tears, and Abby wondered where he had been keeping her. She was clearly afraid of her surroundings.

Abby didn't fancy their chances. Eddie might be outnumbered, but they had no weapon other than fists. She caught hold of George's sleeve and began skirting the room away from the door, guiding him with her, conceding defeat.

"Go." The path to the door was clear. "We only came for Erin. We won't follow you." She prayed in that moment that the sirens were still a distance away. That he would leave while he had the chance, and they could get to Erin. As much as she wanted to keep hold of the little girl, Abby could see no other way. She could only hope that the lengths he was going to in order to escape meant he wouldn't harm her.

"Thea, go to the green door. We have to leave the house." He edged around the table, keeping it between them, with the knife always pointed in their direction.

Abby watched as Thea tentatively moved towards it. "Daddy, I'm scared. Things will get me out there."

"I'm here, peanut. Nothing can get you out there while I'm with you." He took her hand as he reached her. "Any hint that one of you is following me, and someone will pay. I promise it won't be me."

With the little girl swept up in his arms, he was gone, and Abby could breathe again. She still held George's sleeve and felt him tremble. His eyes were glazed as he stared at the now-empty space.

"C'mon. Erin needs us." She shook him back to life.

He mutely followed as she sprinted across the room, heading for the doorway Eddie had appeared through. The stairs going down confused her for a moment, but she didn't stop, taking them two at a time. As soon as she burst through the door, Thea's words and demeanour made sense. It was a child's room, with no real windows, and locks on the only exit.

Where was Erin?

A low moan snapped her attention to behind the door. "Erin. Oh, fuck, what did he do?"

Erin's hands were steeped in blood. It bloomed over the bottom of her T-shirt and pooled by her side. "Thea?" Her voice was barely a whisper.

"Shush. Don't worry, sweetheart. Help's coming. We'll find her."

George took in the scene, and stalked across the room. He threw a towel towards Abby from the bathroom. "Press this as tight as you can to the wound."

Abby gingerly removed Erin's hands, wincing with her as the perforation in her side opened. "I'm so sorry, love. Here, help me hold this." She pressed her hands against Erin's, holding the towel in place.

Erin's eyes rolled back with the pain, as sweat gathered on her ashen face. "Keep your eyes open, Erin. I need you to stay awake for me."

George slipped the belt from his jeans. "Here, help me get this around her."

Abby took it from him. "Listen to me, Erin. Focus on my voice and stay awake for me. I need you to hold on tight to the towel and lean a little forward."

Erin did as instructed, her face etched in agony as she moved. Abby looped the belt around her, and George tightened the buckle over the towel as she helped Erin keep it in place.

Erin leant back against the wall and grabbed for Abby's hand. "We have to go after them. He's crazy."

Abby shook her head. Erin's palms were clammy and her fingers had turned to icicles. She dragged a blanket from the bed and wrapped it around Erin's shaking shoulders. "We're not going anywhere. Not like this. The police will be here soon. George, you need to call again and get them to send an ambulance."

"Too. Late." The words were obviously an effort, but Erin wasn't giving in. "He'll hurt her."

"She's right, Abby," George said. He took his phone out. "Who knows what he might do if the police corner him. Maybe we should go after him. I've seen what he's capable of, remember?"

Erin looked up at him. "What?"

"It doesn't matter now." He squatted down with them.

"We're not going anywhere. Look at her." Abby was firm. "Erin, I'm not leaving you."

"George. Please go," Erin beseeched him.

Abby could tell she was close to tears and any strength she had left was waning. The battle between wanting to stay and wanting to do as Erin asked raged inside her. "I'll go."

"No." Erin gripped her hand tighter. "You can't get hurt."

"And neither can George."

Erin nodded in recognition of what she was asking.

George dialled nine-nine-nine and waited for it to connect. "Then we'll go together."

CHAPTER 47

"Which way?" Erin clutched tighter to George, one arm looped around his neck, the other holding tight to the makeshift compression covering her wound.

Abby ran ahead out of the house and craned her neck in the direction of the lane. "Would he have taken the road?"

Erin shook her head. "He's on foot." She pointed towards his car at the side of the house. "Head for the river."

She continued the laboured half-run, half-walk, with George as her crutch. Abby led as they circled the house and picked up the trail towards the river. "Can you see them?"

George shifted her arm to his waist, giving him more height to scan the area. "Nothing. I don't know how quick he'll be able to move in this though."

The river flowed fast, lapping the banks higher than normal, and engulfing them completely in some places. The ground had turned marshy underfoot, and water quickly seeped into Erin's shoes. It frustrated her that although Eddie might be moving slowly, they were slower.

"This way," Abby called back. "The river runs out of town in this direction." She slipped her way up a bank to higher ground. Erin gritted her teeth against the pain as George practically dragged her to the top. They had a better view, and Erin squinted against the sun looking for movement ahead, as the fear gripped tighter with every minute that ticked by.

"Over there." George pointed to fresh skid marks on the bank ahead. "It looks as if someone came this way not long ago.

A high fence halted their progress, and they were forced back to the marshy water, now ankle deep and precarious. Erin kicked her way through it in annoyance. The river curved out of sight, and Abby continued ahead at a jog, seeking out the best route and calling back instructions.

Numbness spread through one of Erin's legs. It cried out for a rest, but the fear tightened every other muscle in a battle with the pain and propelled her on.

"Fuck." Abby stopped stock still ahead, and Erin felt her stomach drop in dread. "The bridge, George," she shouted. Then Erin could only watch as she sprinted and disappeared around the bend.

"What bridge?" She could barely breathe and could now only drag her useless leg. George had most of her weight and gasped along beside her.

"For the hikers," he panted. "It's a crappy old rope thing. Not far." He shifted her weight to his other side. "Can you make it?"

She stood as upright as possible. "Don't stop now, George."

They rounded the bend finally and stopped as Abby had. Eddie clung on to the rope bridge near the opposite side of the river. He had Thea thrown over his shoulder. Erin could hear her sister's terrified cry. It was enough to let her forget the pain momentarily and drive her forward once more.

She watched as Abby waded deeper into the water, arms outstretched for the wooden ladder that led up to the bridge. It was merely two lengths of rope set at different heights, strung from one side of the river, to the other. A badly designed tightrope meant for convenience, which should never be attempted when the river was high.

Abby's reassuring calls to Thea drifted back to Erin, and she clung on to them as if they were meant for her.

"Abby, be careful." George called out the words she was thinking but unable to force out.

Then the world slowed down.

First the knife dropped as Eddie's legs swayed back and forth, trying to keep up with the violent tremble of the flaccid rope as he sidled sideways, unbalanced with Thea's weight on one shoulder. Erin watched as Thea's small hands reached out for safety before gravity did its job. The rope finally escaped, slipping from under the soles of his shoes until Eddie's feet met nothing but thin air.

His body tilted backward, and the hand not holding Thea reached out uselessly as it lost its grip. His shout was barely audible over the smack of his body on the water before it sucked him under.

Erin never saw whether he resurfaced or not. She didn't care. Her full attention was on her eight-year-old sister, who had managed to break free from him in the fall and was now clinging on to the bottom rope.

"Hold on, Thea," Abby called to her as she climbed the ladder.

"Erin!" The little girl screamed her name, and it tore a piece from Erin's heart.

George waded them closer to the bridge, and Erin joined in Abby's chorus of reassurance. "We're coming for you, Thea. Just be brave and hold on tight."

Erin knew there would be little strength in her, having spent her whole life in a single room. She'd never tumbled and run in the outside world, climbed a tree, or ridden a bike. All she could hope was that the instincts that made her reach out for the rope in the first place told her how to hang on.

They did. She saw Thea's face screw up with determination as she tried to hook a leg back over the rope.

Abby reached the top of the ladder and stepped tentatively on to the bottom line, but the give in it sent a vicious shudder Thea's way.

"Stop," Erin shouted. "She won't be able to hold on if you shake it." The rope was currently tucked under Thea's arms, but it swung wildly every time she tried to lift her leg back over. "She needs to get her leg wrapped around it, then she'll have better grip until you can reach her."

Abby stepped back on to the ladder, tears of frustration streaked across her face. "Fuck. Fuck. Fuck."

"Thea? I'm here for you, sweetheart. We're coming." Erin's throat was raw, and she swallowed back her own tears, attempting to maintain calm and do the same for Thea.

"Hurry, Erin. I'm slipping." She was crying now, her face red with exhaustion and fright.

They were almost out of time. "Listen to me, Thea. You can do this. I just need you to get your leg up so Abby can come and get you. Try one more time for me, sweetheart. One last big stretch."

Even from their distance, Erin could see the quiver run through Thea's body as she struggled to hang on. She watched as her thin leg swung back and made one last valiant effort to sling itself back over the rope.

Then the world stopped.

CHAPTER 48

At first, all that penetrated the vacuum was a scream, followed by a splash.

Erin's legs buckled, but somehow she was still moving. George hauled her from the water back to the bank, and his gruff shouts gradually infiltrated the muffled fog in her brain.

"Abby. Stay with her. I can run faster." Then he was gone, and Abby was at her side.

"Help me up." The air felt thick, and her body failed to gain traction. "Help me." She pleaded with Abby, useless on her own.

Abby sidled in close and wiped at her face. "Erin, you can't. George has gone after her. He can do this. You need to let me take care of you right now." Erin watched as Abby shrugged out of her jacket and yanked off her T-shirt. "Take a breath for me and brace yourself." She undid the belt buckle and peeled the saturated towel from Erin's side. Erin couldn't bring herself to look, but Abby's face said it all. She quickly pressed her T-shirt against the wound and redid the buckle.

"Now get me up." Erin turned on to her knees and grabbed at a branch for leverage.

She saw the panic in Abby's eyes as she cast a glance in the direction George had gone. "Please, Erin. Help will be here soon. I don't want to make it worse." She gestured towards Erin's torso as she put her jacket back on.

Erin was undeterred. Her sister needed her. Thea needed her. She was the only family Erin had left in the world, and she'd be damned if she wasn't going to fight to the very end for her. She couldn't sit in a useless heap wondering if George had reached her in time. "I need to get to her, Abby. Please." She pleaded with her again. "I can do it with your help."

"Are you sure?" Abby seemed sceptical, but Erin was already finding her feet. Fresh adrenaline coursed through her. She wasn't sure if it was from the renewed pain after the dressing change or abject shock. She didn't care. All she cared about was Thea, and it was the boost that could help get her to her sister.

"We can do this." She clasped Abby's hand and stood upright.

Abby manoeuvred her into the same position George had. They made slow progress and took it in turns to call out to George. They were still unable to see him ahead. The river veered sharply and the foliage thickened. Sirens rang in the distance, and Erin had a moment of panic that they wouldn't be found. It was more worry for Thea than herself. "They don't know where we are."

Abby craned her neck back and stopped. "Only George has a phone. So, we can either stop here and I go back to let them know, or we keep going?"

"Keep going." The choice was simple. Their eyes darted from the water, to the banks, searching for any sign of movement.

"George," Abby called out in relief as they rounded the bend and he came into view. Knee deep in water, he didn't move or reply, only stared a few feet further out, his face a mask of shock. "George, what are you doing? Can you see her?"

They reached him and followed his stare.

Erin sank into the water as Abby let go of her arm. She could only watch as Abby pushed George out of the way and waded through the sludge towards the patch of green, monkey-adorned material.

"George, help me!" Abby screamed at him as she turned the small figure upright, the paleness of her face incongruous against the filthy water. The terror in Abby's screams finally jolted him into action, and he waded out to meet her. He took over as Abby struggled in the reeds, scooping Thea up in his arms.

At the sight of her, Erin felt the last vestiges of strength seep from her body along with the blood. She no longer felt the pain, only the hopelessness of loss as she watched George lay the last of her family carefully in the mud.

She tried to stand, but her legs were lead. Abby sank down beside her and held on tight, as they crawled together to reach the bank. A high-pitched bell rang through Erin's ears, and she tried to blink away the white spots. Her body gave in first, collapsing beside the limp form of her sister. Then, as she grasped a lifeless hand in her own, the darkness won.

CHAPTER 49

They never found his body.

Divers scoured the murky depths for days to no avail, while a police bulletin went out to the public asking, "Have you seen this man?"

Nobody had.

Erin avoided the news. She focused on recovering and regaining her strength after weeks hooked up to machines.

She didn't do it alone.

Abby and George rarely left her side, giving her updates only when she asked for them, as well as care and support even when she didn't. Not once had she opened her eyes to find the chair beside her bed empty. Even Ann and Simon had made a shy appearance.

George came with tales of the latest drama with his now-official girlfriend, Emily. Apparently, playing the hero had sealed the deal for him, but she was feisty and cut him little slack, something Erin reminded him he should be used to, having Abby for a sister. They poked fun at his budding relationship woes, and that brought them some light relief.

Eventually, the nurses stopped arguing with Abby over visiting hours. Night after night, when the lights went out, she climbed on the bed with Erin. Now they simply brought her tea and a blanket and closed the door.

When Erin was tired but couldn't sleep, she would close her eyes and Abby would lay close. She'd read to her or simply hold her hand and stroke her hair until the drugs worked their magic and she drifted away.

At the centre of them all and never out of their thoughts was an eight-year-old girl, comatose and fighting for her life.

Erin's sister. Her family.

The first few days had been the worst. Erin's wound had become septic, and she'd lost a piece of her liver to surgery. Unable to leave her bed, she had relied on Abby and George to be her eyes, ears, and voice. To hold Thea's hand and whisper messages of love to her in Erin's absence. They even video-called between the two hospital rooms, merely so Erin could watch her a while and feel her close.

Tears sprung free again as she now held Thea's hand. She was finally mobile, courtesy of a wheelchair, and the nurses allowed her free access to the room, day or night.

She willed Thea to wake up every second of the day and stared endlessly at the monitors, afraid the rhythm of her heartbeat would change.

"Hey, beautiful."

Erin looked up at the sound of Abby's soft voice and smiled. She wiped away the tears and accepted the tissue she offered gratefully.

"Hey, sweetheart."

Abby pulled up a chair beside her and stroked a hand gently down Erin's back. "No change?"

Erin shook her head. It was a daily question, yet still no easier to answer. "The doctors say her vital signs are stronger today. They seem positive that the therapeutic hypothermia has limited the potential for damage to her brain."

"What about the seizures?" Abby motioned towards the machine they'd been told would monitor and record them. Sometimes the seizures weren't physically visible even though Thea showed no signs of paralysis.

"None. That's four days without one. They keep reminding me how resilient kids are." She smiled wryly. "But until she wakes up, I'm not sure how reassuring that is."

"She'll make it," Abby repeated her own daily reassurance. "If she's anything like her big sister, she's tough and brave. She'll wake up when she's ready."

Erin leant into Abby and accepted her reassuring arm. "Any news?"

They both knew what she meant.

"A few possible sightings that came to nothing. And as long as you're both here, I've been assured they'll keep a police officer outside your rooms."

Erin shivered. The thought of Eddie showing up at the hospital haunted her constantly, despite the guard outside her room and Abby's comforting presence in her bed.

"They told me the longer they go with no leads, the more likely it is that it'll be a dead body that turns up." Abby squeezed her tighter and enveloped her in a full hug.

Erin's heart broke for the small child that lay in the bed and the lost child inside of her. Both now orphans. It was up to them to make a new start, make their own family. All she needed was for Thea to wake up, and Erin would dedicate everything she had to doing exactly that.

"So, you're out of here in a few days, I hear?" Abby pulled away, unable to hide her smile. She brushed the hair from Erin's face and cupped her cheeks. "Which means I have a question for you."

"Uh-oh. I'm never sure I'm ready for your questions."

Abby smiled. "It's good to keep you on your toes. Are you ready?"

Erin would have been lost these past weeks without Abby at her side, and she dared not think what might have happened had she not met her and George. It had occurred to her more than once how in the moment, the path taken sometimes seemed so random, and then boom, you discovered the reason you were meant to go that way.

"Only if the second question involves offering me coffee."

Abby chuckled. "Deal."

Erin leant in and pressed a tender kiss on her lips. "All right then, go for it. But make sure it's an easy one."

EPILOGUE

Erin bounded up the castle steps and sang a cheerful hello to Ann and Simon en route to the kitchen.

Today was a good day. In fact, it was a fantastic day.

She practically skipped through the kitchen door, paying no mind to the other staff as she slipped her arms around Abby's waist and planted a kiss on the back of her exposed neck. She inhaled her citrus fragrance, and when Abby turned to meet her lips, she tasted the remnants of coconut.

"Thai green curry?" Erin sneaked a look at the pot.

"Ten points. You're getting good at this." Abby draped her arms around Erin's neck and matched her smile. "It went well then? Are we to have a new teacher in the village?"

Erin beamed and squeezed her close. "Very well. They said they'd call me later today with a decision. I'm quietly confident." She took Abby's hand and tugged her towards the large walk-in larder. "But before I tell you about that, I need to talk to you a minute."

Erin didn't miss the roll of the eyes that came from Brian, Abby's new trainee chef, and she poked her tongue in his direction as they disappeared into the cupboard.

"What's up?" Abby seemed concerned.

Erin closed the door. "Nothing." She pinned Abby against the shelves with her lips and showed her how perfectly fine things were. Breathless, they only broke apart when an impatient knock came at the door, and Brian called out that he needed Abby.

Erin laughed but didn't let her go. "I need you more."

Abby chuckled and kissed her again. "Good job I'm the boss."

And she was. Abby had found her ambition. It turned out to have been in the castle all along. She'd secured a business loan and purchased fifty-one per cent of the castle from her parents. She'd paid nowhere near the actual value, but it offered them a little security, and when the time came, she and George would inherit the rest. Her parents had resisted at first, reminding her it would one day be hers anyway, but pride had played a part. Abby had felt the need to earn it for herself rather than morbidly coasting until the day her parents departed.

It also came with George attached. Too young to get decent credit, they had still done it together, and his name shone proudly above the door along with Abby's. He had enrolled in business school part-time and would take over as manager eventually. Between them, they planned to put Cornfield Castle on the map, not only as a hotel, but as a restaurant and venue for all occasions. And by buying their own stake, it meant they could run it how they saw fit, and any responsibility they shouldered no longer came with the resentment of working solely for their parents. It had seemed so obvious once the idea had taken shape. In the end, her parents were delighted with their decision, and George had found a new strut in his step now he could call himself a castle owner.

But before Abby and George had made the commitment, Abby had asked Erin to make one of her own. She had invited Erin to come home with her. To stay.

Home.

For the first time, that word meant something to Erin. There was no hesitance in her answer, no question it was where she belonged. With Abby, and even George, she was safe and loved. It filled her with such an abundance of excitement for their future that not a moment of uncertainty had entered her mind. She was sure of Abby and the new adventure they planned to take together. She was sure about it all.

And it was everything she wanted to offer to Thea.

The knock at the door came again, this time more insistent. Erin stole a final few kisses. "Is it ready?"

Abby grinned triumphantly. "It's perfect."

"Right, I better go get her." Erin squeaked with anticipation, and Abby grinned along with her.

Abby kept her for one last kiss and a final few words of encouragement. "Deep breath, sweetheart. It's all going to be okay."

Erin returned her smile. "It's going to be wonderful."

~ ~ ~

They each held a hand and counted the ninety-four steps up to the tower along with Thea, eventually guiding her up through the trapdoor opening, with George close behind.

She put her hands to the blindfold, but Erin caught them quickly. "Hang on. Angus's still trailing behind." He took his time, but his interest was obviously piqued and eventually he joined them.

"Okay, we're ready. Are you?"

"Yes," she squealed in eagerness. "Hurry."

Erin whipped the blindfold off. "Ta-da." She swept her arms around the room.

Thea's eyes went wide as she scanned the space, then a little worry clouded them and Erin thought she was about to cry. Before she had a chance to reach out, Thea darted to the window seat and gazed out. "We're in the tower?"

"Well, yeah, silly. Where else would we be after ninety-four steps? I thought the doctors said your brain was supposed to be fine?"

Thea threw her a stern look but only for a moment. "No more downstairs?"

"Nope. It's only upwards for us now, kiddiewinks."

George flopped into an armchair. "I can't believe I'm finally getting to see this place, and it's been converted into a kid's playroom," he huffed.

Abby moved to Erin's side and slipped an arm around her waist. "Aw, what a shame for you, George. If only you'd seen what I had going on up here before." She waggled her eyebrows in his direction.

"Ew...yeah, maybe I'm better not knowing."

They all watched as Thea circled the room systematically, touching all her new things. The easel and art supplies, bookshelves filled with all her favourites. She bounced on the oversized beanbag and grinned her approval. "But I don't have to live up here, right?"

"Of course not." Erin pointed to the trapdoor that was now minus the "trap". "See, the door is gone, and here..." She pulled a long chain from her pocket. The ornate key Abby had given her hung from it. "This is yours now." She looped it over Thea's head. "It's a key for the downstairs door."

Thea ran her fingers over its ridges and beamed up at them. She understood its significance, and the tears that brimmed, Erin was sure, were happy ones. She held up a hand and Erin dutifully high-fived her. Then she spun on the spot and giggled, falling back on to the beanbag.

Erin clutched Abby closer, her own tears threatening. She swallowed them back and instead stole a calming kiss from Abby.

"Erin loves Abby," Thea's singsong voice rang out, making Erin blush.

"Yes, she does, cheeky monkey." Erin launched at her, assaulting her sides with tickles until they both rolled from the beanbag into a heap on the floor.

The laughter subsided, and Thea climbed into her lap. "I really get to stay here? With you and Abby?"

Abby joined them on the floor and ruffled Thea's hair, much to her annoyance. "I'm afraid so, princess. You're stuck with us."

Thea looked between them a moment, then shrugged. "At least I have George for when you're being all kissy and gross."

"You sure do, partner." George beamed her way. "It's nice having someone who agrees how gross you two are," he said, pointing in Abby and Erin's direction. Thea leapt up before Erin had a chance to get in another round of tickles and started on a second circuit of the tower.

Abby sidled closer to Erin on the floor. "By the way," Erin shivered as Abby's breath caressed her ear lobe, "I love you, too."

"Good job." Erin grinned and linked their fingers, squeezing tight. "Because you're stuck with me, too." She leant in towards Abby's waiting lips. "I'm yours to keep."

###

About Wendy Hudson

Originally from Northern Ireland, Wendy is an Army kid with a book full of old addresses and an indecipherable accent to match. As a child she was always glued to a book, even building a reading den in the attic to get peace from her numerous younger siblings.

Now settled in Scotland, Wendy loves to explore the country that inspired her writing in between travelling to as many new countries as the calendar will allow. Summers are all about camping, hiking, sailing, and music festivals. Followed by a winter of avoiding the gym, skiing, football, and not dancing at gigs.

She's always enjoyed writing and turning thirty was the catalyst for finally getting stuck in to her debut novel, *Four Steps*.

CONNECT WITH WENDY

Website: www.wendyhudsonauthor.com
Facebook: www.facebook.com/wendyhudsonauthor
Twitter: @whudsonauthor

Other Books from Ylva Publishing

www.ylva-publishing.com

Four Steps

Wendy Hudson

ISBN: 978-3-95533-690-5
Length: 343 pages (92,000 words)

Seclusion suits Alex Ryan. Haunted by a crime from her past, she struggles to find peace and calm.

Lori Hunter dreams of escaping the monotony of her life. When the suffocation sets in, she runs for the hills.

A chance encounter in the Scottish Highlands leads Alex and Lori into a whirlwind of heartache and a fight for survival, as they build a formidable bond that will be tested to its limits.

Collide-O-Scope

(Norfolk Coast Investigation Story - Book 1)

Andrea Bramhall

ISBN: 978-3-95533-849-7
Length: 291 pages (90,000 words)

One unidentified dead body. One tiny fishing village. Forty residents and everyone's a suspect. Where do you start? Newly promoted Detective Sergeant Kate Brannon and King's Lynn CID have to answer that question and more as they untangle the web of lies wrapped around the tiny village of Brandale Stiathe Harbour to capture the killer of Connie Wells.

The Red Files

Lee Winter

ISBN: 978-3-95533-330-0

Length: 365 pages (103,000 words)

Ambitious journalist Lauren King is stuck reporting on the vapid LA social scene's gala events while sparring with her rival—icy ex-Washington correspondent Catherine Ayers. Then a curious story unfolds before their eyes, involving a business launch, thirty-four prostitutes, and a pallet of missing pink champagne. Can the warring pair join together to unravel an incredible story?

Between the Lines
(Cops and Docs - Book 3)

KD Williamson

ISBN: 978-3-95533-825-1

Length: 370 pages (118,000 words)

Cool, detached psychiatrist Tonya Preston prefers dealing with her patients more than her family. When her path dramatically crosses that of irrepressible rookie cop Haley Jordan, she's thrown out of her comfort zone. A simmering attraction draws them close. But will it be enough when work, family and a confronting police case start to tear at them?

Mine to Keep
© 2017 by Wendy Hudson

ISBN: 978-3-95533-882-4

Also available as e-book.

Published by Ylva Publishing, legal entity of Ylva Verlag, e.Kfr.

Ylva Verlag, e.Kfr.
Owner: Astrid Ohletz
Am Kirschgarten 2
65830 Kriftel
Germany

www.ylva-publishing.com

First edition: 2017

Credits
Edited by Andrea Bramhall
Proofread by Amanda Jean
Cover Design by Adam Lloyd
Print Layout by eB Format

Printed by Amazon Italia Logistica S.r.l.
Torrazza Piemonte (TO), Italy

12740040R00176